# THE TANKER DERBENT

# YURI KRYMOV

**Fredonia Books**
**Amsterdam, The Netherlands**

The Tanker Derbent

by
Yuri Krymov

ISBN: 1-58963-684-8

Reprinted from the original edition

Fredonia Books
Amsterdam, the Netherlands
http://www.fredoniabooks.com

# CONTENTS

## THE MORSE KEY

THERE WERE two of them on night duty at the Caspian Shipping Line wireless station—Tarumov, the operator, and Beletskaya, whose job was to pass on the radiograms to their destination. Tarumov was a youth of twenty, but he had the reputation of being the best operator on the line. They said he could tap out over a hundred signs a minute. When questioned on the subject he would smile as much as to say: "What do you take me for—a man or a machine?" He knew every screw and wire of his set and could do without the help of a technician. If he noticed anything wrong he would whistle, bite his nails and then get to work behind the control panel. Beletskaya would laugh. "If you get electrocuted, Arsen," she would say, "I'll die of fright. Think of me, at least!"

They were both the same age and had been working together for quite a while. Beletskaya was in charge of taking in and sorting the telegrams. It was a wearing, monotonous job which required no special knowledge. Arsen liked to watch her when they were by themselves in the transmitter room. She went efficiently and unobtrusively about her work, her lips moving slightly as she read the telegrams. Her hazel hair would fall over her eyes and she would toss it back with a jerk of her head. On such occasions he thought her very attractive. At the end of the shift she was just as fresh as at the beginning except for a slight trembling of her hands.

At the station they called her Musya. She looked quite young, liked a bit of fun and had a glib tongue. Tarumov sometimes saw her home after work, and she calmly hooked her arm in his.

He knew she was married but had never heard a thing about her husband—for all the world as though he had never existed.

Once, as they were going along the sea front, he saw a couple kissing on a bench and looked away.

"What on earth do people kiss for?" Musya whispered mischievously, looking him straight in the face. "Some pleasure it must be, and I don't think!"

He answered in a rough tone to hide his own embarrassment:

"Then don't you kiss your own husband so often. Show more sense than the others."

Musya was silent for a while.

"I've not seen him for a long time," she said with what might have been a sigh or a yawn. "I don't know how long."

"How's that?" he asked, wondering whether she was joking or telling the truth.

"He's fa-ar, far away," Musya drawled out. "He's chief engineer on the tanker *Derbent*."

A change soon came about in the relations between Musya and Tarumov. He caught himself thinking of her even in her absence. He liked to touch articles of clothing or other things belonging to her and it gratified him to hear their names mentioned together, which often happened at the wireless station.

He sometimes felt irritated at himself without any reason: there he'd gone and fallen in love like a schoolboy with a workmate, another chap's wife. And nothing but dreams could come of it.

And sometimes, watching the stack of papers mounting on her table, he would get a sudden scare; suppose she got fed up with the job and left it, and that was the end of it all. He could not imagine another girl sitting in her place. But Musya had no intention of leaving. She was as merry and as untiring as ever. And  when she left him at the crossroads after work she would shout:

"Thank you, my cavalier! Don't get run over by a tram!"

There was not much work that evening. At 11 p.m. Tarumov tapped out the weather report: "In the Astrakhan area, medium-clouded, dry, wind north-east, up to three points. In the Makhach-Kala-Krasnovodsk area, possible light showers, wind not more than five points. Forecast for the next twenty-four hours—further drop in wind, light cloud." In the log-book he found reports from ships that were behind schedule because of bad weather. There had been no reports at noon.

The gale veered off to the south, its tail trailing between Krasnovodsk and Baku. Towards evening the gale signals were taken down and the first steamer left the freight docks with a hoot of triumph.

After sending out the weather report, the operator switched over to reception.

Judging by the morning's reports, no tankers would be arriving within the next two hours. The call wave was idle. Faint, hardly audible singing filtered through the headphones like the scratching of some tiny delicate insect on the diaphragm.

Tarumov turned the vernier and the sound grew louder and fuller, the melody could be clearly distinguished, interwoven in the accompaniment on a piano. Another turn, and the amazingly clear female voice died away in a long hum of applause.

The operator switched on the loudspeaker and pulled off his headphones. The loudspeaker spluttered, shaken by an earsplitting din out of which strident voices detached themselves like shouts for help. Beletskaya left her place by the telephone and came over.

"Have you gone crazy?" she asked in alarm. "Suppose somebody calls you up?"

She leaned on the back of his chair, breathing in the back of his neck. The applause subsided. The female voice started singing the same simple homely lullaby again.

"A lullaby," Musya whispered. "She sings fine, doesn't she? Move up a little, Arsen."

She sat down on the edge of his chair, with her arm round his shoulders to keep her balance. Her face was so near that he could see the moist glimmer of her teeth between her half-parted lips. He slowly let his head drop back towards her and her hair tickled his cheek. This she did not notice; her eyes were fixed on the loudspeaker. He was not listening to the music, he was thinking that they had never yet sat like that, so close, and that they would get closer and closer until ... until they were man and wife. "That's the way it happens," he thought with joy, "yes, just like that." Another thunder of applause brought him back to his senses.

"That'll do," said Musya. "They're cursing you somewhere at sea. You'll get yourself into trouble."

He turned the switch and cast a side glance at Musya. She clasped her hands at the back of her head and stretched.

Her eyes were friendly, caressing. It seemed she already knew that he liked her and yet she didn't hold aloof from him. On the contrary! Perhaps the time had come to speak to her!

He slowly put his headphones on and tuned in to the ships' calling wave. Silence. Musya had gone to her table; her hands were deftly running through a heap of papers, sorting and stapling them. Nothing could be heard in the transmission room except the hum of the gas stove on the other side of the partition. He looked at his watch: 1.50 a.m. Suddenly he thought: "If there's a call from sea before two, I'll tell Musya today." He felt surprisingly cheerful and yet apprehensive. He remembered how when he was a kid he and his friends used to toss a stick into the air to decide important arguments. They went about it seriously and in complete silence. The stick spun in the air and fell either flat or on its end. One way was as good as another.

1.54 a.m. Only six minutes left. It didn't look likely. Better think of something else. But what? Musya's husband was on the *Derbent*. That ship had been in the news a lot recently. Her crew had started the idea of Stakhanovite trips, and had been the first to put it into practice. Now there was emulation between the *Derbent* and another tanker—the *Agamali*—a jolly fine crew she had too—and there was still no telling who would come out on top. There had been a radiogram from the *Derbent* that morning: she was towing some ship that had engine trouble. Musya had seen the message and not said a word. The day before there had been a gale. She never even as much as mentioned her husband. And once—that was on the day of the *Derbent*'s Stakhanovite victory—she hadn't even gone to the wharf to meet him. Tankers don't stay in port for more than three hours. So they'd cooled off towards each other. Well, that happens sometimes.

What was her husband like, he wondered. A ship's engineer, Vlasov was his name—no—Basov. No longer on the young side probably, and sparing of words like all ship's engineers. And Musya liked a bit of fun.

1.56 a.m. Some ship's radio was tuning in; there was a faint click and a humming in his phones. If only they would start calling! He dipped his pen in the ink and brought the log nearer. He must talk to Musya today. But it was awkward on duty; he must see her home and then...

1.57 a.m. Loud and clear the signals broke into the quietness of the room. Their unaccustomed monotony puzzled him; as though a hand was playing about with the key. Dot, dot, dot. Dash, dash, dash. Dot, dot, dot... S.O.S.... He pulled down the wires of his phones and the steel half-circle dug into his skull. The loud crystal hammering beat madly at his temples:

"S.O.S.... S.O.S.... S.O.S.... *Uzbekistan* calling. 42.36, 18.02 south of Chechen Island. Fire on board. Unable to control it... S.O.S.... S.O.S.... S.O.S...."

The operator started writing. He felt as you sometimes do in a dream, when in the middle of lazy fantasies somebody shouts one word in your ear and everything seems to be full of dreadful forebodings. The hammering went on:

"S.O.S.... 42.36, 18.02 south of Chechen Island. Tanker *Derbent* had me in tow. Cut tow-cable. Following previous course. Answers no signals. Situation desperate. ... S.O.S...."

"Musya, the rescue service!" cried Tarumov. "Quick, Musya!"

He heard her voice muffled by his earphones:

"What's the matter, Arsen?"

"Don't say anything. Here's the message."

Her hand reached over his shoulder and seized the log-book.

He heard her rattling the phone-rest.

"Shipping Line," she said calmly; "give me the rescue service. Look sharp!"

The wireless rapped out again:

"S.O.S. *Uzbekistan* calling... Cargo heavy oil. Number ten tanks burst. Losing stability. Fire on quarter-deck, boats hard to launch. 42.36, 18.02. *Derbent* heading away ... not answering signals ... S.O.S. ... S.O.S. ..."

A pause. Musya was phoning the message through. She had her back turned and her hand cupped over the mouthpiece. She was speaking in a low voice so as not to hinder reception. A splendid girl! She clapped the receiver on the rest and came over to him.

"The scoundrels!" she exclaimed angrily. "Abandoned their comrades! Listen, Arsen!"

"What?"

"Can you hear anything?"

"No."

"Arsen, why are they sailing away?"

"'Dunno. Carrying heavy oil too, aren't they. 'Fraid of catching fire, I suppose."

"The rotters! Saving their own hides, eh?"

"H'm, h'm..."

"Arsen, are you listening in?"

"Yes. Don't talk to me."

He pressed his hands on his headphones till his ears hurt. The ether in alarm was discordant with a bustle of signals.

"*Bolshevik* calling *Uzbekistan*. Thirty miles away. Coming to you. Baku, Makhach-Kala, Krasnovodsk, send all freight ships to 42.36N 18.02E south of Chechen Island. ..."

Tarumov switched over to transmission. Behind the partition the dynamo wailed as it revved up. The glass of the transmitter lit up with the yellow glow of the valves. He put his hand on the key and started tapping. Blue sparks flew from the contacts. The loudspeaker whistled.

"All freight ships ... proceed 42.36, 18.02. ..."

Then he switched back to reception. Ships' wirelesses squeaked once or twice and were silent again. A tense, businesslike silence set in during which he seemed to hear the rattle of anchor chains, the hiss of steam, the foaming of water churned up by screws. And suddenly the hoarse tonal wireless piped out with great distinctness:

"*Derbent* calling *Uzbekistan* ... *Derbent* calling *Uzbekistan*... I am coming. Shall approach from starboard, am putting out boats. Assemble crew. Keep calm. Over. ... *Derbent* calling Baku, Makhach-Kala..."

"Musya, ring up the emergency station," Tarumov bawled out, missing the connected sequence of the signals, "D'you hear, Musya?"

"*Derbent* calling Baku, Makhach-Kala... Going to rescue crew of *Uzbekistan*. Have full load of heavy oil. Risk fire in spite of precautions taken... Send rescue ship 42.36, 18.02."

Musya ran up to the table.

"The emergency station's waiting on the phone," she said. "Have you finished?"

She grabbed the paper and hurried to the telephone. Tarumov saw her put the receiver to her ear and look at the paper. Suddenly she leaned against the wall, bit her lip and shut her eyes tight. She stood like that not more than a few seconds. Then she opened her eyes and spoke into the phone in her usual voice: "Ready? Here's a telegram: Tanker *Derbent* calling Baku, Makhach-Kala..."

Tarumov leaned his chest against the table. Again the ships' wirelesses began crackling. In the noise they were making he was afraid to miss the hoarse piping of the station. His ears were ringing with tension and his thoughts were confused with the snatches of Morse messages.

"It's bad luck that there's no steamer in the vicinity. Why are they calling freight ships? Tankers easily catch fire. The *Derbent* is a tanker. Cut the cable and sailed away, then went back. Strange! It'll be harder for her to save the men now. The wireless operator was the last to leave his post... Who's operator on the *Uzbekistan*? Valya Lastik—just a boy. Perhaps he's got suffocated? Perhaps they all have? No, the *Derbent* will put out boats and pick them all up. But why did she go away? And not answer the signals? And why did she go back? A dangerous cargo she had—Krasnovodsk oil. Very volatile, and highly inflammable—like petrol. What were they saying about that tanker? Oh, yes, Stakhanovite runs! Ahead of shipment plan. And Musya's husband, Basov, is chief engineer on the *Derbent*. She got a scare when she read that radiogram... A strong wind blowing, sparks flying and heavy seas... The chief thing is not to miss any calls. They said the ship was losing stability, heeling over. So when the superstructure was on fire and the ship was about to capsize, Valya Lastik was still at his wireless. His clothes were singeing on his back and he was choking from the smoke of burning oil and paint. And him a mere kid..."

The ships were silent. Barely audible music once more filtered through the phones. Tiflis? Erivan?

"Farewell, my camp, for the last time I sing..." The gipsy girl's rending cry seemed to come from behind the blind wall.

A lousy receiver, no selectivity! With a turn of the regulator the operator tried to get rid of the song. He was cross at the gipsy who knew nothing about Morse or the distance to rocky Chechen Island and its breakers. But at last the applause died down and all was quiet again.

The ships' call wave was silent.

Turning round, Tarumov saw Musya. She was standing behind his chair, her hands pressed to her breast. Her face was pale. He had the impression she might collapse.

"No news, Arsen?"

"No."

"You know, I can't work. Do you mind if I stand here a little?"

"Of course not." He moved up, making room for her on his chair. "Sit here. Don't get excited."

He felt his superiority over her because he was calmer. But at the same time there was something that vexed him.

Musya sat on the edge of the chair and a cold shudder shook her frame.

"I'm shivering," she complained. "It's cold here."

"It's the excitement, Musya."

"No, it's really cold here. Listen, Arsen."

"What?"

"Last year the petrol ship *Partisan* was burnt out. Do you remember? They were carrying Krasnovodsk oil. It's explosive, isn't it?"

"Nonsense!"

"No, tell me the truth!"

"Nonsense, I tell you!"

"Ah, you're only fibbing. I'm awfully scared, Arsen," she admitted. "Suppose something happens..."

He put his arms round her and drew her closer, amazed at not feeling the slightest shyness. He saw Musya's pale face resting on his shoulder in miserable apathy. And to cheer her up he said:

"Your husband is not taking part in the rescue work. He's in the engine room, it's not so dangerous there."

Musya sighed.

"You mean Basov? He's not my husband any more."

"What do you mean?"

"What I said. We've parted. For good..."

She was silent a while.

"You know, I don't think he ever loved me at all. But perhaps he did in his own way, I can't say. He's so—queer. He just went away and that was the end of it. Don't think I'm afraid for him! There are forty-five of them on the *Derbent,* and if anything happens..."

He patted her shoulder, thinking that the man must have hurt her somehow and she was miserable and couldn't forget. And it made him proud to think she was confiding in him and looking to him for sympathy, as though she had united with him against that unpleasant man, her former husband. Then the page of the log-book caught his eye and he read over the words of the telegram: heading away ... not answering signals. He imagined the vivid glow of the fire and the silhouette of the ship treacherously sailing away into the dark. Basov, the engineer, he thought, had something to do with that.

He pictured him huge, red-faced, and fierce, standing on the stern, roaring like an ogre as he slashed at the tow line. The crew had gathered on deck bewildered, but no one could make up his mind to go near him. Then he remembered that there was a captain on the ship, and that the engineer Basov had to obey him just like the rest of the crew, and he was vexed that the scene he had conjured up so well did not fit reality.

Musya suddenly straightened herself out and stood up with a jerk.

"Ugh! What misery!" she said in a low, bitter voice. "Isn't it over yet? See you don't miss anything, Arsen!"

She went slowly over to her place by the table, sat down and started fingering the papers. He saw that she had forgotten all about him and had no idea what an impression her words had made on him. Turning away, he saw his reflection in the varnished table top—his ruffled hair and the dark patches of the phones on his ears—and he thought it would not work out between him and Musya. The level-pitched cheerless hum still sounded in his ears like the impetuous sea wind blowing through his earphones. Now and again he started at the crackle of atmospherics and reached out for his pen, but no signal came.

The rectangles of the windows turned blue, the stars grew larger and pale—it was getting light. A green flash lit up the roof of the bakery on the other side of the waste tract—that was the first tram leaving the petrol harbour.

There was a sudden crack in the headphones. Tarumov pressed them closer and snatched up his pen. Musya at once jumped up and ran over to him. He just had time to wonder quickly how she knew when the tonal wireless boomed out:

"*Derbent* calling Roads... Call back rescue ship... *Uzbekistan* sank 42.36, 18.02... Crew rescued and taken on board ... Provide medical aid at landing ... Cases of burning..."

After a second's pause came the short, hurried line: "For political assistant of the *Derbent*—Basov."

"Capital!" shouted Tarumov, throwing off his headphones. "They've picked up the crew. Do you understand, Musya?"

She seized the book and rapidly read the message, her lips moving.

"Basov signed it," she said quietly. "See what a chap he is! I tell you—he's very queer."

Tarumov answered without thinking:

"That Basov of yours is no doubt the real stuff, a wonderful chap. Just imagine, they had Krasnovodsk oil in their tanks. It goes up like petrol!"

"And you said it was all nonsense," said Musya with a miserable smile.

"Does it matter what I said! That was because you were so cut up. You'll see each other again now and everything will be grand. You'd only fallen out a little. It happens, you know. But gosh, what fine fellows! Pitching seas, sparks blowing about in the wind and they just sail up and pick them off! There's sailors for you! Pity the *Uzbekistan*'s sunk, but the men are more important."

"Some of them have burns," Musya said in a low voice. "Perhaps they—what do you think?"

"It's all right. Probably got singed a little. Listen, what kind of a chap is that Basov?"

"Why, you know. He's chief engineer."

"It's funny. Why didn't the captain sign the radiogram? Ah, it doesn't matter. Splendid of them, wasn't it? Call back rescue ship. That's our sailors for you! Aren't you proud of them, Musya?"

"Of course, but some have burns. I'm afraid."

"Afraid! Ah, think of something else! Why, Musya, fine chaps they are..."

He beamed with happiness and ruffled his hair in excitement. Looking at him, Musya too began to smile.

Then he suddenly looked at the log and became plunged in thought.

"Only why did they first sail away?" he wondered again. "First sailed away and then went back?"

## COMMANDERS

### I

Yevgeny Stepanovich Kutasov was superstitious like many old tars. Before sailing out to the off-shore fishing grounds in spring he would drop a pinch of snuff on the sand as a guarantee against losing his tackle. When he got becalmed and the sail hung like a rag on the yard, Yevgeny Stepanovich would whistle softly through his teeth to call a wind.

Sometimes a breeze did come and swell out his sail. The boat would heel and race along. Yevgeny Stepanovich would not exult or even think much about it: the breeze had come and that was that. On other occasions the glistening surface of the calm waters stretched away to the horizon, merging with the scorching sky, and whistle as he might, he could not rouse even the slightest breath of air. Then, not giving in to dismay, Yevgeny Stepanovich would ply the oars.

Sailing alone was Captain Kutasov's favourite pastime. He loved to stop at a beer bar and chat about his old profession with old tug pilots. He had long given up sailing himself and worked in the records department of the Caspian Shipping Line. It was a quiet job; his six-hour days glided comfortably by in the midst of file boxes filled with musty records of shipments of years gone by. The windows of the room looked out to the sea. Over the flat-roofed houses the blue surface of the anchorage was puffed with smoke from ships. The hum of the ventilators clearing the air of the dust of the archives reminded him of the muffled throb of steam engines he used to hear on the bridge of his ship.

But that was only one side of his life. As he sailed off the coast on his free days he would gaze after steamers making for sea until they disappeared beyond the horizon in a curly transparent puff of smoke. Then he would cast a glance at the shore from which he was separated by a narrow strip of polluted water and feel a vague yearning like homesickness. But reminiscences were fraught with danger and he was afraid to look into the past.

Sitting at home one day over a cup of tea, Captain Kutasov tore a leaf off the calendar. It was a blurred picture of a Red Army soldier in a helmet menacingly pointing his bayonet at some ships steaming out to sea. Under the picture he read the inscription: "1920. Soviet Power established in Odessa." He looked at his wife. Natalia Nikolayevna was reading a book, her fresh round face the picture of calm satisfaction.

If she knew all that happened that night, just fifteen years ago, would she be so calm? Would she still love him? And he started recollecting—hastily, with a feeling of dread and shame, vaguely hoping to find some excuse for himself now.

The *Vega* was lying in the docks, waiting to be loaded. The Whites had placed sentries at the gangway, and the thump of their rifle-butts on the planks of the quay could be heard on deck. At supper in the officers' saloon someone pronounced the word "evacuation" and they all started talking at once, but in low tones as though afraid of waking somebody sleeping in the next room.

"You can't fight rifles with your fists," Yevgeny Stepanovich said. "If we refuse to take them they'll kill us. . . . Will you shut that door!"

"I won't take them," said Greve, the chief engineer, turning white. "They can kill me if they like! They've had their beating and the filthy swine are avenging themselves on the Jewish women. I saw them myself. . ."

"For God's sake, Greve!" said Yevgeny Stepanovich, raising his hand. "Everybody here agrees with you, but what's the use of shouting? Don't you know the portholes—"

The navigation officer banged on the table.

"Dismiss the crew," he wheezed angrily, "open the sea-cocks. That's all there is to it. Agree?"

Greve bit his nails.

"We can't do that now; they'll notice it, and that'll be the end of us. So we must do it at night. Listen, tonight."

Yevgeny Stepanovich glanced around. They all seemed to have gone out of their wits that day, there was no persuading them. "All right," he said submissively. "Tonight."

A disgusting shudder shook his bulky frame. He wanted to go home, to get some tea, to calm himself, and to see his wife. The streets were dark and deserted. The wind was sweeping the snow in gusts along the pavement. People are changing before your eyes, thought Yevgeny Stepanovich, even Greve. At home, contrary to his expectation, he felt no better. Natalia Nikolayevna listened to every noise coming from the street, and kept peering anxiously into his eyes. What could he tell her? That he was going to dismiss the crew of the *Vega* that night and open the sea-cocks?

Outside things were already happening. The tramp of feet could be heard through the shutters. Something heavy was moving slowly along the street, something so heavy that it shook the window-panes. And above it all came slow heavy thumps, like blows of a blacksmith's hammer on an iron slab.

Yevgeny Stepanovich put on his coat to go to the port. His wife clung to the breast of his jacket and blessed him with tiny hurried crosses on his shoulder. He tore away her hands, looked into her quivering features and felt his resolution waning.

He rushed out on to the porch. He could not recognize the street. A tide of people streamed past him in the dark; glowing cigarettes flickered. They were all moving in silent haste, filling the whole street, their countless feet pounding on the ground. The Whites were retreating. Yevgeny Stepanovich crept after them along the pavement, stunned and subdued.

On the quay the bright globes of lamps hung swaying from the posts. Yevgeny Stepanovich made his way through the dense crowds of soldiers and refugees to the gangway where the guards barred the way with crossed bayonets. But seeing the captain's cockade on his cap they let him pass.

He stood on the deck of the *Vega*, the sailors gathered around him. They were waiting for an order, but he only screwed his eyes so as not to see the epaulettes of the guards shining in the hard lamplight.

Greve appeared unexpectedly at his side, his face haggard, sallow and fierce-looking.

"It's started sooner than we thought," he said tensely. "We must get away, captain. The lads are waiting for an order from you."

Yevgeny Stepanovich started.

"Wait a little, there's a good chap," he muttered indistinctly. "You can see what is going on. And perhaps we should take them after all?"

"Why did you come at all?" Greve said in a grieved tone. "A-ah, a fine captain you are!"

At this moment the human tide swept past the sentries at the gangway and crowded over the deck of the steamer like a stampeding herd. Dark figures of seamen were lurking on the foredeck. One after another they slowly swung their legs over the rail, crouched down, dropped noiselessly on to the quay, and still crouching, dashed along its dark parapet like schoolboys playing leap-frog.

Yevgeny Stepanovich heaved a sigh of relief. The crew had left the ship without waiting for the order. But he was at once seized with another fit of blood-freezing terror. He snatched his cap from his head and tore the tell-tale cockade off with his nails.

"Captain, that's desertion! Stop it!"

He cowered at the peremptory shout. He gazed bewitched at the mad staring eyes.

"I'm not the captain," he said in a lisping, faltering voice that was not like his, "and I know nothing, nothing at all."

"So you don't know, don't you," the voice rang in Yevgeny Stepanovich's ears. "You don't know, you rascal? I'll make you know!"

A violent blow knocked him off his balance and his limp body fell sprawling on the deck. Through a gathering tear he saw the shining top of a jack-boot and above it the stripe of an officer's breeches and a hand hastily unfastening a holster.

"Don't! Don't!" screamed Yevgeny Stepanovich, grabbing at the boot with both hands. It tried to wring itself free from his contact. "Don't!" he gasped out, catching the leg at last and pressing his bleeding face to it.

Lying flat without raising his head, he could feel that the danger had passed.

"Where is the captain then?" roared the officer. "Do you hear, you boot-licker!"

"He's over there." Rising on all fours Yevgeny Stepanovich pointed somewhere in the direction of the quarter-deck. He rose to his feet and pressed his hand to his face. Disorderly and bareheaded as he was, he would have no difficulty in leaving the ship. Going down on to the quay he heard the swelling menacing hubbub of voices. He turned round for the last time to see what was happening on the *Vega*.

A shot cracked out and sent a shudder through his whole body, like the lash of an invisible whip burning into his sweat-sodden back. Yevgeny Stepanovich knew what had happened. He pushed his way through the crowd, gasping and holding his handkerchief to his bleeding face. He did not stop until he was out of the harbour. Leaning against a lamp-post, his body trembling, he wept for a long time staring at his blood-stained fingers. The pain was not great, but he exaggerated it and uttered drawn-out groans which helped him to overcome the powerless loathing he felt for himself. The tail of the retreating army was still straggling along the main street. Yevgeny Stepanovich could hear the distant boom coming out of the darkness.

"Just wait, you scoundrels," he muttered, turning in the direction of the wharf. "You'll not get away." The madness which had made him so powerless was now gaining control of him. But the unknown that was advancing from the steppe, shattering the air with its iron punches, might be still more dreadful. ... They might break into his home any minute, beat him up, outrage Natalia Nikolayevna, while he could only entreat them or look on while they outraged her. He knew he would not have the strength to resist that. How fine to become quite inconspicuous, to give up his captaincy!

In his walnut sitting-room the paraffin lamp was burning and the clock on the wall was ticking as before, just as though he had never been away.

To Natalia Nikolayevna's questions he gave but short, laconic answers. "They killed Greve. ... They wanted to kill me but I escaped. They killed Oscar Karlich."

He could not bear her looks of love and devotedness. The careful touch of her soft hands as she bandaged him burnt into his soul.

He stayed at home a few days, sitting in his arm-chair, hardly moving. Seldom did he go to the window and pull aside the curtain. Outside everything was quiet.

Once he saw a soldier in an unusual uniform with a helmet on and no shoulder-straps, but a scarlet stripe sewn on his chest. He was standing with his legs apart like a man who is his own master, reading a leaflet pasted on the wall. Yevgeny Stepanovich looked at the soldier and at the passers-by. They took no notice of him and elbowed him as they passed. He understood that the war was over. The alarm had passed, leaving an apathy that was like a permanent weariness. But he had to live. One day he said to his wife, reddening and hiding his eyes as though owning up to something shameful:

"I should like to go away from here—for good."

Without a moment's thought she answered:

"As you like, my dear. But where shall we go to?"

She looked at him with that lingering sympathetic look that makes words superfluous.

"There's the Caspian," said Yevgeny Stepanovich. "I should think the freight turnover there is as big as ours. And it's hot there too. I like heat."

They set out as soon as the snow had melted and a warm breeze blew in from the sea. In Batumi they went to see the Botanical Gardens and bought tangerines wrapped in leaves. Yevgeny Stepanovich became himself again. He felt less conspicuous, smaller. He presented himself at the Caspian Shipping Line, unshaven, in civilian clothes, with a pince-nez and a tie with both ends flying loose in an old-fashioned way. There was no telling him from an obscure clerk. He nodded gravely as he listened to the cheerful young commissar impressing on him the importance of accounting in socialist economy. He liked everything: the commissar, the sea in the bay, the brightness of which was new to him, and even his new job.

Fifteen years' sedentary work made Yevgeny Stepanovich old and sluggish and rooted many habits in him. The new things he came across at every step got him in an inextricable muddle. In the petrol harbour his curiosity was excited by big flat-bottomed ships. They were tankers. Everything about them seemed to be unnatural, chaotic, and not where it should be. The cargo space was divided into compartments called tanks instead of holds. The hatches in the deck were only the size of manholes with round inspection-holes in them. At sea the hatches were battened down and the ship was as air-tight as a beer bottle. There were diesels in the engine-room instead of steam engines. The capstans and the rudder were worked not by steam but by electricity and the fire hose spurted out carbonic acid gas instead of water. The deuce take them! Everything had been much more wisely and conveniently arranged on the *Vega*. He used to laugh at the ignorant skippers and had been the first among the captains to study the steam engine. Now it was beyond him why they needed motor vessels and radiotelephone on the Caspian instead of the old Morse transmitters, and electric cranes instead of steam winches.

One day after lunch, when the clatter of the calculating machines had died down and the restrained voices in the records section had toned down to a whisper, Yevgeny Stepanovich was summoned by Godoyan, the head of the Caspian Line. Going upstairs, with a gait like the rolling of a smooth steep-sided bark, he was a prey to forebodings. Perhaps he had got reports muddled up and it had been noticed? He stopped at the office door and straightened his jacket.

Godoyan was sitting at his desk, poring over papers. His spectacles flashed as he raised his head.

"Captain Kutasov? Take a seat, captain. What's your job?"

His voice was soft and quiet and his head seemed small and delicate beside that of the stone bust on the desk. Yevgeny Stepanovich felt his spirits returning.

"I'm records inspector."

"You're a deep-sea captain aren't you?"

"Yes."

"What ship did you sail in?"

"The freight steamer *Vega*, ten years."

"Oh, that's a long time! You're past master at the job, I should think."

Godoyan adjusted his spectacles and smiled. Yevgeny Stepanovich smiled too. The head of the Caspian Shipping

Line was obviously a fine fellow. Serenely smiling Godoyan went on:

"You're a good worker, captain. I suppose your practice as a navigator is a great help to you?"

"No, I don't think it's of much help. You see it's quite a different matter here —statistics."

"Well, in that case,"— Godoyan heaved out the words with a sigh of relief, like an interrogator who has established the case for the prosecution—"in that case, there is no reason why you should be sitting in an office. That's clear, I think."

"What should I be doing then?" muttered Yevgeny Stepanovich with a drop in his voice. The thought of a mistake in the reports again flashed through his mind.

Godoyan rose and slapped on the papers.

"We'll find work for you, captain! The tanker *Derbent* is being put through its final tests. She'll leave the ship-yard in a few days. That would be a good job for you, wouldn't it? We're short of experienced captains."

It came so unexpectedly that Yevgeny Stepanovich was at a loss what to answer. He knew that he should have refused without any hesitation, but Godoyan's eyes seemed to paralyze his tongue.

"I think it would be better for me to stay here," he started pleadingly, trying to give his voice an earnest softness. "It's not so easy for me, you know, at my age..."

The expression on Godoyan's face changed instantly. It became mocking, as though he had suddenly realized that the man before him was not the one he was looking for.

"You want to stay in the office? Well, you ought to know." He looked wearily past Yevgeny Stepanovich and added: "Why, it's something really big that I am offering you. Ah, captain!"

Yevgeny Stepanovich felt himself turning red. He wanted to raise some objection. Had he done badly at the small job he had been entrusted with? Yet he wanted that spirited young man to smile amicably at him again, as at his equal.

"What's the *Derbent*'s tonnage?" Yevgeny Stepanovich asked to his own surprise. "Just as though I'm ready to accept," he thought, alarmed.

Godoyan smiled.

"Eight thousand gross. Not enough for you?"

"No, that's not it, but—well, I must know," Yevgeny Stepanovich answered with a forced smile. For the last time he felt a twitch at his heart, realizing that he was saying just what he ought not to. But Godoyan rose, stretched out his hand and shook his with a strange alacrity.

"So that's settled!" he said merrily. "Well, I wish you success. Another man would have jumped at the offer. But you... Ah, captain!"

Yevgeny Stepanovich smiled as he wiped the perspiration from his brow. The quiet room in the records section, the reports and the figures dwindled away into the distance as though blown out of his mind by the free, sweeping wind that was whistling in his ears.

## II

The man had travelled a long way and the boredom of it drove him to strike up acquaintances in the train. He offered a young lady in the next compartment a bunch of flowers and helped her to arrange her things on the shelf.

"I love travelling," he said in a free and easy tone. "There's nowhere you can make so many interesting acquaintances. When you're travelling you rest, and yet at the same time you seem to do something useful,—you get nearer to your destination. As a result your mind gets more receptive, your interest in people is aroused. One gets far more sociable on a journey. Take you and me: we didn't know each other an hour ago, and there you are listening to me as though I was an old acquaintance. But suppose I spoke to you in the street—you'd be offended. By the way, it's about time we introduced ourselves—Kasatsky, navigation officer."

They were standing at the open carriage window. The derricks of the oil-fields were already looming on the horizon and the sea glittered like steel in the distance. The navigation officer Kasatsky politely turned aside as he drew on his cigarette so that the smoke would not go in the girl's face. She looked at him with curiosity and apprehension. With curiosity because his movements, like the expressions he used, were quick and unexpected and because she was unable to make even a rough guess at his age. With apprehension because at times he stared intently at her as though sizing her up, and even when he looked out of the window she felt his eyes still on her, taking in her every movement.

"I've been half-way round the world and spent a good deal of my life on ships. A sailor's thoughts are always for his port of destination. There a new page in his life starts. What can be more wonderful than a night in an unknown southern port? You sail in, and the harbour lights close round you. They are reflected in the water and shine in the depths of the sea like pools of light. The ship glides towards the quay, you hear voices speaking in a strange tongue, you see fantastic silhouettes of buildings and clusters of trees you have never seen before. You'd like to plunge straight away into the heart of that town where you are to spend but one single night. And because you have only one night at your disposal you feel as though you'd only just been born and that unknown town was some wonderful toy in your hands. I assure

you, it's a remarkable experience—nothing but curiosity and light-heartedness."

"Yes, it must be fine," said the girl. She closed her eyes and passed her tongue over her full lips. "Tell me something else. You're not a poet by any chance, are you?"

Kasatsky took off his cap and ran his long fingers through his hair. She noticed with amazement that his hair was quite grey.

"I used to write poetry when I was young, but I gave it up," he said with a merry laugh. "I did a bit of self-criticism and wasn't satisfied. I gave it up, like a lot of other things not worth mentioning. Do you like poetry?"

"Yes. I love it. But do go on, please. You're going back to sea. I envy you."

"No need to. Our life has its troughs and its crests like every other life. Now it's going to be a trough for me, and a filthy one too. I'm going to the Caspian to sail on an oil-tanker. The Caspian is an inland sea. No strange towns, no new runs. It's beastly hot. The coast is a desert and the cargo is fire. I've been posted to the *Derbent*, one of a new series of tankers. They are gigantic floating cisterns, you know, sort of naval doss-houses. They call them that because seamen don't stay long on them—they find all sorts of pretexts for leaving them. It's hard to put up with the deadly monotony—the same runs over and over again, with your duties laid down and learnt by rote like a boring play. And the intervals are short. Three hours at the pier to fill up. You don't know what you're envying."

"Poor fellow," the girl said sympathetically. "And you like distant voyages. But why are you going there?"

"Yes, it will be hard on that ship," he went on in a melancholy voice, as though he had not heard her question. "On land people are stunned by events. Whoever they are, each new day has some little touch of novelty for them. I shall only have the wireless and an occasional newspaper. But there may be some kind of surprise in store for me too. Not long ago the tanker *Partisan* was burnt out on the Caspian. Perhaps you heard about it? Such things do happen..."

He spoke slowly, with half-closed eyes and a sad face. The girl sighed.

"Don't be so gloomy," she said, giving his hand a friendly pat.

Kasatsky immediately livened up.

"I've just been trying to picture my future life. On big holidays the ship will lie at the pier and the stay will be lengthened by half an hour or so. There'll be more women there than usual. They all have their anxieties—husbands, fathers or brothers whom they see for no more than three hours every five days. But nobody'll come to see me. I'm all alone." He was silent for a while. "Alone in the wide world. Sorry. Am I boring you?"

"Not in the least," she replied. "Look, the sun's going down!"

The sun was sinking behind the brown hills and the clouds above it were all pink. The girl leaned against the window frame and the wind played in her hair. The navigation officer looked at her out of the corner of his eye, intently, searchingly.

"Strange, the way man is," he started off again. "He never stops dreaming. At sea I shall dream too; of the land, as though someone were waiting for me there."

From the compartment where the girl had her place came the clatter of dominoes and loud laughter. A dark-faced youth peeped out and shouted, "Zhenya, come and join us. We're having such fun!"

The girl answered crossly:

"No, I won't. Play by yourselves!"

Kasatsky said hastily:

"Couldn't we go and have a drink of something? It's so hot here."

They went through a few coaches without talking. He supported her on the buffer, gripping her arm tight above the elbow. In the dining-car he ordered wine and cigarettes. She drank a glass calmly. He asked her who she was. She smiled.

"I'm a student in an oil institute, as a matter of fact I'm already an engineer."

Something like a twitch of impatience clouded his face. For a few minutes he seemed to be collecting his thoughts.

"Technique," he said, "how it changes the face and the soul of a profession. Take my profession, for example, that of seamen. The sail was invented by men of the bronze age. It must have been a goatskin, stretched on a wooden cross-piece. These men were daring sailors. Their craft was dangerous and probably seemed attractive to them. Sailing progressed for a thousand years, but the sail remained the same, dependant on the will of the wind. Man fought with the elements, the sea was for him a mysterious, menacing thing. It fed him, cast up treasures for him, sometimes killed him. The sailor's life has always been surrounded with the haze of romantic adventures. Then Fulton, an American engineer, fitted a steam engine to a sail schooner. Ships began to sail against the wind. They were still not manœuvrable and were as slow as a tortoise. The screw was something like a corkscrew. It was taken for granted that a thing of its length would bore into the depth of the water and propel the ship better.

"One day there was an accident; bits of the thread broke off the screw. It happened far out at sea, it was impossible to repair the damage. The rest of voyage had to be made with what was left of the screw and—the speed of the ship was doubled. That was how blade-screws appeared. The sea surrendered one position after another. With the invention of wireless communication the mysteries of shipwrecks disappeared. You only have to look at our tankers now. One can hardly call them ships. A better name would be speed factories. It's not a gale or a hurricane that's needed to sink them, but a downright meteorological catastrophe. And they're manned not by sailors, captains, and navigators, but by workmen, technicians, and engineers. It's hardly a hundred years since Fulton's time, and the sea has already lost its power over man. That's the way of things!"

Kasatsky drank some wine and his eyes shone. He saw that the girl was drinking in his every word; he was conscious of the fascination of his accurate, docile tongue. He grinned as he remembered the dark-faced youth in the girl's compartment: "A Tatar, I suppose," he thought.

"Your friends are waiting for you," he said suddenly. "Perhaps you'd like to go back?"

She shook her head.

"No, you go on. You were talking of the soul of your profession. Has it changed? Has the romance disappeared from it?"

"Yes. Sailing technique was created in the beginning by sailors. They lived on the sea, loved it, and probably met their death on it in the end. But the German engineer Diesel hardly ever sailed any other way than in a first-class cabin. That doesn't prevent the *Derbent*'s diesel engines from developing about thirteen miles at top speed. Models of ships are now tested in special chutes set up in laboratories. Currents and miniature waves are artificially produced in them. The people in the laboratory may never have seen a real storm, never fought with one, never felt its blows. And yet the ships they design can stand up to storms. The romance of the sea is now confined to fishermen's yawls and is enjoyed only by tourists from inland towns. Pity, you know!"

He drank off his wine and pushed his glass aside.

"But I don't agree with you," the girl said suddenly. "Men have hard and thankless toil on sailing boats. They are at the mercy of the sea and they feel lucky when they get safe ashore. That, I think, is all their romance. And for that minute of pleasure, what a life of hardship and monotony! I prefer the romance of achievement. Divers bring to the surface ships lying on the sea-bottom. Ice-breakers cut a way to the Arctic. That's life! And the main thing is that there's no limit to the possibilities of man. Today at the bottom of the sea, tomorrow under the ocean or at the North Pole. Perhaps I'll be the one to do it, perhaps you will. You never know. No, the fight with nature has only just started. How many victories the future holds for us! I liked it when you were talking about screws. But then you went and spoilt it all." She ended with a friendly pout.

Kasatsky bowed his head.

"You're right," he said appeasingly. "I'm a coarse, ignorant sailor, nothing else."

"Oh no, you're not! You're very sensible, indeed! But you don't see romance where you should."

They were silent for a while, then they looked at each other and laughed.

In the girl's compartment the game of dominoes was still going on. The dark-faced youth gave a hefty slap on the seat every time he laid a domino down. The slaps rang out sharp and deafening like shots.

"Not so much noise, Husein," mildly observed a nice old man who had lined up his dominoes in front of him like a wall. "Perhaps somebody's asleep in the next compartment and you . . ."

"I can't see a thing," said the swarthy youth, pushing the dominoes together. "It's dark, and I'm fed up."

He rose, spat out of the window and sat down again.

"Listen," he said leaning forward, "you seem to be a doctor. Are you?"

"Well, suppose I am."

"Well, tell me, doctor, what's drink?"

"Drink? What do you mean? Alcoholism?"

"If you like, it's all the same. What is it? Is it an illness or what?"

The doctor stroked his beard.

"It certainly is. Addiction to alcohol is always attended with poisoning and degeneration of the tissues. It's a serious disease. And it's hereditary, mark you!"

"And how can that disease be cured?"

"Unfortunately there is only one sure remedy," the doctor said smiling, "and that's to give up drinking."

"A fine cure!"

The youth stretched his legs, leaned against the wall and lapsed into silence. He smoked his cigarette down to the stump, so that in the darkness it looked like a live coal between his teeth.

"So you're a drinker, I take it?" inquired the doctor.

"Well, suppose I am."

"Give it up, Husein. You must!"

"Don't you worry..."

They remained silent. After a while, the doctor got out his luncheon basket. He spread a newspaper neatly on his knees and produced bread, boiled eggs, and a chicken. His fingers came up against a bottle of vodka, but he withdrew his hand and quickly closed the basket.

"A wonderful bird," he said, munching a piece of chicken. "Would you like some?"

"No, thanks. Listen, doctor."

"Yes?"

"Can a chap be brought to court for being ill?"

"I don't understand you."

"It's quite simple! Let's say, you're a drinker, or to use your expression, an alcoholic, and you're absent from work two or three times. For that they have you up before a court of honour with a prosecutor sitting at a table covered with a red cloth and all the rest of it. Is that right?"

"H'm. Of course it's right. That is, generally speaking. You see, Husein, we call alcoholism a disease in the sense that it is accompanied by morbid phenomena—poisoning of the organism and so on. But it depends on you to put an end to it, to stop drinking. If you don't, and if you break discipline into the bargain, they'll have you up for trial. Not for being ill, but for not having the will to give up drinking. Understand?"

"Quite simple!"

"You're a member of a collective, Husein, and in a collective, lack of good will is often equivalent to crime. You didn't do what you should have done. Your crime is, so to say, a passive one, but it's a crime all the same."

"That'll do. It's quite clear."

"Perhaps you've been in court for all I know?"

"Perhaps I have!"

"What for?"

"For that very thing."

Husein rose, obscuring the window with his big body. It got dark in the compartment.

"I got a tough sentence," he said in a calm voice. "They chucked me out of the Y.C.L. and dismissed me from my ship. What am I now? A branded good-for-nothing."

"Don't talk rot," the doctor said sternly. "How did it happen?"

"Quite simple. It's like this with me, doctor. I work for a month or two, perhaps even three. I make up my mind to forget the very smell of it—vodka, I mean. Because I know it's my weak point and I say: Cut it out! But all the same, I have it in me, the disease. It's there waiting for the moment I weaken and can't check myself. 'Cause there are times when I'm displeased with myself and think that the others are ready to pounce on me too. And of course there are always rubs, in friendship the same as in work. And then I just rush at people. And it's all so disgusting, so hopeless."

"It's your nerves. What were you sentenced for?"

"Just listen. I'm a ship's motor-man, you know. The engine is the most important thing on a ship, and I'm a valuable man. I know the engine by practice, by experience, by habit, not like a ship's engineer. He started by studying, learnt the engine out of a book and then got his practice. I should like to get to the bottom of everything too, but how can I? The engineer says: Do that, and it's up to me to do it. I started to worry him with questions: What's this for? What causes that? He cut me short: Do your job, he says, and not so much talk! He doesn't want me to know because he knows and he relies on himself. But it got my goat. Why does he keep his knowledge to himself? It seems to me I can understand just as well as him. We had a row when we were in port. And then that moment came on me. In a word, the need to drink. And I went on the booze right away."

"And didn't go back to your ship?"

"No. When I went into that bar I got drunk in a flash and made a beast of myself. I'm not a nice chap when I'm drunk. It's nothing to me to insult a man. And besides, you know, I'm quite strong. My comrades tried to talk me round and that started a brawl. The very thought of it hurts me."

"Did you knock somebody about?"

"Yes, I did. I was tried afterwards, when the ship returned. The whole crew was assembled in the mess-room and I was placed alone, according to the custom. The political assistant was the prosecutor. 'That man,' he said, 'is bringing water to the mill of our class enemy.' Me, mind you! He spoke for a long time, but it didn't make me feel at all ashamed. It just got my back up more and I refused to say anything for myself. It's only just now that I've started to feel any shame."

"But why now?"

"It somehow made sense the way you explained it. You, an ordinary man! Did justice to that leg of chicken—and explained it so well!"

"A queer chap, you are," said the doctor with a smile. "May I ask where you are going now?"

"The personnel section sent me to the new motor-ship *Derbent*. They think the change will help me to give up drinking. I promised I would. What do I..."

"You must. Absolutely," said the doctor clearing his throat. "You've got to take yourself in hand."

"Enough of that. It was fine the way you put it just now. Couldn't be better. Enough of it."

The light flashed on above them. Husein stood in the middle of the compartment, his hands behind his back. He was depressed and seemed to be listening out for something.

"Where's Zhenya got to?" he wondered. "Still with that lanky fellow?"

"Do you like her?" the doctor asked kindly.

Husein did not answer. He lowered his head and went out into the corridor.

The train was drawing near to the station. In the dark sky the lights on the oil-derricks were twinkling like large yellow stars. Zhenya hurried along the corridor arranging her hair. At the sight of Husein she stopped and turned to an open window. He saw her wipe her eyes with her handkerchief. He went up and stood behind her.

"Let's have a look at you," he said roughly. "Has anything happened, Zhenya?"

"Leave me alone," she said in a low voice. "It'll be all right. I don't want anybody to notice..."

Husein took her by the hand.

"Nobody'll see you. It's dark here," he said. "Has he been overstepping the mark? Eh?"

"It's nothing," she said, violently blowing her nose. "The rotter! But please don't say anything."

"I called you before and you wouldn't come," he said reproachfully. "Where is he now?"

"At the end of the corridor. But don't you get it into your head to say anything to him."

"I won't say anything," Husein said. He took a copper five-kopeck piece out of his pocket and tossed it on the palm of his hand. "D'you know what? You just go back to your compartment as though nothing had happened. Understand?"

She stared at him.

"What are you going to...?"

"I'll knock him as flat as a pancake," he said in a low galled voice. "That's all."

"You're crazy!"

"Not in the least."

"Don't!" She clung to his sleeve and whispered desperately. "Don't, please! I'll shout if you..."

"What are you getting excited about?" asked Husein in surprise. "I won't touch him if you don't want me to. But it wouldn't be a bad thing."

"No, no. Don't, really! How beastly of him though. I nearly struck him myself." She shrugged her shoulders.

"Pity you didn't."

"No. Now I'm glad I kept my temper. I tore myself free and came away." She came closer and said confidentially: "I was more afraid of you just now. How savage you looked. But don't go away, he might come."

Husein gave her a sidelong glance and tossed the five-kopeck piece absent-mindedly. She stood and watched him.

"Listen," she said at last. "What did you need that coin for?"

"This?" Husein opened his hand and then immediately clenched his fist and dug it in his pocket. "It's only an ordinary five-kopeck piece."

"So I see," said Zhenya with a grin.

"Your punch is harder with it," he explained reluctantly.

The girl opened her eyes wide and suddenly burst out laughing. She turned to the window, covered her face with her hands. When her laughter stopped she sighed and bit her lip.

"Excuse me," she whispered, trying to suppress her mirth, "but you're such a hopeless ripper!"

She regained her seriousness immediately and said with warmth:

"All the same, I'm very thankful to you. You're a fine pal. We'll get out together just now, and you can help me to carry my things. How wonderful we got to know each other! We can meet somewhere in a few days. Would you like to?"

"Yes," murmured Husein. He carefully freed his hand and looked round. "There's someone coming."

Kasatsky came along the corridor whistling softly. He seemed younger and slimmer by electric light. He went past, his heels tapping out carefully measured steps, his shoulders squared. As he passed Husein, he shot a bright naïve look right into his eyes as much as to say, "I didn't succeed. You have a try now. Don't waste time, youngster!"

"A devilish cheeky mug he's got," said Husein, following him with his eyes. "What kind of a chap is he, I wonder?"

The train sped between long rows of goods trucks, its wheels thundering over the points. Strings of lights and the dark chimneys of the refineries with their tops wreathed in smoke flashed past the windows. Kasatsky sat on his suitcase at the door of the carriage.

"Steppes, heat and smoke," he said to the conductor. "Where's your blossoming paradise? Just look at that smoky town. Exoticism! It's a bare-faced swindle!"

The gloomy silence of the conductor seemed to delight him; he darted mirthful glances at the passengers.

Zhenya observed him surreptitiously and whispered to Husein:

"The fellow hasn't the slightest feeling of shame. He just looked at me and smiled. You know, I'm afraid of him..."

### III

On the night when the new tanker *Derbent* lay for the first time at berth in the petrol dock and its future captain Yevgeny Stepanovich Kutasov slept for the last time in his home, Basov, the *Derbent*'s newly appointed chief engineer, wandered aimlessly along the sea front till dawn.

Judging by the look of him, he was slightly the worse for drink and his mood was a pensive one. Now he would go to the water and light a cigarette, now he would sit down on a bench and gaze for a long time at the stars glittering between the branches of the acacias.

Just before daybreak when the lights in the harbour went out and the moon sank into the sea, he leaned on the sea-wall and spat between his teeth into the lapping waves.

"My life's a wreck," he said in a low voice. "A failure. I'm a failure myself."

And he searched his memory to bring back to life fragments of the past in an effort to find out the reason for his misfortune. He thought of people to whom he had meant something and who had all forsaken him. It was hard for him to reconcile himself with the thought that they all lived somewhere in that town, and yet he had nowhere to go to and was compelled to while away the night on the promenade.

Take Yakob Neuman, the engineer. How smiling he had been during the first days of their acquaintance in the docks. He had then been merry, red-cheeked and loose-tongued, his voice booming like a gong over the moorings.

They had made friends during the winter repairs. The situation in the docks that winter had been alarming. Ships had been coming in for repairs by the dozen, crowding the moorings. The repair shops had been working in three shifts. Here and there on the wharfs and the approaches to them you could see captains, navigation officers, and ships' engineers, treating the work-weary engineers to cigarettes and edging in a word about putting their order through out of turn.

Basov's brigade had been put on to the job of repairing the engines of a big tanker. When the hooter went the brigade assembled on deck, waiting for the dock engineer Neuman, who was late. The engineer of the tanker paced up and down by the ship, occasionally looking at the berth. Basov could see that he was vexed with Neuman at the tanker having to lie idle and was ready to transfer his vexation to him, Basov.

It was two hours before Neuman appeared on the ship. He wearily went up the gangway and sat down on a bollard.

Basov bent down and peered into his face.

"You're ill, you're not fit to work," he said in a worried tone. "Why, your lips are quite pale. And my chaps have nothing to do. What shall we do?"

He listened to Neuman's heavy breathing. He was itching to take the responsibility on himself, if only he could get to work at once.

"I'll undertake to carry out the order," he said quickly; "everything will be all right. You don't need a genius for the job."

The engineer hardly managed to part his inflamed eyelids.

"Will you? Not taking too much on, eh, old chap?" Torn between doubt and hope he looked vaguely at Basov standing in front of him. "You've not been on the job long, you know." After a silence, during which he evidently could think of no other way out, he said: "Well, all right," and went away.

The brigade went down into the engine-room. While the fitters were taking out the defective parts, Basov had time to run over to a tug lying under repair at the next berth. There Bronnikov was also waiting for Neuman.

"Neuman's ill," he said. "Have you got a defect report? Then strip down the engine. We'll manage the repairs ourselves."

Bronnikov stared at him in amazement.

"You must have gone off your head! Me, take the place of an engineer? How on earth can you expect me to?"

"But repairs mustn't be held up," Basov said impatiently. "Blimey, make up your mind, don't be such a funk, Bronny!"

On his way back to the tanker, he could see Bronnikov running about the pier, getting the fitters together. He knew that he would manage the order himself, but he was worried that Bronnikov might get in a muddle because he seemed to be afraid and had so few men.

When the defective parts had been removed, Basov went to the technical section. But it happened that all the draughtsmen were busy and there was nobody who could draw the plans.

"No, I've got nobody," said the head of the section with a helpless gesture, "that's all there is to it. No use asking me." He tried to get past Basov, but the latter did not let him.

Basov looked at his irritated face and shrugged his shoulders.

"Give me some paper, I'll do the sketches myself," he said firmly. "Repairs mustn't be held up!"

He went back to the tanker with a roll of paper and settled down in an empty cabin. Bronnikov came running over from the tug. He was in the irritable mood of a man who is not sure of himself and has let himself be talked into something.

"What am I to do with this heap of parts?" he inquired savagely. "The technical section won't draw the plans."

"We'll do it ourselves," said Basov as he pinned the paper to a drawing board.

He watched Bronnikov without the latter noticing him and tried to look unconcerned. As a matter of fact, he was far from it.

"You've gone out of your mind," Bronnikov said viciously. "We'll be in trouble before we know it!"

"You'll put in the measurements," Basov answered calmly.

They worked on well into the night. Bronnikov calmed down. He went to get the measurements of the details, and ran to the shop for something to eat.

By the time they had finished and left the cabin bright wintry stars were shining in the black sky. From the lighted windows of the dock workshops flowed a deep wavering hum. Now here, now there on the dark high decks of the ships the green sparks of welders flashed.

"We can't release them without Neuman," Bronnikov said in a pleading voice grasping Basov's hand. "There'll be trouble. Give it up, Sasha!"

He was past the stage of irritation and vexation against himself, he was afraid of possible trouble. Basov put his arm round his waist.

"You've forgotten our students' drawings," he said sarcastically. "We weren't afraid to hand them in because they were not working ones. But do you mean to say we didn't learn anything?"

They handed the drawings in at the workshop and parted at the work gates.

Neuman turned up the day the workshop section delivered the finished details to the brigades. He was still pale. He rubbed his hands as though he were freezing and tried to keep his face to the sun.

"I managed to get over it," he said cheerfully. "How are things on the tanker?"

"The technical section was overloaded," replied Basov, "we carried out the order ourselves."

"Capital! We'll have a quick look through them and then hand them in."

"I handed them in on the same day. They'll deliver the details today."

Neuman gave a whistle and looked askance at Basov. There was something elusive about him that made him resemble Bronnikov when the latter was alarmed.

"They've probably not had time to estimate all the details, have they?" he asked in a quiet voice. Basov understood that the cautious inquiry meant, "Are you sure of yourself? Perhaps we can still hold them back. What if you've made a mistake?"

"I tell you they'll be ready today," Basov answered. "They promised to deliver them by two o'clock."

And his answer meant: "Don't you interfere. I know what I'm about and I'm ready to take the risk."

Neuman understood. He slapped him on the shoulder and his face brightened up.

"I have a lot of work up in the management," he said. "You can see to the assembling by yourself. O.K.?"

The workshop delivered the details by lunch-time and the brigades began assembling them. Basov kept an eye on the work. He had an idea that the men could be distributed in a new way. Some of Bronnikov's fitters had not turned up, Basov sent him some of his. Thus they were not cramped in the engine-room.

The first piston was hoisted up and hung on the chains. The gear got jammed. Basov ordered the piston to be lowered on to the grating, climbed on the girders and had the gears cleaned with paraffin. He examined each detail himself, and got covered with machine oil and sweat. Yet he went so calmly about everything that he seemed not to be in the slightest hurry.

The fitters frowned, but obeyed in silence. When the first piston was raised Basov looked at his watch. Three men were working on the crane and seemed to be in one another's way while on the engine the men were fussing about. It was obvious there were not enough of them.

They lowered the piston into place and screwed down the cover. Basov called one of the men down from the crane and sent him below to help to secure the connecting rod. The fitters grinned: it was more like timing than assembling.

The second piston was hoisted. The carriage of the crane glided swiftly along the girders. The fitters were working with speed. The stops irritated them and they were afraid their earnings would be low. Basov timed the whole operation of securing the connecting rod. It took ten minutes.

They dealt with the third cylinder in eight minutes. The fitters worked in silence with a concentration they were quite unused to.

Neuman came into the engine-room. He stood and watched the work but did not call Basov.

They fitted in the camshaft and other details requiring careful adjustment. Basov distributed the men in still another way. He did hardly anything himself in order to be able to observe and direct the assembling. Then he saw Neuman and went up to him.

"Did you see how I distributed them?" he asked in triumph.

Neuman gave him a warm look.

"There's really no need for me here," he said. "Orjoni-kidze said the best organization is where nobody's irreplace-able. He was right."

Basov was touched with the praise, but he realized that Neuman had missed the main thing: the assembling had been done faster than usual.

He wanted to tell him about the experiment. But Neuman was in a hurry.

"You should go to Bronnikov on the tug," he said, "they're held up there."

Basov's physics teacher at technical school used to say to him: "You are clear-headed, but too practical."

Basov said nothing. He himself could feel that he lacked something ... patience perhaps. At lectures on abstract sub-jects he was out of sorts, and felt with his whole being the minutes going by without any use for him. At lectures on heat engineering or on the parts of engines, on the other hand, he drank in every word. That was just what he had missed as a ship's motor-man before going to technical school. It made the engine less awe-inspiring, simple and easier to understand.

In the docks, the labour processes fascinated him. He was interested in the sequence of the operations in the produc-tion of details and often spent a long time in the workshops.

He watched piston rings being turned in the lathe and thought the job could be done more quickly and material saved if the lathe were provided with two cutters. Again, when fitters were filling the cable-box, Basov thought there must be a simpler and quicker way of doing it.

Yet at times what seemed quite simple and haphazard proved to have been thought out in the slightest details. The processes had been elaborated over years and every attempt to change them came up against difficulties. He asked the foremen questions, but they winked to one another behind his back and called him a greenhorn. He would give in for a while, then think it all over again, trying to find a way of saving time.

Basov often thought that the man at the lathe could easily improve work if he knew the theory of cutting and what certain details he made were needed for. A lot of the men liked to get hold of books, and thumbed through them with the helpless envy of a poor man standing before a shop window filled with expensive goods. Some started studying, gave up work, and never came back. The factory lost some of its best workers who were replaced by unqualified labour. The best thing, Basov thought, would be to teach the men.

One day, he went to Neuman's office and found the engineer particularly excited over something. Neuman laid his drawings aside and told Basov to sit down.

"I've just come from a plenary meeting of the District Party Committee," he informed him. "They've decided to organize instruction for all shops in the works. We've got a big job in front of us."

He paced up and down the room and his deep voice made the ceiling ring.

"Here's what we get, comrades, I said: the Young Communists from the workshops go on the ships during the dinner hour to see where their details are intended for, but the engineers chase them away because they have no time for explanations. If the technical section goes wrong in its reckoning there's no blunder of theirs the workshop won't reproduce. Then the fitters curse the draughtsman and the workshop, and at the assembling mercilessly warp the detail, forcing it till they manage to fit it in somehow. Disciplinary measures are of no use in such cases, I said. It's efficiency, not reprimands, that we need. We've got to teach. . ."

He caught breath and then finished off solemnly:

"To put it briefly, we're going to teach them!"

Basov was about to say that he had already thought of that, but he did not. What he was interested in was how they would manage to organize technical training at the works: some of the workmen were capable, others were dull, some had instruction, others were illiterate. You couldn't dream of putting them all in the same group. A few days later, they suggested that he should organize training for the fitters and he agreed. If the District Committee considered training possible, why shouldn't he, Basov, get down to the job?

The examination commission sat in the evening on the stage in the club. Yakob Neuman called out the fitters one by one. They came up from the back of the hall and stood in front of the table, their faces aglow with excitement. Incorrect answers raised a hum in the room, prompting whispers could be heard from the front rows and Neuman knocked on the rim of the decanter with the stopper for order.

It was there that they passed their technical minimum examination, a feat that filled Basov with cheerfulness and confident content. Sitting beside Neuman, he peered tensely into every man's face as he answered, his heart full of the fear that they would get shy or lose the thread of their thoughts. But the fitters answered smartly and showed no hurry to go back to their places, as though they expected more questions. Basov spent many an evening sitting at that red table, but he never wearied of looking at the workmen's familiar faces, which the unwonted excitement lit up as with some inner light.

There was soon talk in the works of a suggestion made by Zakiria Eybat. Basov already knew him.

The small Azerbaijanian, hardly more than a boy, was thin and dark-skinned and had a shock of curly hair. He used to come to the fitters' classes, often asked Basov questions, and sometimes argued with him. He was one of the first to pass the examination with distinction. After his exam he came to the *Derbent*.

"I've something to tell you," he said mysteriously, "It's like this. . ."

He was excited, his eyes were shining. Basov slipped his arm under his. "Let's walk," he said in a friendly tone. "What's the matter, Zakiria?"

"D'you know, yesterday I doubled the speed of processing on my lathe," said Zakiria, with excitement. "I cut deeper. And it turned out fine. But the foreman saw me and got wild: 'Trying to get a bigger pay-packet, are you?' he said. 'You'll ruin the lathe!'"

"Keep cool, Zakiria," Basov said. "We'll fix that..."

"And I've thought of a way of machining pistons too. You know we clamp the piston in the cam with the head propped in the centre of the back mandrel. That makes it hard to work the face according to pattern. I unclamped the head. I allowed for everything and clamped the piston tighter. And it worked. Now I've no difficulty in hollowing out the face according to pattern. Do you see? Before it took me six hours for one piston, now it takes me two and a half. It'll be all right as long as they don't notice it. See that you don't say anything about it."

"Why not?"

"Oh, you don't know our workshop! They'll say I'm ruining the lathe again and there'll be a hell of a row."

Basov's face became clouded; he threw his cigarette overboard.

"You're talking as though you've robbed somebody," he said indignantly. "Your foreman's a scoundrel. You wait, I'll have a talk with Neuman."

Basov went to see Neuman towards evening. There were a lot of people in the office. Bronnikov was telling them something, guffawing all the time. Neuman echoed with roars of laughter.

Basov sat down.

"It's disgraceful what's going on in the machine shops," he said in an irritated tone. "Foreman Lukhnov is kicking up a row with the men because they are raising the productivity of labour. Just listen."

He spoke slowly, trying to remember all the details of his conversation with Eybat. Neuman went on smiling benevolently, but silence came over the room, and the others were listening, somehow on the defensive.

"Why, the lad was right in his reckoning," Basov said. "If you unclamp the head, you can hollow it out according to pattern. The method absolutely must be introduced. And the foreman needs a dressing down to take the meanness out of him."

"Just a minute!" Neuman interrupted. He was not smiling any more; his face had adopted the official, cautious expression that it had when he was listening to customers complaining. "I've already heard about that. For your information"—he looked severely at Basov—"foreman Lukhnov is not being mean, he's teaching the men discipline. That inventor of yours might have wrecked his lathe. Perhaps you'd like the foreman to go and take lessons from him? There, see for yourself:"—he turned to Bronnikov—"we seem to have gone to the opposite extreme with this technical training. They're going to give us a dog's life now for the sake of earning more. And there are chaps who defend them." He nodded at Basov.

"What the devil are you talking about!" Basov said, his nostrils quivering. "The administration's got in a panic because the men are starting to use their brains. I hate to say it, but it's nothing but obscurantism and cowardice. . ."

He looked round for sympathy. But he found none; many faces even displayed a sort of prudish perplexity, as though Basov had committed some blunder.

"These rationalizers are giving us nothing but trouble," Bronnikov put in mildly. "They want to invent gunpowder. As for the working of pistons—you'll find directions in the books. Look them up"—he turned to Basov. "It's not our first year on the job, anyway. Free the head? Who on earth would do that?"

Neuman looked out of the window and drummed on the table. He suddenly swung round, crimson in the face.

"You've no right to accuse me of cowardice!" he thundered, in a burst of passion. "First do the job I've done."

"I'm not accusing you," said Basov in a weary tone. "But all you say sounds so absurd."

He got up and went to the door. He could not understand the hostile silence behind him. He felt as though he had run up against a stone wall.

## IV

The engineers and technicians of the works were having an evening party. Basov arrived home late and hardly had time to change. He hurriedly tied in a bow the bright tie that he had just as hurriedly bought. He felt that it was not a nice one at all, but it was all the same to him. As he passed the hotel he stopped for a second in front of a mirror. An awkward feeling came over him. His suit seemed ridiculous and tasteless. He got himself a beer at a stall close by and it cheered him up. He bought a huge flower in Morskaya Street and stuck it in his buttonhole.

He met Bronnikov going in. The latter stared at Basov in amazement, but said nothing. Bronnikov was dressed in a sport suit and top boots and his white collar set off his slim, youthful neck.

There were a lot of people in the rooms. It smelt of perfume and eatables. Neuman was sitting at a table, plucking at his beard with a bored expression. Basov thought it would be a good thing to seize the opportunity to have another talk about Eybat's suggestion.

A girl in a white dress was setting the table. Straightening herself up, she tossed back her hair with a jerk of her head. Her face seemed familiar to Basov. He went up to her and held out his hand and she introduced herself: Beletskaya. He realized that he had never seen her before.

Somehow, he forgot about Neuman and Eybat's suggestion. He sat down near the wall to get a side view of the girl. His hand went mechanically to his chin and touched his tie. He pulled it away with a start.

While serving as a ship's motor-man before going to technical school he had once stuck inside the lid of his suitcase a small photo cut out of a newspaper. It must have been an actress or a film star. Some of his crew-mates wrote obscenities under the photo, and he went for them as though he had been in love with the girl. Then the photo got wet in a gale, and he had to throw it away.

When the girl in white bowed her head she reminded him of the one on the photo. The resemblance, however, was more in his imagination than in her features. He could not take his eyes off her. Once she cast a glance in his direction, and her calm brows fluttered. Bronnikov reached over the table and took hold of her hand. She snatched it away and laughed. When Neuman spoke to her, he just called her Musya. Basov felt a sort of hostility towards Bronnikov and Neuman.

When everybody rose and went to the table, Basov mechanically followed her white dress, but Neuman sat on her right and Bronnikov on her left. With thoughtful movements of his lips, Neuman poured himself some vodka. Bronnikov leaned over to Musya and whispered something. His tall top boots squeaked under the table.

It was quite an ordinary party. The conversation was in low tones at first, you could hear the clinking of glasses and dishes. Then the voices grew louder, nobody seemed to be listening to anybody. The women refused to drink wine and the men tried to persuade them.

Neuman drank his glass slowly. He leaned his chin on his broad hand and looked with friendly sympathy at whoever was talking. Bronnikov had his arm behind Musya's chair as though embracing her. She was looking curiously around, not listening much to Bronnikov. Then she suddenly turned towards him with a smile, apparently apologizing for her lack of attention. Basov thought they were sitting too close to each other and that their knees must have been touching under the table. He drank a lot without noticing it, and soon got rather tipsy. His eyes were on Musya all the time. Once she stared sharply at him as if to tell him to stop looking at her and turn away. He did so.

Then everybody stood up and there was a jingling of glasses. Basov hurried into another room where it was dark, and grabbing the knot of his tie he ripped it off with furious delight. A button came off and rolled on the floor. He snatched the flower from his buttonhole and crumpled it in his hand. His head was spinning and a bitter taste kept coming to his mouth. He tried to calm himself with the thought that in six hours he would be at the works. He had to go to the Party Committee about Eybat's suggestion. But the thought which he had forced to his mind faded away without bringing him any relief. In the next room was a girl called Musya, with lively, unfriendly eyes, white skin and strong shoulders, and Bronnikov was leaning over towards her: it hurt him just to think of it.

When Basov went back into the room, Neuman was sitting alone at the table. Dancing couples were whirling round. The designers Beyzas and Medvedev had got sentimental and were shouting loudly. They had been addressing everybody familiarly for some time and were most demonstrative in their friendliness. Musya calmly put her hands on their shoulders and they kissed her. She looked at Basov and smiled: It couldn't be helped, it was the custom. He went slowly round the room so as to get nearer to the white dress. And then, somehow, they found themselves next to each other by the window. Musya's eyes shone bright through her eyelashes.

"So that's the kind of chap you are, Basov," she said in a low voice. "Yakob Neuman told me about you. It's not often he praises anybody. He said you're a wonderful worker. But I didn't imagine you like that at all."

Basov said tensely: "I don't know what Neuman meant. I'm just an ordinary mechanic—like Bronnikov."

Musya shook her head.

"No, Yakob knows. He's very coarse, is Yakob Neuman, but he and I are friends. Why were you looking at me like that during dinner? It made me feel awkward."

It was hot, she had probably drunk one too many and she spoke slowly, as though tired.

"I work at the shipping line wireless station. We're really sailors too, but in communications. They say they're going to give us naval uniform. Will it suit me, do you think?.... Now tell me about yourself."

"I don't know what to tell you," said Basov. "I'm only an ordinary chap. But there are such fine fellows in our place. Take Zakiria Eybat, the Aserbaijanian..."

He found it interesting to tell her things.

She was listening with her head a little on one side. Suddenly she clapped her hands like a child.

"Your shirt's torn, and a button's ripped off! O-oh, yo-u!" Her hands touched his neck. They were dry and hot. He did not move for fear she would take them away. Her familiarity, he thought, was probably unconscious.

"I've been looking at you all evening," he said almost in a whisper, "but I was afraid to talk to you. It's the first time it's happened to me, word of honour."

"Really? And I was thinking: he'll certainly talk to me. And I sat down here by myself on purpose so that you would."

He pulled the curtain to, trying not to be noticed. Musya whispered: "They'll see us." They were alone in the semi-darkness. The street lights cast yellow patches through the window. He kissed her on the lips but she immediately drew back.

"Neuman's been telling me a lot about the works," she said, "and I pictured you a serious kind of chap, who thought of nothing but your job. But there's the kind you are—kissing a girl on the lips straight away!"

He offered to see her home, but she shook her head.

"No," she said, "come to the wireless station for me tomorrow. I finish at midnight."

His heart sank for a minute. She wasn't the sort to lose her head, and even when she pressed against him she remembered to arrange her dress so that it would not get creased. She stopped thinking of him the moment she stepped out from behind the curtains. In the corridor she was immediately surrounded by designers, all vying with one another to help her to put her things on. She did not even look back to say good-bye to him.

Basov wandered along the sea front till daybreak. An icy wind was blowing from the sea but his face was burning. That Beletskaya was not the right sort of girl. She had only taken a passing interest in him and that was all. And yet the thought of her melted his heart. She was natural and showed comradely simplicity towards everybody. There were too many chaps hanging round her. Afterwards they'd probably say rotten things about her and about her appearance. Next day he kept away from those who had been at the party for fear somebody would talk to him about her.

He managed to get to the wireless station after wandering for a long time over waste tracts. The radio masts were lost in the black sky, their yellow lights twinkling up on high like stars. A sentry popped out of his box and rattled the bolt of his rifle. Basov stopped at the fence with his back to the wind. Half an hour passed. He stood there motionless, his hands stiff with cold.

Musya appeared in the lighted doorway. His heart stopped beating—she had probably forgotten all about him. They went towards each other like chance passers-by and did not say a word when they met. There was not a soul around, the sentry had tucked his head away in his sheepskin coat. Musya put her arm round Basov's neck and turned his collar down. Standing in the field by the barbed wire, they embraced as if they were to part for ever.

"I had persuaded myself you wouldn't come," said Musya, stepping back and slightly gasping. "I always do when I really want something, so that it won't hurt so much afterwards."

She took his hand and drew him towards her. The lights formed a ring around them. From the sea came the shrill hooting of tugs.

"Why did you think so?" asked Basov. "I love you. Really, can't you see that?"

"In one single day, Sasha?" she said with a reproachful laugh. "No, it doesn't happen that way."

"If I say so, it means it does happen. Now we're together and I feel so fine. Listen: I think we should get married."

Musya laughed.

"A real commander you are! By the left! Forward—to the Registry Office! But you and I have not had a real talk together yet!"

She felt her way in the dark, leaning on his arm so as to be nearer to him. But he did not bother about the road. He kept hindering her by trying to hold her hand in his.

"I was like a sick man at the works today because of you," he said. "They say it only happens once in a lifetime."

They stopped by the stone balustrade on the sea front. The bare acacia branches were shivering in the wind. Waves scurried in from the bay and broke against the tiles of the bathing station. Down below, the pitch-black water hissed angrily as it rushed up the stone wall. Musya rearranged her cap over her sparkling eyes. He seized the moment she raised her arms and embraced her. But she freed herself and dragged him towards a bench. She surprised him by starting to talk about the works.

"You're a very capable man, Sasha," she said. "Neuman has a high opinion of you. But I know he's not quite satisfied with you now. He says you find something wrong everywhere and take it upon yourself to put it right. That irritates people, and then... You support Eybat's stupid suggestion against everyone else. Perhaps I've got things a bit mixed up, but it hurts me to think that you're so open and honest and yet they take you almost for an intriguer. Neuman said..."

"Musya, let's drop that subject," said Basov, dejected. "It's not like that at all. You don't know, Musya."

She bowed her head without answering and dug in the sand with her heel. During the silence that ensued a cloud seemed to creep between them and his happiness waned.

"Perhaps it would be better for you to work quietly like the others," Musya said simply, "you can get on in the world. I'm as good as anyone else but I don't get anywhere, probably because I've got no ambition. But there's a lot I could wish for you. You should work like the others —only better than the others."

Basov stroked her hand as he listened to her. What she was saying seemed strange to him, he could hardly get the meaning of it. She drew her hand away, trying to focus her attention on her words. He was seized with a fit of impatience and said, almost without thinking:

"I'll do my best to put everything right. Don't you think about it. I love you."

Musya cheered up and let him embrace her.

"Darling," she said caressingly, "let's talk about how we'll live together."

Weddings took place from time to time at the works. Basov would play his accordion and observe the newly-married couple. They seemed to condemn themselves purposely to discomfort so that the collective could have a good time. It happened sometimes that after getting married a chap became indifferent to everything and disappeared immediately the hooter went. That was intolerable, and Basov was not sorry that it turned out quite different with him.

Musya came to him after work. She brought with her a small suitcase with her things and a whole pack of dresses. She was very calm and quiet and when Basov looked at her he felt amazed at the speed and ease with which everything had been settled. Musya began by sweeping the floor. She tucked up her skirt just like the cleaners at the works and swept out the cigarette-ends from under the table. She cleaned away the spiders' webs from the ceiling and hung curtains on the window.

Basov looked at her bare feet, which were small and

strong, just like her hands. The waiting on windy nights by the sea had subdued him. He had become shy and looked at her with gratitude in his eyes. He remained like that for their first days together and Musya felt satisfied with him.

"You're a good-tempered chap, commander," she used to say. "It's as if I knew you from my childhood."

Basov did his best to come home early and they would go for walks together. When they went to the cinema he hardly looked at the screen—he took such pleasure in observing her profile. She sat quite straight, with wide open eyes in which the rays dancing on the screen were reflected. That sweet cheerful woman, he thought, was dearer to him than anybody else on earth. Yet he could not talk to her about his perpetual dissatisfaction or his observations at the works. Because she wanted to live just like all the others and had unquestioning faith in authority. Still, it was fine being with her, and he no longer noticed the minutes go by.

Sometimes they had visitors—workmates or hostel acquaintances of Musya's. Musya would put on her white dress and seem changed somehow, as though she had washed in beauty lotion. He shot furtive glances at her and his heart ached.

"I feel like having a lark today," she would whisper in his ear. "Try and put up with me."

Istomin, a communications engineer, used to be among the guests. He smelt of perfume and his smooth-brushed hair reflected patches of light. He was a pompous fellow who talked only when everybody else was silent. Musya would wink to the girls and affect to trip over his feet as she went past him.

"Move up," she would say curtly, "there's no room to pass. Don't sit in the way."

She just called him George and paid not the slightest attention when he shrugged his shoulders in offence. Basov would drink tea and blow smoke rings.

"Musya," he would say good-naturedly, "why hurt a chap's feelings?"

He felt at ease when everybody around him was enjoying himself. That was worth giving up an evening for. He would have liked to play his accordion, but it was an instrument Musya could not put up with. "Buffoon's music," she used to call it. Istomin, on the other hand, was a good guitar player: he could pluck the strings so smartly, with his pink little finger raised. He would shift his cigarette over to the corner of his mouth and gaze at Musya. The girls sang to his accompaniment. Liza Zvonnikova—rather a plain girl—used to whisper to Musya: "Look, you've got him spellbound. He's off his nut altogether. He's ogling like a fakir. You wait, I'll tell Sasha."

She would start tittering and hide behind Musya's back.

"Silly thing!" Musya would say. "Don't be so silly!"

Istomin would sip his tea and gaze calmly at the girls. "It's only a hazard that brought me here," his glance seemed to say. "I'll be going any minute." He would wait patiently for silence.

"There are strange moments in life," he said impressively. "I was going along the street today, and I saw a woman about ten paces in front of me. She was slim and stepped so lightly. I thought—I was quite sure that she was—well, a person I was thinking about that very minute. I called her, and she turned round. And just imagine—she was a complete stranger!"

The girls listened with their mouths half open. Musya smiled unruffled.

"You've just made all that up, haven't you?" she said.

Basov listened to the conversation and studied Istomin. He remembered that Musya had one day said about Istomin: "What I like in that chap is his independence. He knows what he's worth and won't be trifled with."

Basov tried to make out what Musya could like in him. He was amazed when Istomin said, "I never trust women. They are so fickle. A man must be mad to trust them."

"What the devil does he mean! How vulgar! He'd do better to play his guitar."

When he was alone with Musya after the party he wanted to dissipate the unpleasant impression. She was combing her hair in front of the mirror and in it he saw her face — pale, tired, all the recent animation gone out of it.

"Nothing but gossip and insinuations," he said in a conciliating tone. "How commonplace that chap's talk is. Really, he doesn't speak the same language as we do. Doesn't he bore you?"

Musya's reflection in the mirror stretched and yawned pleasurably.

"He was speaking plain Russian, Sasha. Do they speak another language at your works?" She sighed and slipped off her dress. "What can you do about it? It's merry with him, and I wanted a bit of fun. You can't re-educate him!"

## V

In January ten tankers came in for repairs on a single day. The workshops were overloaded. The rumour got about that part of the work would have to be left to the ships' crews. The convenient expression "with the crew's resources," casually uttered by somebody, was heard here and there over the works. It was said with a smile that might have been indicative of spirit or of embarrassment—like that of people obliged to admit their shortcomings.

At the production conference Neuman unexpectedly declared that half the ships would have to be transferred to other docks. One could not make the men work round the clock, working overtime was not a way out. The engineers cast glances at one another as much as to say: he's admitted it. The director stared at the ceiling with a strained expression on his face as though it was all he could do to contain himself and hear Neuman through. Then he exploded:

"I can see what the feeling must be like in the workshops when the chief engineer talks like that! We've got to put a stop to that kind of rubbish."

Neuman put his hands on his hips and scowled with stony savageness.

"I'll put in a report. I've got figures to back me," he thundered in reply. "It's easy enough to do the talking when others do the work."

Those men seemed to hate each other, the way they shouted. But Basov knew they would presently come to an understanding and go and have a smoke together in the corridor. He thought of Musya. She would be waiting for him all night, listening for his footsteps outside. He waited till there was a pause and then flung out so loud that everybody turned round:

"I think we've got to work under pressure. All hands to the job, that's all about it. What's all the talk for?"

Neuman stopped squinting at the light and sat down in silence.

The engineers started talking all at once. Voron, a brigade-leader, who had been injured when a boiler burst, turned round on his chair with an effort and smiled at Basov. After the meeting Neuman stopped Basov at the door.

"You can spend the night in my office," he said with exaggerated politeness. "There are two divans there."

Basov nodded and turned away. He very much wanted to go home. On the piers, in the dancing lamplight, black figures were moving about, harassed by hooting trucks. Going down into the engine-room of the tanker, Basov saw the fitters' grimy faces looking up at him from below. The brigade-leader called to him:

"Are we going to have to stay here long?"

He put his lips to a hanging kettle and noisily drank some water. Letting go of the kettle he ran his hand over his sweating face and winked at Basov. The latter answered:

"Yes, we are."

Towards morning he went to Neuman's office. It was cold there. The branches of an acacia were beating against the blue panes of the window. He lay down on the leather divan and thought of Musya for a while before going to sleep.

The wind was howling in the chimneys, the trams had already started running. She probably hadn't slept much that night...

He saw Musya next evening when she came home from work. She clasped her hands at the back of his neck, pricked herself on his chin and started laughing. It didn't look as though she was angry with him.

"I rang Neuman up yesterday evening and was told you were staying the night there," she said. "You know Neuman got me wild." She stared at his hands, the nails on which were black with oily grime. Then she knitted her brows and became engrossed in thought.

"I asked him how long he was going to keep you and he just laughed and said: 'He'll stay here as long as he's needed!' I clapped the receiver down. I could have punched him!"

Her face darkened with the blood mounting to it and became dejected and hard.

"He doesn't like you," she went on. "None of them like you, for some reason, or else they're afraid of you, I can't make out which. I don't think you'll ever be a success, Sasha. Whether you'll be happy is another matter! Perhaps you're happy now. They use you to stop holes, but you say it's an emergency job and you're satisfied. It's a pity though, a crying pity. Don't get angry..."

Tears were actually rising to her eyes and she squeezed his hand till it hurt. In his bewilderment he did not know what to answer. As was often the case, he found what she said strange and meaningless.

"Musya darling!" he cried forcing himself to be cheerful. "Stop this panic! Who's doing me any wrong? I can bite too, you know!"

He drew her to himself and stroked her hair, but she obstinately struggled free.

"It seems to me you live in a kind of newspaper style, Sasha," she said. "Others live differently. I want you to get on in life."

He did not come home next night, nor the next again.

Then Musya went on night duty and had to leave when he came home. She seemed to get used to it and not to notice his absence.

"That emergency job of yours is lasting a long time," she would say, jokingly. "How long d'you think we've got to live? I'll soon be getting old, commander."

By the end of January the tankers left the repair docks. Neuman made a speech at a meeting of the workers. He spoke of sleepless nights, bad supplies and strength of purpose. His speech was excited and heated, he got long applause. Basov was sitting next to Eybat.

"I had a talk with Neuman and Gladky, the workshop foreman," he said. "They're still against it. We'll see what the workers say!"

Eybat looked depressed.

"Drop it, Sasha," he said. "It'll be just as Neuman says. What am I? Nothing but an ignorant fitter."

"Scared, are you?" Basov said drily, shaking the other's hand off his shoulder. "There's a rotten streak in you, Zakiria."

He looked round the room figuring out which of those present would support him. Brigade-leader Voron came limping along the passage, breathing with difficulty. Gravely and proudly he dragged his crippled body like a bullet-riddled standard. "He'll be on our side," thought Basov.

The director spoke of the experience of the winter repairs and of the importance of the coming shipping season. Then came Basov's turn.

Basov tried to be brief. The works could economize time and resources. Everybody knew about Eybat's suggestion, but it was getting musty in the chief engineer's brief-case; it had to be taken out of there (he had no intention of offending Neuman, but it sounded spiteful and provocative). There was a good lot of workers and new machines in the works. If the men learnt to save seconds there would be no call for emergency jobs.

The foremen listened with frozen smiles on their faces. The designers whispered to one another. Bronnikov grinned, moving his lips as though about to speak. Basov sat down. He suddenly felt quite clearly how out of place his speech had sounded. Everybody wanted to speak about the difficulties they had overcome and what they had achieved. And suddenly there was he declaring it could have been done cheaper and quicker.

The room got noisy. Voron rose with difficulty and shouted out:

"He's talking business. We must find out why they don't give..."

But Neuman leaned over towards Voron and whispered something to him. Bronnikov rose to speak and immediately the atmosphere became more cheerful.

"The mechanic Basov proposes saving seconds and then we'll have to spend weeks repairing the lathes. As for the suggestion he spoke of, it is hardly practicable, it's even dangerous. What's that he's saying about the cams holding the piston? The foremen will have a fit when such suggestions reach the workshops."

Basov bent down and his face darkened. There was no doubt about it, the meeting was out for fun. Features were softening, losing tenseness, the audience was getting noisier. One of the designers remarked in a bantering tone:

"They wanted to do us out of the premium! Let them have it, Bronny!"

Basov gasped and stood up.

"You don't want to let the worker have his say? It won't work! We'll see our ideas through!"

Among the indifferent, puzzled faces that turned round at his shout he saw some openly hostile ones that eyed him with unconcealed malignant joy.

"You won't give yourselves the trouble!" he thundered. "You hide behind printed rubbish! What did we teach the men for?"

Then he immediately cooled down and his excitement gave way to apathy. He felt ashamed of his outbreak. As he went towards the door he heard Neuman say:

"That's bordering on hooliganism. He's got to be put in his place."

Basov went home, sat down by the table and dropped his head on his arms. For the first time he felt himself alone. All those men, mechanics and workshop foremen with Neuman at their head, worked hard and conscientiously; there was no doubt about that. But for some reason they were all obstinately clinging to the monstrous, antiquated set-up in the works, with its emergency jobs, its chaos and its repetition of the same old mistakes. Basov felt as though he had run too far ahead and suddenly looking back, felt himself all alone.

Musya saw that there was something wrong with him. She sat down by him and looked into his eyes. "Anything happened?" she asked. "Why don't you say something?"

Basov came to himself again. He told her what had happened. She listened in silence. She neither asked questions nor showed indignation. She was all eyes, as though studying his features for the first time. When he told her how Eybat had tried to persuade him not to speak, she could no longer restrain herself. She clasped her hands in dismay and anger.

"He himself tried to persuade you?" she inquired. "Did he? Really, I never saw a man like you before!"

She was laughing, but her lips were quivering. Then she took his hand in hers. Her face became wretched and imploring. It was entreating, ingratiating, menacing. Basov had never seen her like that before.

"Sasha, darling, chuck it all! Can't you work like everybody else, without trying to be original, without making a fuss? You worked at night and they gave you no credit for it. Didn't the others get premiums? You've not the sense to take what you've a right to. You can't get on with people. And now you've got to jump up with that suggestion. You've got all the top ones against you, and they'll pay you back, you can be sure. Why do you do yourself harm? Really, you're queer, very queer. Just an old crank."

He listened to her, weary and indifferent, busy with his own thoughts. It takes great persistence, conviction and indifference to one's own fate to convince people that one is right. There he was torturing his own wife. He was impatient, hot-headed. But did he want to strain his relations with his comrades at the works? He couldn't even give a name to the truth which had possessed him. He had studied the labour processes and come to the conclusion that the machinery was not being properly used, that the work could be done better. That was all.

"Are you unhappy with me?" he asked pensively.

"I'm anxious. Somehow I've no confidence at all in what tomorrow's going to be for us. You're so queer..."

## VI

Before the opening of the navigation season new tankers came to the docks—serial-built giants for the shipping of heavy oil. The diesel engines had been constructed by the Sormovo works and were designed to develop a maximum power of 1,400 h. p. But when the first tanker—the *Derbent* —was being tested, the test shop did not manage to get more than a thousand out of it. The matter remained at that.

Bronnikov made a report at a conference. He gave a detailed account of all the defects of the engines and stated the opinion that the planned power could not be achieved in any case. Then he opened Nemirovsky's manual and read out:

"The ceiling cruising power of an engine is generally between seventy and seventy-five per cent of the designed power." If that was the opinion of the expert Nemirovsky, well....

Bronnikov's opinion was somehow quickly accepted and when the second tanker showed 1,000 h. p. everybody was satisfied: it was clear they would not get any more out of them.

Then, contrary to all expectations, the third tanker, the *Agamali*, developed 1,380 h. p.—almost the designed power. Basov, who had the job of regulating that tanker, reported the fact in a memo to the chief engineer. He asked for two days extra in order to reach the exact designed power and suggested that supplementary work should be carried out on the ships already taken into service.

Bronnikov was called to the management. He was worried, for he anticipated an unpleasant half hour. The *Agamali* was lying at her berth, with white puffs of smoke rising from her gigantic funnel to the mast above—Basov was trying to get the designed power out of her and menacing with his obstinacy his—Bronnikov's—calm and contentment. It was obvious, he thought, that Basov wanted to get promotion and big pay. Whatever the case, Bronnikov hated him that minute.

In the dining-room Bronnikov was stopped by the designer Beyzas.

"Heard the news?" asked the latter, and in his eyes Bronnikov could read curiosity and anticipation of a row. "They've managed to get the designed power out of the *Agamali*'s engines. That means we've deceived the shipping line. Ugh, we're in a spot!"

When Bronnikov presented himself at the director's, the latter was having an argument with Neuman.

"Don't you try to justify yourself," the director was saying heatedly. "Tell me straight: did we deceive the shipping line? Who's wrong—the Sormovo works or us?"

"Ask him," Neuman cut in coldly, pointing to Bronnikov. "I've already told you what I think."

On his way, Bronnikov had had time to think the situation over and prepare his defence. He recalled all the defects he had found while regulating the *Derbent*'s engines. The port engine had given a hundred and five revs in gear, the starboard engine a hundred and three.

"How can you talk of deception?" he said with restraint. "The works turned out these tankers in a hurry, and you know yourself how we took them over. There's nothing surprizing in the engines having different capacities."

"But there's that Basov, he undertakes to get the designed power out of them!" said the director with sudden ill-will. "So it can be got out of them. It can, I tell you!" The director suddenly banged on the desk and fixed his round, awe-inspiring eyes on Bronnikov. "Look, he writes that there's not enough compression in the cylinders. Why isn't there full... er... er... compression?"

Bronnikov hung his head, trying to keep control over himself. Neuman said in a confidential undertone:

"There's more than meets the eye in all that, Ivan Danilovich. We had a rotten business with that Basov, Ivan Danilovich, a very unpleasant argument."

The director cooled down as quickly as he had flared up. He thought for a while, seeming to forget to take his eyes off Bronnikov.

"Leave everything as it is," he said wearily. "If necessary the *Derbent* can be regulated by the crew. We can't bring the tanker back into the dock." He went slowly through some papers; Bronnikov glanced with relief at the door.

"Oh, there's still another question," the director suddenly remembered. "The line needs an engineer. For that ill-fated *Derbent*. They suggest we detach one of ours—just for one trip, they say, but you understand what that means. Still we can't do anything about it—we're taking over a new fleet. Whom would you propose?"

Bronnikov was sorry he had not been able to slip out. However, the director was looking at Neuman. Would Neuman really suggest to send him? Perhaps he would. It was he who had regulated the *Derbent*'s engines, and made a mess of it. It would be awkward for him to refuse now. He started thinking of reasons to refuse: lack of practical experience, a touch of tuberculosis discovered in his lungs two years ago, a sick old mother, nervous strain. . .

"It's a works we run, not a technical school," said Neuman angrily. "Whom can we send?" He sighed and looked at Bronnikov. "Got to be a Party member. We'll send Basov," he added, after a pause.

Bronnikov slipped quietly to the door and half opened it, trying not to make a noise. Outside he stopped for a while, pale with excitement. The director didn't seem to have any objection.

He brightened up and hurried to the workshop. In his joy he even forgave Basov the unpleasantness he had occasioned him. If that crank hadn't been there, it was hard to say how the matter would have ended for him, Bronnikov.

Basov did his best to appear satisfied. As soon as he was able fully to realize the necessity of the transfer, his permanent calm and bright mood would come back to him. Somebody had to be sent to service at sea, they had chosen him. Perhaps it wouldn't have happened but for that clash he had had with the chief engineer. But then somebody else would have been sent, Bronnikov, for instance; and Basov, of course, would not have felt indignant, or sorry for Bronnikov.

Musya listened without interrupting him. She folded her hands on her knees and looked sideways at him. When he stopped talking, she shook her head as though throwing a burden off herself.

"How unfortunately it's all turned out," she said controlling herself. "You're unlucky."

He had been expecting reproaches and a painful explanation. But there was none of all that. Musya opened the chest of drawers and took down some clothes hanging on the wall.

"You've got to get ready," she said. "Let's see what we must do."

She showed no surprise at all. She did not talk to him or even pay the slightest attention to him. She heated some water in the kitchen and got the tub ready for the washing. Basov stood beside her, watching the flakes of lather pearling down her bare arms. At that minute she really meant more to him than anybody on earth. He had entered a strange period in his life, when every achievement held prospects of further failure. He had got the tanker's diesel engine up to designed capacity, and as a result he was forced to leave the works. Neuman, Bronnikov and many others had become alien to him. Dull, helpless people think out limits to achievements to hide their helplessness. They make use of old, worn-out standards and false science. They league together, raise a fuss about imaginary dangers and stubbornly defend their own comfort.

Musya came back into the room and sat down by the window without putting the light on. She wrapped herself in a fluffy shawl and hunched her shoulders as though she felt a chill. Basov wanted to console and cheer her. Really, there was no reason for them to be downcast. How many famous captains, engineers and navigators there were in the fleet! Musya wanted him to get promotion. Well, they had given him the engine-room of the *Derbent*. The main thing was to understand the necessity of it. Somebody had to go to sea. If it wasn't him, it would be somebody else. What had they to be cut up about?

"That's the end of my life as a land-lubber," he said merrily. "I'll have to go down below and stir up the ghosts. Honestly, I'm even pleased, Musya. Is it because a thing's hard that you must refuse to do it? You'll receive our calls at the wireless station. You and I'll see each other once every five days. Yes, every five days..."

Musya nodded but said nothing. He could not see her face in the dark. He wondered what he could do to cheer her up for the farewell. The weather was mild, there was a fragrance of acacias, the air over the bay was blue. In the Water Transport Workers' Club, sailors were dancing a tango with students from the Industrial Institute to the accompaniment of a concertina. He wanted to take Musya there. The moon rolled over the flat roof of the house opposite and the light shadows of the clouds crept along the walls.

"Darling!" he called affectionately. "Look! What a moon!"

Musya slowly raised her head. Big shining tears trickled down her cheeks, wet the corners of her mouth and fell on to her breast. She bit her lips and dried her eyes with the corner of her shawl.

"You never did love me," she said with conviction. "I never meant anything to you."

It was so quiet in the room that he could hear her spasmodic breathing and the rustling of her dress. He stretched out to touch her shoulder, but she drew back.

"But that's not what I'm crying over. Don't get that into your head! I'm just sorry for you because you're such a failure. Why do you try to cheer yourself up, to deceive yourself and others? I've always been something secondary in your eyes. You've turned our life into one long hurry, you lived uncomfortably, as though in temporary lodgings: overtime, getting ready for circles, meetings and sleep. We've never lived like human beings. But all that doesn't matter, and I never breathed a word to you about it. You were working so much! But did you really work? You got the whole workshop against you, everybody shunned you. That's not what they do to people who are worth something. I'm sorry to say so, but to me you're just a failure, a weak, ridiculous fellow. They've got you out of the works. That's an insult! And you're satisfied. If you showed the slightest little bit of spite or got into a rage about it, it would be easier for me. Another chap will come instead of you, some bluffer, some good-for-nothing, and he'll draw a good wage..."

Her tears had dried but her voice was watery and trembling, she was in a hurry to load out in front of him all she had on her heart. And in the darkness it seemed that it was not Musya that he had before him, but a stranger, a stupid, cold, spiteful woman. He shouted wildly at the top of his voice:

"Shut up!"

She looked at him with fear and shielded her face with her hands as if she thought he was going to strike her. And at the same time she looked at him with some kind of strange hope. He controlled himself and raised a glass of water to her lips. She drank a little and pushed his hand aside disappointedly.

"Fancy saying such things," he said sadly. "They shun me, that's a fact. But it takes all sorts to make a life. It's only because I never left them in peace. In some shops they work badly, and I see that they can do better, much better. I think every workman will soon realize it. But for the time being they still go by old standards. But those standards were set up by men, and everything has changed since then. And I..."

Musya looked attentively at him, with sadness in her eyes. The way people look at a sick relative. He stopped in the middle of a word, as though he had come up against a wall. Perhaps they had really never meant anything to each other?

"Enough, Sasha dear," she said. "It's our last evening, you know. There's something else I wanted to say. That oil fleet—why, even sailors desert from it! They hide their qualifications, steal papers—I don't suppose you knew that. And we'll see so awfully little of each other."

Then she fell silent and smiled a guilty, frightened smile.

"D'you know what? I need you, darling, but what can I do when you're the way you are? I want something out of life, really, I do. Don't get angry!"

An amazing apathy suddenly came over him. Musya's fingers were stroking his hair and tickling his face. He felt the touch of her moist lips on his cheek. He rose quickly.

"Well, after all, we're not tied together," he said indifferently. "You can do as you like."

He left the house, and spent that night, his last night ashore, wandering about the town.

## RIFF-RAFF

### I

THE GREEN water swishes ceaselessly along the sides of the ship. Snow-white sheets of foam fall lazily aside. Countless bubbles scatter over the waves and burst noiselessly.

> *A little French girl called Nellie*
> *Was selling bouquets of camelia*

The steel deck is scorching under the sun. Sunshine sparkles in the waves, sunshine burns on the polished copper railings. The devil knows what the words of the song mean! The wind wafted them from no one knows where, and they stuck like sweet glue on Husein's lips. As soon as he gets drowsy, he starts humming them. He squats down by a hatch and gazes into the distance. When his hand-rolled cigarette has smouldered down to white ash it will be time to go down to the engine-room again.

The stream of air in the ventilation shaft is humming, the waves are rolling, rolling. It was like that yesterday, it will be like that tomorrow.

> *An English boy of good breeding*
> *Of her bright blue eyes was dreaming*

Husein is not thinking of the words of the song. He is wondering if there's a way of leaving the *Derbent* before the end of the season. Pretend to be ill? Start a brawl in port? No, that's no good. Not much prospect of leaving on good terms either. And yet there's not a man on the ship that you could really make friends with. On the first trips he got to know the whole crew, treated them to smokes, suggested games of dominoes. Sheer boredom drove him into every corner of the ship where there was the sound of voices or movement. After the first few trips the attraction of novelty wore off and the boredom became chronic.

Dogaylo, the bo'sun, scurries over the deck all day and his eyes of an anxious old man are always looking for something to be put in order. He's always in a hurry and never answers questions.

Husein tried to make friends with Alyavdin, the second mate. He began to tell him how he had been expelled from the Y.C.L. for drunkenness. But Vera the stewardess ran over the bridge and Alyavdin whispered: "We'll put that on the asset side," winked, burst out laughing and rubbed his hands, and Husein did not finish his story.

He tried to make up with the Y.C.L. chaps. They get on well together but keep to themselves too much. There are five of them: three electricians, one motor-man and the assistant engineer. They are demobilized Red Fleet men and service in the navy has given them love of discipline, remarkable tidiness in their dress and that deliberate businesslike concentration typical of people who are used to responsibility. Husein has a great liking for these young fellows and even goes rather out of his way to ingratiate them. One of them, Kotelnikov, an electrician, asked him all the details about that unfortunate spree of his, listened with a look half serene, half squeamish, as though it was something that might soil him. His curiosity vanished with the last question.

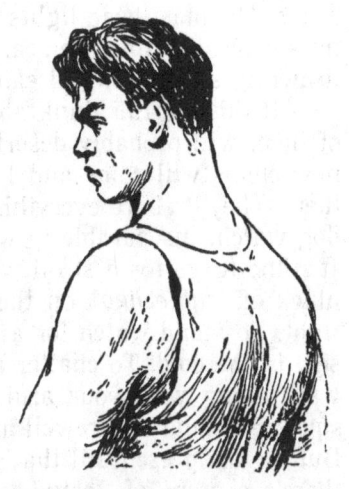

"Show by your work what you're worth," he said in a monitorial voice, "though I shouldn't think much will come of it. You don't just come in and go out of the Y.C.L. like that."

He looked round for a pretext to put an end to the conversation. Husein could have hid in a mouse-hole. Since then he has avoided the Young Communists. The others take no interest in his fate. O. K. He won't take any interest in them. Why should he?

It is thirty-eight hours' sailing to Astrakhan, and the return trip, light, takes thirty. Always the open sea, the blue sky overhead, and the bouncing wind. Captain Kutasov reads thick books in his cabin, wipes his red neck with his handkerchief and sighs with melancholy the while. Kasatsky, the navigation officer, lets down his venetian blind and hooks his door fast. He always smells of vodka but never stumbles and never raises his voice. He never favours Husein with a glance either. Alyavdin, the assistant navigation officer, plays a gramophone in his cabin. Saxophones croak, violins wail, cymbals ring. In the narrow passage between his berth and his clothes press, Alyavdin taps away, learning the steps of the latest European dances.

Husein doesn't read books, doesn't buy the latest gramophone records or straw-coloured ties. He doesn't dare drink vodka. Coming off watch, he purposely takes a long time over his shower just to kill time. The lather bubbles, the fine jets of water prickle his shoulders—the sea water is bitter. The mast-head lights flash like stars, damp cool darkness comes in from the sea. He sits on a hatch, humming a drawling stupid song, dreaming.

"All this riff-raff think about is how to get ashore. A lot of them will probably desert before the season's over. Then new chaps will come and I'll be able to make friends with them. They'll share everything alike and be together on the dog watch: inseparable in work, in misfortune and in rows. It's fine to go for a stroll with a friend on the sea-front, to pluck off *Yablochko** on the guitar, to dance in the moonlight. To stand watch for a pal in bad weather, on a rough sea, in the cold. To chatter away to your heart's content, to walk along with your arm round the other's shoulder, to squeeze a hand in farewell and promise friendship till death. But for the present all that's only a dream. On the *Derbent* there's a crew of forty-five—sailors, motor-men, navigators—but there's no real friendship."

There was Kasatsky escorting the captain over the spardeck, his hand under the captain's elbow, a dazzling naïve smile on his face. Kasatsky, the first mate, is the only one who can smile like that. Yes, that was the way he was smiling when he squeezed the girl on the buffer plates in the train.

"Pooh, Yevgeny Stepanovich! Take no notice of it," Kasatsky was trying to persuade the old man. "They kick up a row at the administration because we're a trifle late. It's time you got used to it! And besides, you're in their good books, my dear fellow."

What a friendly pair, the captain and the first mate. But an hour later Kasatsky was on the spar-deck again, this time with Alyavdin.

"The old man got a rocket by wireless," said Kasatsky composing his face into his official smile. "He's a decent old chap ... but so funky, lazy and weak-willed. If anything goes wrong he'll put all the blame on us. You'll see."

* The Apple—a Russian folk-song, popular among sailors.—Tr.

They nearly bumped into Husein as they went past.

Alyavdin, the second mate, would be whispering to someone else shortly. No, there was really no friendship on the *Derbent*! Only a crafty show of it—walking arm in arm, polite compliments and the cautious sting of venomous wit under the cover of a dazzling smile. He had no use for such friendship.

But Husein's worst luck was that his immediate chief was impossible. If he had the choice he would have chosen Kasatsky or Alyavdin. Basov, the chief engineer, was worse than either of them, even worse than any other of the forty-five men on the *Derbent*.

Basov went down to the engine-room during every watch. He looked like a man perpetually suffering from toothache, his eyes were bloodshot. He would stand, with a slight stoop, his elbows away from his body, as though rooted to the steel plating. Mechanics, fitters and motor-men would scatter in all directions from that motionless figure. He stood under the dim light of the lamps, bearing on his shoulders all the responsibility for the wildly thundering six-cylinder engines of the *Derbent*.

A belated motor-man appeared on the upper platform. His hands slid down the greasy rail of the ladder, his legs, still woolly with sleep, bending under him. As he reached the bottom and turned about, the chief engineer loosened the tight pressure of his lips:

"Had a good sleep? If not you can go back. We'll do without you."

The weak sounds of his voice were completely drowned by the din, but you could guess his words by the movements of his lips. The chief engineer had once been a rank-and-file motor-man himself. So the crew said. He could have had a little more heart for the chaps. Probably the sleeplessness that made his eyes so red had dried up his heart too.

"Son of a bitch!" muttered Husein with a look of hate at the broad back. "And a Party member too! Bloody sweater!"

Husein was never late for his watch himself. The chief engineer never had a harsh word for him. But they avoided each other and looked on each other as enemies. It would come to a clash one day, no doubt.

Towards the end of the watch, Basov went to the upper platform, where the electric motors were. There it was relatively quiet, hot and moist. The dynamos were humming softly behind the panels. Basov bent over the railing and listened to the beat of the engines. And strange to say, from all the corners of the engine-room the mechanics, motor-men and electricians assembled without the chief calling them. They went up the ladder, half naked, in shorts and grease-stained sleeveless vests. Streams of grimy sweat were running down their heat-flushed faces. Those who got there first leaned over the rail beside Basov. The others hung about in the rear.

"The port engine's doing a hundred and three revs," said Basov; "the starboard one—a hundred and five. I'm sure we could get a hundred and ten out of both."

The lads nudged one another pulling wry faces. The ship was only just off the stocks. Husein was infuriated by such boasting.

"Why don't you, then, Comrade Chief Engineer?" he asked provocatively. "There's nothing to it. Get down to the job and see it through!"

He looked round at his comrades, expecting approval from them.

Basov said calmly: "I can't do it by myself. And it's not so simple either. But you and I together will see it through all right."

He livened up and raised his head.

"The motor-men know as well as I do what's wrong. First, the injectors get fouled. That means the fuel flow to the cylinders is irregular. Secondly, the piston rings are no good. That's why there's not enough compression. The inspection engineers live ashore. But here on board we have sailors..."

Husein pushed forward, unconsciously leaning his elbows on his neighbours' shoulders. Ashy shadows crept over the chief engineer's face. He slowly lowered his head, as though preparing to rush at an invisible obstacle.

"Some motor-men are afraid to breathe on an engine because it was regulated ashore. This is not the place for the like of them. They should go and sail on lighters. They're not sailors! Regulate your engine yourself, time and again, and she'll show you what she's got in her and send her acceptance report to the devil. Am I right or not?"

He cast a glance over the men standing silent around him, and the light in his eyes went out. He wiped his forehead and trod on his cigarette end. The motor-men, electricians and fitters filed towards the door. Husein was reluctant to go. Before him was Basov's back with the shoulder-blades bathed in sweat. Had he turned round, Husein would have had the courage to speak up. But Basov hurried back to the engine-room and the last Husein saw was the stubbly cropped back of his head.

Freezing on the spot, he resumed by force of habit his defensive attitude to the indifferent world: "Trying to win authority. Ugh, putrid!"

There was nobody Husein could talk to, so he listened eagerly to others. He knew the chief engineer was not liked on board.

"They've gone and dumped a commissar on me," sighed the captain. "Today he told my political assistant the loading could be done quicker. Tomorrow he may start checking on me for all I know."

The captain's eyes filled with morbid senile fear, but Kasatsky's dazzling smile came to his help.

"Yevgeny Stepanovich, my dear fellow! Our esteemed engineer is not quite right,"—his finger went up to his forehead—"is it worth while getting alarmed?"

It did Husein good to see that he was not the only one to be miserable. There was another man near him fenced in with the same blank wall of hostility. But Basov did not seem to notice it. During loading he kept looking at his watch. He tried to interfere—poor ridiculous, incongruous chap with inflamed, bloodshot eyes. What could you do with such riff-raff? You got better chaps on freight ships, where the work was easier, the shore spells longer, and premiums more frequent. But here you got whoever happened to be at a loose end on shore when the tanker was launched. A lot of them were alcoholics, sick men, good for nothing. They smoked on the cargo deck against orders, they crawled about lazily like sleepy flies. That day Kozov, a motor-man, had been inspecting the lubricating pump. He just lifted the cover a little, got his fingers greasy, winked at Husein and twisted his face in a comical grimace. Husein had turned away. Wasn't it all the same to him? Let the engineer overwork himself, the motor-men take it easy, the sailors smoke on deck. Let the five Y.C.L. chaps have meetings. The tanker was not fulfilling its plan, it was at the bottom of the list for the season. What did it matter!

## II

They arrived in the roads behind time again. An icy spring north wind was piping in the rigging, snatching flakes of foam from the crests of the waves and dashing them on to the deck. It blew over from the horizon a curtain of clouds which screened off half the sky and rolled overhead shedding a drizzling rain.

In the wireless cabin Volodya Makarov had a job keeping awake and kept rubbing his eyes with his fists. He sprinkled sea-water on his face, sat down by his set, and sighed into the microphone.

"Astrakhan," his voice rang out. "Astrakhan roads! Why are you delaying our lighters?"

The sun appeared in the east—a leaden disc, wreathed with billowing rain-clouds. On the spar-deck the canvas cover of one of the ship's boats had blown loose and was flapping in the wind with a hollow noise.

"Astrakhan," Volodya said, "we radioed our arrival in time, where are the lighters?" He turned away from the microphone and started swearing with annoyance under his breath. Kotelnikov, the chief electrician, looked in through the wireless cabin window.

"Got them, Volodya?"

The operator nodded without speaking and reached for the headphones. He switched over to reception and started writing.

"I'd sack the lot of them if I had my way," said Kotelnikov sullenly. "The captain, the mates and all those shore rascals. They should all be sacked and new ones appointed!"

The operator was writing, bending over his paper, the tip of his tongue sticking out.

"They say there's been a mistake," he explained. "The tanker *Agamali* has taken our lighters. So who would you sack, comrade?"

"The lot of them. Do you call them commanders? Invalids with no brains left, that's what they are. We're becoming a laughing-stock. That trick with the lighters has saved the *Agamali* four hours. She passed us at sea, now she's going to have a six hours' start on us. But nobody bothers about that. They're laughing at us in the dispatching office, on the ships, and in the duty shop. We've not had a kopeck premium, it's a fact!"

Volodya drew a three-cornered sail and a hook-nosed head wreathed with smoke in the margin of the log-book. Then he cocked his head on one side and admired his drawing, sucking his pencil.

"There's me been barking into that phone for half an hour," he said grinning, "and I could just as well have shouted down the ventilation shaft. The devil take them! Who appreciates my work here? In a single month we've dropped behind by no less than half a million ton-miles. What can I do about it?"

"It's a fact."

"Yesterday they started taking oil in without pumping the ballast water out of the tanks. The captain shook like an old woman when they reported it to him. Then I heard Kasatsky giving his account of it to a government official—it appears it was the pumps that were to blame."

"It's a mess, Volodya."

"Couldn't be a bigger one!"

"The political assistant is a decent chap," said Kotelnikov, "he'd carry the cargo on his own shoulders if necessary. But he doesn't know a thing about navigation and he's afraid to interfere with the captain's orders. Besides, he's got T.B. I don't think he'll last long."

Meanwhile Volodya had been drawing a diver in full rig-out. He even smiled with self-satisfaction at his success.

"D'you know what, Stepa?"

"What?"

"Let's clear off this ship altogether." The operator lowered his voice and ran his tongue over his cherry-coloured lips. "I know where I'll go. To Epron. They're raising ships now that sank at Biryuchaya Kosa. There's a job!"

"They won't let us go," murmured Kotelnikov, looking anxiously around. "How can we leave the tanker? It would mean we got yellow sooner than the non-Party chaps. No, chuck that idea..."

"There's work for you there too," Volodya went on unruffled. "I found out. Perhaps we'll not bother about papers? But no, they'd probably take our Y.C.L. cards away from us."

"Don't talk nonsense!" Kotelnikov made a move as if to go. But he remained by the window. He was embarrassed and interested. Volodya's proposal had the effect of a magnet on him.

"Suppose we try through the District Party Committee?" he said doubtfully. "But no, they won't let us go."

"Rot! We're not slaves just because we carry out orders. I'd like to see them keep me here against my will!"

"No, deserting's not the thing," said Kotelnikov, firmly, though without any warmth. "Perhaps we'll be able to arrange things. Besides, I'm chairman of our ship's trade union committee. Still, find out about Epron, just in case." He had a strained smile as he said the last words.

Steps rang out hollow and uneven on the spar-deck and were lost in the wind. Somebody strode with long paces past the cabin, bent forward as though pressing on in the face of a strong wind.

"Basov," Volodya whispered. "He didn't hear us, did he?"

"Dunno." Kotelnikov backed away from the window. "Well, enough of this panic-mongering. It's not the thing for Young Communists. There are the lighters coming alongside!"

### III

Pale green waves with brown oil patches swept over the roadstead like terrified light-footed beasts. The lighters greeted them with a creaking and a cautious dipping of their steep rusty sides. The black, toy-like tug dropped the dripping cable into the water, gave a deafening hoot, and churned away through the waves, leaving a swirling foamy wake behind.

The *Derbent*'s pumps were at work. The deck vibrated slightly and rose gradually above water level. Basov was standing on the bridge by the railing, his elbows pressed to his sides to keep warm.

"This sea's not shaped right," said Dogaylo, the bo'sun, who was standing near Basov. "I'd even say it's settled most awkwardly this Caspian."

He stuck forward the toe of his huge top boot, which looked as if it had been moulded in cast iron with the leg itself.

"Our sea's drying up, feeding the soil. You know the old Devichya Bashnya* in Baku? It's two minutes' walk from the sea now. There's a legend that wicked Khans locked up a poor girl in it and she pined away with grief. The tower stood in the water then. The sea withdrew, laying bare the

* The Maiden's Tower.—*Tr.*

rocks. It's just the same in the Astrakhan roads: the water used to be deep here. Now it's dangerous for a ship with more than twenty foot displacement to come closer in than the Tyulen Bank. There's water all round, as far as the eye can see, but it's not navigable."

The bo'sun's voice was high-pitched, soft, and musical. Basov looked with astonishment at the bo'sun's Adam's apple, which seemed to burst out of his pea-jacket collar, and said in a tone of assurance:

"We'll dredge it soon and then tankers will be able to go right to Astrakhan without any trans-shipping."

Dogaylo gave a quiet laugh, looked at Basov with mild pity, and slowly took off his cap. The wind ruffled the sparse fluffy hair on his egg-shaped head.

"Nothing's hard for you, you can do anything. But I should think that before you educated people racked their brains over that and gave it up. The reason here is treacherous currents and alluvion: they'll play havoc with your work and clog your channels with sand. No, you'll not have it your way!" He pronounced the last words triumphantly with another steady look of disapproval at Basov. The latter was not inclined to argue. He moved away along the bridge.

When all was said and done, Basov had had his own men at the works. Men like the fitters, Voron, the brigade-leader, and Eybat, the little turner. On the *Derbent* there were so many sections, rooms and mechanisms. There were a lot of men with different jobs to do. But Basov had no friends. He looked at those around him, but as his eyes met theirs, faces got bored, pupils narrowed and disappeared between eyelashes. The men scattered in front of him, all sluggish and incomprehensibly alike. Their diligence seemed to be put on, their seriousness—preposterous. They moved in silence, as in a dream, along the narrow passages in the engine-room, swallowed the hot air and sat down wherever they happened to be. They turned the fly-wheels in silence, the muscles bulging on their wet backs. Before the change of watch they gathered on the upper platform, listened to his explanations and stared at him as if he had been a curiosity from another land. Sometimes he would turn up unnoticed and would see the motor-man Husein squatting and swaying as he hummed to himself some trashy song, or two other motor-men Kozov and Gazaryan goggling wearily at the light with smoke-black rings round their eyes.

"Do you call them a crew? They should be sent back to where they came from and new ones mustered instead!" one of them would say.

"Ah, my dear fellow! Do you call them sailors?"

And they complacently agreed with each other, as though the pair of them were the only real sailors on board, and the *Derbent* could do with many more like them. They lied to each other and lied each to himself. In fact, they had long given up any concern for ton-miles or the number of revolutions of the engines. . . .

Floods of water splashed on to the decks out of the open cocks. Streams ran on all sides, covered with a rugged coat of dust. The sailors moved over the wet slippery steel deck, pushing with difficulty their mops wrapped in soaking cloths. Dogaylo fussed about among them, like a shuttle flying to and fro. One of the sailors, the clean-shaven Khru-lev, climbed up on the stern with his guitar under his arm and a cigarette behind his ear. Tossing his fair curly mop from his fore-head he started thrumming the strings:

*The doctor asks: where's the
pain?
For sev'n men my heart's
aflame.
Oh! What a dame!*

Basov paced the quarter-deck. His gaze mechanically

followed a gull circling over the waves. The bird dropped like a pinkish white ball and skimmed the water with its wing. Khrulev plucked a last wailing twang from the strings, yawned, and cast an indifferent look at Basov.

By the entrance to the engine-room, in the monotonous hum of the engines, Basov pictured to himself that little world encompassed by the blue line of the horizon, diminutive and colourless like a bloated eye, in which everybody was satisfied with his own insignificance but despised the others for theirs. "My dear fellow, do you call them a crew!"

At the works Basov had been considered a good organizer, but the works had existed before he came and would go on existing after he had gone: here everything had to be started from scratch. How? He was tortured by his powerlessness, his unavailing efforts to improve things. But it was not in him to be indifferent, to take it easy, to shut himself up in his cabin. His tenacious brain, though racked and stunned with fatigue, kept aching and goading him: he had to act, to give everything a new start, keep the men on board when the ship berthed, overhaul the engines, increase the revs. . . .

### IV

Yevgeny Stepanovich Kutasov stood by his cabin window and watched his wife laying out her purchases on the table: a bundle of newspapers, a bottle of wine and some coffee.

The town lights shimmered through the half-drawn blinds. They were sometimes blacked out by dense smoke, as though clouds had fallen to the earth and were creeping along the streets.

"The Solntsevs asked to be remembered to you," said Natalia Nikolayevna; "Dynnik too, and Simochka and her husband. Are you listening, Yevgeny?"

Shouts and the squeaking of crane cabels came from the pier. Long, shaggy shadows like spiders' legs, crept across the window. The names his wife had mentioned were those of old colleagues from the records department.

"It's very kind of them," said Yevgeny Stepanovich. "Will you give them my..."

Somebody came hurrying along the corridor and knocked at the door.

"Who's there?" asked Yevgeny Stepanovich. "What do you want?"

"Everything's ready for loading, Yevgeny Stepanovich. The pipes are laid. May we start filling?"

"Yes." Yevgeny Stepanovich hesitated for a minute by the door, fingering the bolt. The steps got near the end of the corridor. Suddenly Yevgeny Stepanovich flung the door open and shouted after them:

"Just a minute, my lad. Ask Kasatsky. It's his watch, he's the one to ask."

"Aye, aye, captain! Ask Kasatsky," came the answer.

Natalia Nikolayevna observed her husband attentively. After a short pause she asked:

"Who's Kasatsky, Yevgeny?"

"Well, er..." Yevgeny Stepanovich stopped to think. "He's the first mate. He has great respect for me and we understand each other. What I like about him is his inborn tact and his great culture. He seems a man you can rely upon. So together we manage to wriggle through in this bedlam."

"The reason why I asked you," said Natalia Nikolayevna, "is that I have a feeling there's something wrong here. In the management there is a lot of talk about the *Derbent*. Aren't you too trusting towards your men, Yevgeny?"

Kutasov looked round at the door, then at the window. His face changed instantaneously, the serenity of old age giving way to a faltering distressed smile, while the corners of his mouth creased in wearied grievance.

"I'm rather uneasy myself, my dear," he said, lowering his voice confidentially. "I sometimes have a feeling that something is really happening around me. These men, you see, when I see them stand in front of me and listen to me, I don't believe they could deceive me. But when I'm alone..."

"Don't get excited. When you're alone?"

"Everything seems different. I'm not so trusting as I seem. Yesterday we were shockingly late and we sent a radio message about the weather being unfavourable. There was no bad weather to speak of, just a moderate wind. Kasatsky is an expert in the art of persuasion, and he always takes it upon himself to write such telegrams. But this time it was really not the thing."

Natalia Nikolayevna boiled with anger.

"Then why were you so crazy as to agree? Don't you see that it's not right, it's ignoble! Why did you give in?"

"Sh-sh. Don't shout, please. I gave in because we were, in fact, in an awkward spot. The devil knows why we were late! For some reason they kept us waiting for the lighters in the roads. The pumps were working badly. That's not my responsibility. Everything is so slack here, as if some kind of general decay had set in. The personnel department were in too much of a hurry getting the crew together. It's most unsatisfactory."

He lapsed into a gloomy silence, scratching a stain on his sleeve with his nail.

"I'm fed up with it, Natasha. And the worst of all is the constant alarm. The ship is manned with riff-raff, a rabble, soakers. And it's a new ship, with a maze of complicated mechanisms, and an inflammable cargo in the holds. If anybody were to shout 'Fire!', I think my heart would burst. The political assistant is a sick man. Kasatsky wriggles out of everything. Basov, the chief engineer, tries to get the motor-men up to scratch. But there you are, the chap has taken a dislike to me, I don't know what for. It seems to me that I'm friendly towards them all, always have a good word for every one. But he looks at me with hate in his eyes and hardly answers my questions. Kasatsky says he's abnormal, but that's not true. Perhaps he's keeping an eye on me.... So you say there are some kind of rumours?"

In the mirror opposite, Yevgeny Stepanovich saw his own sad, aged face. He felt so sorry for himself that he could have wept: weren't they all deceiving him, playing mean tricks on him, spreading rumours? Yet he asked for nothing and wished nobody any harm. Was it his fault that he knew nothing about diesels and pumps? That he was sensitive and could not be harsh with the men?

Yevgeny Stepanovich could feel creeping on him that soft-hearted mood that could come over him only in the presence of his wife, and which always ended in mild self-accusation on his part and protests on his wife's.

"I just can't force anybody else's will, Natasha," he began, pitiably. "Conflicts hurt me, and I am satisfied when I give in to others. Unfortunately, that is not what life demands."

He expected objections which would fit in with his own character and relieve him of his feeling of dissatisfaction with himself. Then he would have felt lighter at heart, like a child that has had a good cry on its mother's breast. But suddenly Natalia Nikolayevna seemed to be in a hurry.

"Oh, I was forgetting," she said rising. "A clean handkerchief, Yevgeny. I've been holding it in my hand all this time. Here, take it."

She stroked his hair and kissed him. Then she hurried away, as though afraid he would begin to speak again.

"You'll get over it all, somehow," she said mildly. "Please don't forget to put on your sheepskin coat for the night watch. The nights are still very cold. Well, it's time. And you know, Yevgeny, I think you should go on the bridge now."

V

Before sunset, Bredis, the political assistant, went out on deck. His lips, parched with fever and his illness, looked like dark half-healed wounds. Round burning red patches on his sallow cheeks gave a deceptive impression of health. He blew on his cold hands and looked round.

On the edge of the sea, a yellow strip of coast was bathed in the rays of the setting sun. The sea shone with dazzling brightness and the sky was a transparent blue. Martles flashed black as they soared above the masts. On deck, Dogaylo was tinkering about near the windlass.

Bredis could hardly stand on his feet. How blinding was the radiance of the sea, how satiating the smell of heavy oil, how irritating the hammering on iron! He tried to remember the bo'sun's curious name, but it had slipped his memory. Hell, how awkward it was! He couldn't remember people's names, he didn't know what was happening on board. He was bordering on despair. His illness was no excuse. It was his job, as political assistant, to see that the plan was fulfilled—and there was no reason why it should not be. That duty was so simple, so concrete, yet at the same time so unachievable... His many years' experience in leadership, his knowledge of men, and his skill in persuasion were of little help in circumstances so new to him. The lack of qualification in the haphazard crew, the unaccustomed mechanisms, the bad service from the shore people, and lastly his illness which kept him in his cabin—everything seemed to conspire against him in that decisive period in his life. He could feel his strength dwindling and did not know what to do.

The chief engineer came out of the engine-room. He looked to the west and then up into the cloudless sky. He did so deliberately, as though enjoying the vastness that stretched before him. Fearing he would go back, Bredis called him.

"You here?" asked Basov in surprise. "What are you up for? You have a temperature, Bredis."

He went up to him and held out his greasy hand.

"I was looking for you," said Bredis with animation. It had occurred to him that the chief engineer was just the man to speak to about the situation on board. "If only you knew how sick I am of my cabin!"

Like a man tortured by a fixed idea, he at once started talking about the *Derbent*'s arrears. He had reckoned that the ship had transported over twenty thousand tons less than it should have done. The lag was made up of small hold-ups in loading and unloading, and it increased at sea because of insufficient speed. Filling up at berth number 80, the tanker had gone aground because they had not cast off in time. An hour had passed before the tugs came, and it had taken another hour to get off the shallows.

Bredis was bewildered by the number and variety of the causes. Nobody seemed to be to blame, there was nobody you could pounce upon, nobody you could accuse of not doing his job. The captain was so alarmed that the very sight of him made you pity him. But the delays were accumulating, and all the petty causes made a gap it would be hard to bridge.

"Who's to blame for it?" asked Bredis, overcoming a fit of coughing. "We, the Party members. I am to blame—I shouldn't be lying up at a time like this, I should keep an eye on everything. Yes, of course I'm to blame. And so are you, and the other Communists! We should have fought against it!"

"There aren't so many Communists among us," Basov replied, laughing. "You and I and then five Y.C.L. members. That means that you and I are the chief culprits."

He smiled gloomily and savagely, the corners of his mouth twitching. You would have thought he was going to clench his teeth and start swearing viciously, or do something violent. Bredis felt uneasy.

"I can see you've been worrying yourself to death," he said softly. "I didn't mean you, really..."

Basov waved him off.

"Don't you be in such a hurry to accuse yourself, old chap. It's other people's business to say whether we're to blame or not. They'll kick us out of the Party and that'll be the end of it." He looked his companion in the eyes with a pitiless grin. "They'll put reliable chaps in our places. But that's not what I'm thinking about now. They're new engines we've got, aren't they, and the loading mechanisms are in order. That means the men are to blame. We can still straighten things out before the end of the season; we will not only catch up our arrears, we'll overfulfil the plan."

"It's fine to hear you say it," Bredis said impatiently, "but I don't understand what you're relying on. Letting things take their course?"

"It's an amazing lot of men we've got here," Basov went on unhurriedly. "You see, they don't feel that their job is part of their lives. They're as indifferent as statues. They wouldn't care a damn if everything was on fire. Perhaps Kotelnikov's right, and they're nothing but riff-raff. But other ships, in the same circumstances, carry out their tasks, day in day out. Take the *Agamali*, for instance. She has on board a lot of demobbed Red Navy men—splendid fellows they are. They made fun of our chaps not long ago, when they were buying bread at the stall on the pier. Slow-coaches, they called them, floating coffins. The radio operator said they nearly came to blows. That's fine. Then they got premium money on the *Agamali* and we shan't get any. That's fine. In a word, our chaps must be given to understand that they're as bad as they make 'em."

Bredis smiled and shook his head, like a musician detecting a false note.

"Just a minute, man. What you're saying is not quite the thing. According to you, it's only a matter of ambition and of earnings. That's not the way to look at it. At the front we fought to death, my dear fellow, even though we got no premiums. We staked our lives for freedom and for the Soviet power. And here it's just like at the front, the same war, if you like. If we don't deliver oil, there'll be no petrol, no lubricants. Nothing to drive the tractors and planes. Is that clear? You've got to get it into their heads that they must work for all they're worth. Why, what are the chaps in charge of those engines of yours? Your own brothers, workmen, proletarians, not riff-raff.

"Even if they're not educated, they'll instinctively understand revolutionary talk. It's their consciousness you've got to develop, not their ambition."

He was shivering with fever, and was shifting from one foot on to the other to overcome the pain. Basov listened apathetically.

"What you say is not new to me, nor to them either, I should think. It seems to me it's harder sometimes to ship heavy oil than to fight at the front. They know the country needs fuel, but they still don't feel any responsibility for their job. They go to sleep on watch, behave disorderly in port. On the last trip some beast left a rag in the lubricating pump. It's no use my talking to them about the importance of oil shipments until they have some sense of shame!"

"What, do you despise them?"

"No, I don't. They're on our side, of course. Though with Alyavdin, the second mate, it's a different matter. But still, they're such a motley lot, it's hard to get on with them. And with our commanders too."

"It's hard everywhere," Bredis agreed thoughtfully. He pulled out his cigarette case and then fumbled for a match. "Listen, Basov. Perhaps you're right. If we could organize emulation. . ."

"We will," Basov replied with unexpected amusement in his voice. He smiled, grasped Bredis's hand and took the match away from him. "By the way, it's dangerous to smoke on deck. You can get blown up."

"Oh, hell!" Furious with himself, the political assistant crumpled his cigarette. He went red to the roots of his hair. "Fancy me forgetting!"

"Worse than at the front, eh?" asked Basov, laughing.

"Aye, perhaps it is!"

## VI

While they were in harbour, Husein managed to get away into town. He met Zhenya at the agreed place. He suggested going to a cinema and then to the beach: he only had three hours at his disposal, but he thought they would have time to go to a café and then to a sports field where a competition was going on. Zhenya preferred the industrial exhibition. In the end they stayed on the boulevard.

Not many people were there at that early hour. Birds were chirping in the bushes, the acacias were shedding their white petals. Zhenya, in a yellow blouse which seemed to blaze in the sun, looked very attractive. She gave Husein no peace, making him tell her about life on the tanker. The sight of her bright lips tortured him with the desire to kiss her.

"So that chap in the train is on the same ship as you?" she asked. "How did you welcome each other? Did he recognize you? I can imagine how stupid you both looked!" She laughed.

It was quite out of place to recall the adventure in the railway carriage. Husein got embarrassed and hid his hands behind his back. She was a real girl—good, and trusting. He spoke to her in a rough and ready way but did not dare to touch her hands. They chatted on merrily, not noticing the time go by.

"I've often thought of you since we parted," she admitted, without any embarrassment. "I think your life is a very interesting one. I read about oil shipments in the *Bolshevik Kaspia*.* The country depends on them for fuel supply. On the whole, matters don't seem to stand too well, though certain ships are doing more than their task. How are you working, Mustapha? I should like to be in your place. For the time being, I'm still a student, still getting ready for life, but other people around me are already in the thick of it. And I should like to take an active part in life, to work with people, and have responsibility. I've been thinking of you a lot. You seem so fiery and tenacious, so fearless. Perhaps you're destined to become a famous sailor; there are quite a number of them already in our waters. I'm romantic,

* *The Caspian Bolshevik*—newspaper.—*Tr.*

94

Mustapha," she added with confidential earnestness. "You mustn't laugh at me."

Husein was astonished at the unexpected turn of the conversation. The girl was interested in oil shipments and his work. She would even like to be in his place. Romance? Where was the romance in their lives? He could not help laughing.

"This is a boring conversation, Zhenya," he said like an adult explaining to a child the absurdity of it. "Our work is hard and dirty, and the worst of it is, it's all in vain. The tanker's not fulfilling its plan, we've not mastered the mechanisms, and everybody on board is at loggerheads with the others. The commanders are no good and the crew still worse. *Beachcombers*, riff-raff..."

"Beachcombers?"

"Yes. It's an English word, you see. In English it means an unemployed sailor, a vagrant. We have no unemployed, so we use the word in another sense. Beachcombers are idlers, riff-raff. D'you understand now? Between you and me, I'm a bit of a beachcomber myself"—he added unexpectedly with sincere unconcern—"and as for being famous—ugh! They know me well enough in the militia stations."

"How dare you speak like that!" She flung the words at him in her vexation. "You ought to be ashamed of yourself."

She blushed and seemed offended. Husein was sorry for what he had said.

"Why, I'm talking to you like a friend," he said, embarrassed. "I exaggerated a little. We'll get over it all. We're a long way behind schedule now, but if we pull ourselves together and set the engines right... The port diesel engine gives a hundred and two revs, the starboard one a hundred and five.... I'm sure we could get every bit of a hundred and ten out of both..."

He remembered that the chief engineer had used those very words, and it gave him an unpleasant feeling. "Nothing but boasting," he thought, with his usual malice. But Zhenya raised her head and smiled.

"You see," she said conciliatingly. "What rubbish you talk about yourself! When you squeezed that coin in your fist, I got goose-flesh. I was horrified and thrilled at the same time. You were so calm. But now you go and spoil it all. You, a beachcomber!"

"Can't a chap have a joke?" Husein grinned with self-satisfaction. "But talking about those diesels. If we manage to raise the speed to thirteen knots, we'll ship what we're down for. Our chief engineer is an intelligent chap, though he's a bit of a bully. By himself, of course, he can't do anything. But with us motor-men, it's a different matter. To set the engines right, we'll have to work when we're in harbour, that is, go without shore leave."

"A great pity that would be!" Zhenya struck in bravely. "What about it, if you've got to?"

"That's just what I say. We certainly will. But all's not well with our motor-men. Some of them are afraid to go near the engines because they were regulated ashore. There's no room for the like of them on a tanker. They're not sailors! (Basov again, came the fleeting thought, but without any malice this time.) Regulate your engine time and again, then she'll show you what she's got in her. That's the way it is, Zhenya. But you just forget about the beachcomber stuff. I was only joking just now."

Sitting beside him was a pretty and decent girl the like of whom he had never met before in his life. Her eyes, which a minute before had shed burning scorn on him, now probed him, as though testing the earnestness of his words. And he suddenly felt an unbearable regret that the victory he had conjured up and of which he had spoken with such shameless assurance would probably never be a reality.

## THE CHALLENGE

### I

Soon, the electricians, on their return from shore, spoke about another brush with the men of the *Agamali*. Confusion could be seen on their faces, their cheeks were burning.

"They're leaving port two hours after us," Kotelnikov related, "and they said: There you are, we're giving you two hours' start. You can expect us towards evening, we'll catch up with you and take you in tow...."

"No!"

"Their very words! You won't lose anything by it, they said, and it'll be a feather in our hat!"

"Internal combustion tortoises, they said," put in Volodya Makarov.

"Who's tortoises?"

"They meant us. Making fun of us, the rotters!"

"The bo'sun said...."

"I don't give a damn who said it," snapped the irritated Husein. "But really, boys, will they overtake us?"

"They oughtn't to...."

"We've got to get ready," Khrulev gibed hoarsely, shaking his curly mop. "Hey, chairman of the ship's trade union committee, smarten the crew up!"

Everything went on as usual that day: watches were changed, weather reports came over the wireless, the men had their lecture in politics. Only the sailors often went up on the spar-deck without any need and looked back south where the land disappeared behind a line of blue. After twelve, a hardly perceptible spot appeared there. It grew slowly, poised at the meeting of the sky and the sea like a speck on the clear line of the horizon. Dogaylo was the first to notice it as he went about the spar-deck looking for something that needed putting in order. He gave a long low whistle and went down to report what he had seen. On deck, the electricians were cleaning the collector of the electric motor.

"The *Agamali* is coming!" Dogaylo announced in an exultant falsetto. "Going all out! She'll overtake us by evening, you bet!"

The electricians ran to the spar-deck and Dogaylo jogged after them, laughing to himself.

"P'raps it's a gun-boat," suggested Protsenko, one of the electricians.

"You don't say so! Then, where's the smoke? There isn't any. No, old chap, that's no gun-boat. It's a motorship."

The motor-men and sailors off duty appeared one after another on the spar-deck. They shaded their eyes with their hands to look at it and then went away without a word. Dogaylo walked up and down the deck as usual. But from time to time he would look at the *Agamali*. On the navigator's bridge, Kasatsky raised his binoculars to his eyes to watch the approaching ship. It kept on growing as though blown nearer by the damp whistling south wind. Kasatsky lowered his binoculars; a frozen smile stretched the corners of his mouth.

More members of the crew kept coming on the spar-deck, hurriedly searching the horizon for the ship's silhouette and estimating the distance between the ships. They all did so in silence, without looking at one another, as though just by chance, trying to hide their uneasiness.

Just before the sun went down, the *Agamali* veered sharply to the right, and showed the *Derbent* its white superstructure and its short funnel sending up thin puffs of smoke at the stern. The end of the watch came. The sailors ran to the fore-and-aft bridge and stood by the rail. The motor-men formed a group round Husein. He was standing with his heavy hands on the rail, and you could see the vein pulsing on his dark motionless face over the left brow.

Basov appeared on the bridge as the ships came level with each other. He looked from the motionless Husein to the navigator Alyavdin, who was stamping nervously with excitement, and to the faces of the sailors, motor-men and electricians gathered on the bridge. Dogaylo went tramping past towards the ladder leading to the stern.

"We must salute our model," he drawled ironically. "Tell her we respectfully make way for her and wish her happy sailing!"

He climbed up the ladder, a few men following him out of curiosity.

"Don't! Stop it, Dogaylo!" came a weak protest from Alyavdin, but the bo'sun did not hear it. He went to the flag at the stern and untied the knot. Three times he dipped the cord, and the broad red flag, fluttering in the breeze, obediently slid down the staff and dropped at his feet.

From the bridge it was easy to see what was happening on the deck of the *Agamali*. Motionless figures could be seen on the bridges. Others were dragging a cable over the deck, its steel coils straightening out like a spring. The flag on her stern was still waving in the breeze, nobody was in any hurry to dip it in reply to the salute.

"They're up to mischief," observed Dogaylo quietly as he came back. "See, they're dragging a cable up. Want to take us in tow, indeed."

The men on the *Agamali*'s deck seemed to be carrying out some serious job thought out beforehand. They threw the end of the tow line overboard, and it dangled zigzagging over the water. The ship was already ahead, showing her round stern. Silence reigned on deck.

"The cads!" said Dogaylo, shaking his head. "Did we arrange a race with them? We've not got the engines they have. The engineer'll tell you. A rum lot they are!"

Eyes were turned towards him, some of the men started smiling. His sing-song voice had a soothing influence on them. Khrulev, who had kept aloof so far, went up to Husein, swaying his body as he went, and tapped him on the shoulder.

"Pick up the tow line, Mustapha," he said, looking round as though inviting the others to join in the fun. "Your engine won't get us anywhere anyhow. Don't miss your chance, old chap."

Husein started as though he had been stung and raised his clenched fist. His face was contorted with the insult.

"Get away, you parasite," he madly roared, advancing on the sailor, "or I'll wring your neck!"

Khrulev backed away, thrusting his hands out in front of him.

"Keep your hands to yourself," he said in a low hasty voice. "I only said it for fun. See that, boys?"

They were immediately surrounded by a noisy ring of onlookers. Volodya Makarov's round freckled face peeped over Husein's shoulder.

"Don't start a fight, Mustapha," he shouted angrily. "Do you call him a man? If you spit in his face he'll just wipe it!"

"What's going on here?" shouted Alyavdin authoritatively. "No fighting, boys!"

Basov came quickly up to the noisy group on the bridge. He could hear Volodya's boyish voice shouting:

"Why do we stick on the shallows at the piers? Why do we only do eight knots light? Tell me, somebody!"

"I'll give you the answer, Volodya," said Basov, elbowing his way to the radio operator. "We'll take the shine out of them on the next trip."

They were all looking at him now, and his voice wavered for a second with the tension. A thought flashed through his brain: he must not make a mess of it now. He looked for the political assistant, but he was not there.

"What's the bawling for?" Basov inquired roughly, and meeting Husein's roving eyes he turned towards him. "Of course, the *Agamali* sailors don't consider us as men. And if you find that funny"—he swung quickly round to Khrulev —"it means you agree yourself that you're not worth your salt."

"He's not the only one," said Volodya in a thin voice. "They don't care a damn for anything. It's their fault if we're racking ourselves for nothing."

Somebody behind Basov turned round and he felt his hot breath on his neck. Basov spoke up in a firm voice:

"We can take the shine out of them. They may be at the top of the list now, and every living thing in the petrol dock can curse us. All the same, we can beat them. The first thing is to get the engines in order. The second—to save time in port. . ."

"And when will we have time off?" somebody put in with a sneer. But the others immediately silenced him. Basov did not even turn round.

"Save time. Treasure every minute. The officer on watch during loading must see that we pull off from shore in time so as not to get stuck on the shallows. We must put the auxiliary diesels in condition at sea. Why, we'll have the water boiling under us if we want to!"

"There won't be any sticking on the shallows in my watch," declared Alyavdin with unexpected heat.

"What's the use of talking? Let's get down to it," said a low voice at the back.

"Shall we get down to it?" asked Husein, looking doubtfully round at the faces of his neighbours, as though he did not yet believe that they could get down to it at once, just like that.

"Ah, come on you chaps, let's do it!" Volodya said, snatching his cap off his head and clutching it in his fist.

Kotelnikov was biting his finger nails.

"What we need is to enter into emulation," he said tensely.

"Ugh, that'd be a big handful," said somebody. "Suppose it doesn't work?"

"We will enter into emulation," said Basov. "We'll challenge them over the wireless. But that's not the question now. Once we make up our minds, all the engine-crew will have to work when we're in port."

There came a short silence. Kozov stuck his hands in his pockets and gazed at the smooth surface of the sea. Gazaryan, one of the motor-men, hung his head and muttered: "How can I go without shore leave when my mother's ill? She's old, I can't..."

"That's hard lines," Kotelnikov observed tartly with screwed-up eyes. "Why, there was nothing wrong with her before! Did you get to know by wireless?"

"You can wallow in the bars, we'll do without you!" shouted Husein with a threatening glance at the motor-man. He was so wrought up that his face kept quickly changing; now it was beaming, now menacing. "Anyone who leaves the ship in port is a rotter!"

"Everybody will stay, don't you worry," said Basov. "Nobody likes to be spat upon. And if anybody does go ashore, well, it'll be one less in the way." He nodded to Husein and went towards the engine-room. But Volodya Makarov ran after him.

"Alexander Ivanovich, the chaps will be working in the engine-room, but what about me? My wireless cabin's in order."

"You've got no business in the engine-room, you're not a mechanic," was Basov's hesitating answer. "Anyhow, damn it! It's not a question of mechanics now. Come by all means!"

## II

Husein woke up in the dark. The bulkheads were vibrating from the throb of the engines, which was regular and monotonous like the pulsing of the blood in his ears. He raised himself a little in his berth and jumped down. He had a fancy that he was late, that the ship was lying in the harbour. But the eye-like port-hole was dark and empty, and through it he could hear the splash of the waves and the soft whistling of the wind. He dashed out into the corridor, almost knocking down a man who was going past.

"Come," said Basov, worriedly, "I've been looking for you. We've just left Zhiloy Island behind. It's time to begin."

They went past the galley with its hot walls, past the row of cabins, to the engine-room entrance. There Basov stopped.

"Nearly all the crew's gathered in there," he said, laughing. "It's a good start, though we don't need them all to regulate the engines."

"Why not?" asked Husein in surprise. "You said yourself..."

"Yes, I did insist on having all hands on the job. It's better for the first success to be the fruit of a general effort. Then everybody'll have the right to be proud, and there won't be anybody near the engines who hasn't an interest in them."

"That's true," Husein agreed. He felt pleased at the chief engineer consulting him and not the others, marking him out, as it were, from the rest of the crew. "You've got the right idea there. But I shouldn't think there'll be work for everybody. Shouldn't we send useless ones away?"

"Plenty of time to send them away," said Basov, "but I don't think there are likely to be any onlookers."

In the engine-room the men were standing in groups on the platforms, talking to one another and trying to make themselves heard above the din. At the sight of such an unusual gathering Husein was embarrassed. He knew every one of those men and considered more than half of them good for nothing. They had not the least spark of initiative; they always tried to get their watch over as quickly as possible. You had to keep an eye on them all the time. And it was with such chaps that Basov wanted to put the engines right!

Going down the ladder behind the chief engineer, Husein felt everybody's eyes riveted on him and it made him feel awkward, as though he was trying to pass for what he was not.

"You'll replace the piston rings," Basov said to him. "Take five fitters and motor-men. And keep your eyes open when you raise the pistons."

Husein's embarrassment increased: the chief engineer had two assistants, and yet for some reason he preferred to put his trust in him. And how could he, Husein, "keep his eyes open," being only a motor-man himself and never having been in charge of men?

Basov laid out on his hand the diagrams of the indicators. The crew clustered round him, and Husein stood for a while not knowing what to do. He could not hear the chief engineer's voice for the din of the engines. Gradually he was overcome by the melancholy thought which always came to him in moments of inaction: the chief engineer would raise the number of revs of the engine, put in a report and get credit for it. What business was that of his, Husein's? He had only made a fool of himself the day before on the bridge.

Suddenly, he saw Basov waving to him, and feeling himself once more the object of general attention he flushed and arched his brows fiercely. He stared vacantly at the diagrams Basov was holding out to him.

"See here," Basov said, poking at the sheets with his finger. "That's the first stroke of the piston. Here the lack of compression gives a distorted curve. And there's a correct diagram—that of the fifth cylinder. See the difference? Where must we change the piston rings then?" He held the diagram out to Husein and put his hand on his shoulder.

Zadorov, Basov's assistant, looked over from the side and prompted him impatiently.

"In the third and fourth, of course."

"I don't need you to tell me," Husein snapped. "We must change them in the third and fourth cylinders, Alexander Ivanovich."

On the upper platform, they were fitting rings on a spare piston. The five-foot long cylindrical body of the piston was lying on the platform, blocking the way into the workshop. Kozov, Gazaryan, and two fitters were struggling to lift it in order to slip the rings over it. They were crimson from the exertion and were shouting at each other as though ready to come to blows.

"The lads are straining themselves while the crane's having a rest," Basov joked. "Go up to them, Mustapha."

Husein hurried up. As he approached, the men dropped the piston and straightened up.

"The crane's out of order," Yakubov, a fitter, explained coolly. "Probably the chain's jumped. What are you looking at? We've been told to have it done by the time the ship berths, and we're trying to do it somehow..."

He smiled good-naturedly, mopping his broad, kindly face with his handkerchief. Husein had always had a liking for that artless young fellow, but for some reason he got wild this time.

"Somehow, anyhow!" he growled and tugged fitfully at the pulley blocks. But the chain would not move.

"Someone'll have to climb up on the girders and fix it," said Yakubov, by no means put out by Husein's shouting. "But I'm afraid of falling."

The others did not move a step but just looked expectantly at Husein. He did not feel much like climbing up to put the chain right either. It might be easier, he fancied, to lift the piston by hand. But he noticed Basov looking up at him and made haste.

"Make the hook fast, boys," he said in a businesslike way, "I'm going up."

To get up on the girders near the ceiling of the engine-room one had to crawl in from the outside, through the glass roof. Husein went out and ran up astern. A cold wind swept out from the coast in the darkness. On either side of the ship the lights of the harbour were reflected like golden garlands in the water. Husein slipped through the open hatch, hung by his hands, and felt for the girder with his feet. He was surrounded by the sickly heat from the engines. The men stood below craning their necks to watch him. Husein crept on all fours along the girder, clinging to the iron with his fingers, and whistling. When he got to the crane carriage, he put the chain on the gears and shouted down, his voice sounding hollow as though he was shouting into a barrel:

"Pull away there! Have you all gone stiff? Heave!"

Basov was standing below looking at the diagrams, and it gratified Husein that he was not watching him, as though he trusted him with the whole job. He swarmed down the chain itself and, landing on the platform, started to help the fitters.

The Young Communist electricians came out from behind the distributor switchboards. They had finished their running repairs, the *Derbent*'s generator being kept by them in exemplary condition, but they had no intention of going away.

"What shall we do?" asked Kotelnikov, biting his nails. "This is the most vital part of the ship. But I must say I haven't got a clue about diesel engines."

"We must give the lead," Volodya said anxiously. "It's up to us to set the example."

Kotelnikov frowned. "You want to be in charge everywhere," he said. "Just help the chaps, that's all, even if it's only by handing tools. That way you'll give an example to those who are doing nothing."

"D'you think he knows what to do?" said Protsenko sizing up the embarrassed Volodya. "Ah, you silly chump!"

Kotelnikov was the first to go down to Basov.

"Alexander Ivanovich, we've finished our job, we've come to give you a hand," he said. "We'll do anything you tell us, even if it's only carrying things, it doesn't matter."

The fitters were fussing round the raised piston, fitting on the rings. Husein had a fancy that the work was being done sluggishly, as in a slow-motion picture. The rings did not fit in the grooves, and the latter had to be cleaned out with a chisel. He heard the mighty throbbing of the engines calm down and the horn wail above deck. He had to get three pistons ready, and they hadn't finished the first. He took a tool out of Yakubov's hands and set to work. Chunks of slag flew off under his chisel.

"Go easy, Mustapha," Yakubov suggested mildly, "or the rings'll lie loose."

They rolled the second piston out of the workshop and, securing it on the hook, hoisted it in the air. Leaving off his job, Husein kept an eye on what was going on at the engines. Men with monkey-wrenches had got to work on the cylinders. Cautiously gripping the hot pipes, they were unscrewing the cylinder covers. Husein saw Kotelnikov among them, but before he could voice his astonishment, Volodya came up from somewhere.

"Haven't you finished yet?" he inquired in a whimpering voice. "We've only got two hours left. You chaps!"

"You do it quicker if you can," Husein snapped crossly. "Here you are, I'll look on."

The metal rang under his chisel, and his perspiring shoulders were covered with black dust from the slag. Yakubov, the fitter, fumbled in his pocket for his cigarettes. Then, with a gesture of indifference he set to work on the last ring.

"Doesn't matter, we'll have a smoke at sea," he said winking to Volodya. "Pass me a hammer, old boy."

When they had finished with the pistons, Husein threw down his chisel and went to the ventilator. The cold jet of air tickled his sweating back, he began to feel a dull ache in his arms. Now that he had done the job, it looked as if everybody had forgotten all about him. The motor-men were taking off the cylinder covers, examining the injectors. They were all in just as much of a hurry as Husein himself, even those whom he had considered useless slow-coaches.

"I've exerted myself and got the job done, but has anybody noticed it?" The thought occurred to him, but did not goad him as before. It rather struck him as dull and repulsive, like a healed scab that you want to scratch off with your nail. He pulled himself together and ran to the engines.

The crane carriage moved slowly along under the ceiling. The finished piston glided through the air to the ringing of the taut chains. Below the men moved about, tugging at the tackle like drivers at a beast of burden.

The piston stopped over the opening and was lowered: the head slid into the shaft of the cylinder. Husein pressed the rings with his hands as they went into the opening. When the last one was in its place, he straightened himself up and rubbed his hands.

"The cover!" he ordered the motor-men. "We're finishing the third cylinder, Alexander Ivanovich."

Basov looked at Husein's animated face and smiled. He was elated at what was going on around him, above all at the new expression on the men's faces. The sluggish torpor seemed to have disappeared and been replaced by an expression of impatience and feverish curiosity, like that of a chap who has put his heart into a serious job for the first time. But he had his doubts. It might be nothing but the excitement of novelty—a bright but unenduring flame that would go out at the first failure.

Basov did not want to think of that, he did not want to believe that the wonderful enthusiasm could disappear from Husein's face. When the horn blew, announcing that loading was over, Basov went calmly to the control panel.

The crew had bunched together in front of the indicators. Husein was standing at the air cock, his hands on the wheel. Suddenly his assurance melted away. Perhaps the speed indicator would show a hundred revs just as before? The crew had gone without shore leave and several of them were now on their second successive watch. It was Husein who had first shouted about emulation and got the lads wrought up. Now they would make a laughing-stock of him.

A signal rang down from the chart-house. Basov gripped the fly-wheel and looked at the indicator. Husein sighed and closed his eyes.

"Open up, Mustapha," said Basov's voice.

Hearing the heavy throb of the first strokes, Husein plucked up courage and went to the indicator board. The arrow showed "Slow astern," then "Slow ahead." The ship was turning, pulling off from the pier.

Husein could no longer hold out. He turned away from the dials. A cowardly thought flashed through his brain: Suppose we fail? Well, what of it! I'll have a laugh with the others. But in a moment he had forgotten everything but the swelling pulse of the engines.

The needle crept quickly round the dial. Without stopping, it passed the hundred and still went on.

Hundred and five ... hundred and seven ... hundred and ten...

There was a buzz of excitement all round. Those behind stood on their tiptoes to see better. The engines were thundering at full speed.

"Hundred and twelve!" Volodya shouted triumphantly in Husein's ear. "Look, Mustapha!"

"Y-yes," Kozov drawled with an air of importance, and a sarcastic twitch of his nose. "We'll show the *Agamali* now, Alexander Ivanovich!"

Husein went out on deck and sat down for a rest. The lights of the harbour were receding in the dark. The wind was hurling down puffs of smoke which blew about the deck, clinging to the hatches like pieces of grey cloth.

Husein saw the chief engineer come out of the engine-room and stand in the patch of light coming from the door-way.

"Will he come up, or not?" Husein thought, turning away. He thought that if Basov came and spoke to him, something very important would happen, something that would change his whole life aboard. He heard steps behind him and started as he felt Basov's hand on his shoulder.

"They gave a hundred and twelve today," Basov said in his usual worried voice. "The chaps are going mad in the mess-room, they never expected anything like it. But that's only the beginning. The engines must be maintained in that condition. That's much harder, and that's where we can come a cropper. I mean it needs constant attention and we'll have to spend more than one spell in harbour in the engine-room."

"The injectors often get fouled," Husein answered in the same dry, inexpressive tone. "It's dark now, we can't see what the smoke's like. So far it's been black, there was a lot of soot in it, but the puffs seem clean now."

"The smoke's only a detail," said Basov in a reverie. "Nothing but smoke." He laughed. "Is it your turn on watch now, Mustapha?"

"Yes, I'll go just now," Husein answered, rising. "I've had a bit of a rest."

Nothing particular had happened. They exchanged a few words about the job and were about to separate. Basov— probably out of absent-mindedness—had been more familiar with him. It has obviously just escaped him, for he was generally like that only with the Young Communists.

"I wanted to thank you too," Basov said suddenly. "If it hadn't been for your help—I can't do anything alone," he added simply.

"What are you thanking me for?" muttered Husein, bewildered. "Was I the only one?" He peered into the chief engineer's face, but the latter was in no hurry to go. He held out his hand.

And then suddenly it happened—the thing Husein had been vaguely expecting. He clasped the engineer's hand and squeezed it with such force that the fingers cracked.

"Oh, Alexander Ivanovich!" he said, from the bottom of his heart. "My dear friend!"

### III

The telegram sent by wireless to the *Agamali* ran as follows:

"We challenge you to socialist emulation in the fulfilling of the shipments plan. Radio agreement.

"Chairman of the ship's trade union committee,
*Kotelnikov*."

Kotelnikov himself was fidgeting impatiently behind the operator's back while he was tapping out the message.

"Perhaps they won't even talk to us? It's a bit thick on our part, you know. Why, we haven't made up our arrears yet."

Volodya switched off the transmitter and swung round on his chair.

"In that case we'll catch up with them unofficially, and they'll have to acknowledge that. Isn't it just the same? We're throwing them a challenge, we the forty-five men on the *Derbent*. Smart, isn't it? A grand thing emulation is!

I just couldn't wait for them to send us those lighters. I fancy I fairly got on the nerves of those thick-headed toughs in the harbour today. Anyhow, they sent us the lighters in time."

"Will we beat them?"

"Of course we will! You know, Stepa, I think you and I were all wrong in our opinion of the crew. D'you remember, you called them riff-raff?"

"I don't seem to remember..."

"Tricky aren't you! And then I tempted you with a job in Epron. You can easily forget what you don't want to remember!"

"That's a thing of the past."

"That's better! Did you see the way those motor-men worked in port? That's something new! The most remarkable thing about it was the commanders had nothing to do with it. D'you happen to remember who started it?"

"Yes, Mustapha Husein."

"He used to be in the Y.C.L. But why isn't he now? D'you know?"

"They say he was chucked out for drunkenness. I don't know exactly."

"It's not right, Stepa, the way we shut ourselves up from the rest and don't know the chaps at all. The emulation started spontaneously, without us, we just joined in."

"You wanted to take the lead yesterday," Kotelnikov taunted him.

"Chuck that—We must do away with our silly offishness, we've got to work with the lads. Then we may be able to lead them."

"We need more open meetings," said Kotelnikov. "Above all, we must really get down to the job. We kept the electrical installations in order and imagined we were setting an example, considered ourselves as little models. Cheap, that is, Volodya! We've got to be wherever things are not going right. If you can't repair the engines, you can hand the tools, get the men organized, show them the aim of it all. It's not an easy job, Volodya, getting people organized. No, it's not."

The *Agamali*'s crew were in no hurry with the answer. That evening during supper-time Volodya came running into the mess-room.

"The chairman of the trade union committee is wanted on the wireless," he announced solemnly. "Get a move on, Stepa!"

The wireless-cabin filled up with men. There were sailors, electricians, the donkey-man, and motor-men. Even Alyavdin, the navigator, came. They conversed in low voices, almost in a whisper, as if the one who had called the chairman of the committee was there in the cabin, behind the switchboard. Husein was listening with his mouth half open to the tapping of the key and the whistling of the loudspeaker.

"Were you sending a message then?" he asked softly. "And now him? What did he answer?"

"Go to the devil!" hissed Volodya. "You'll get me mixed up!"

From far away came at last the perfunctory answer:

"Agree if you are in earnest. Our conditions: ship twenty-five thousand tons above plan, cut down delays in loading and unloading, carry out repairs en route. Over."

The cabin got noisy. The telegram went from hand to hand. Alyavdin shook his head.

"It'll be good if we make up our arrears," he said, "but twenty-five thousand above plan—excuse me, it doesn't make sense."

"But they suggest it," retorted Kotelnikov, frowning. "It makes sense to them."

"Our engines are not theirs."

"They're of the same series. Our heads are not their heads, that's the point!"

"I can tell you something about that." Pronin, the donkey-man, who so far had not said a word, came forward: "Do you know who regulated the *Agamali*'s engines?"

"How should I know?"

"But I do. Our engineer, Basov. He used to work in the docks."

"You've got something mixed up. It's impossible!"

"No, I haven't. I know what I'm talking about. It was him."

Husein smiled triumphantly.

"Yesterday we managed to get a hundred and twelve out of the engines. You all saw it, didn't you. Basov says we can get every bit of a hundred and fifteen."

He snatched the telegram from the table and ran out. Khrulev watched him go with an evil smile in his eyes.

"What's he up to?" he said, winking to Alyavdin. "Gone to the engineer now to grovel to him, I suppose. The bootlicking beachcomber! You know he was in court for hooliganism, don't you?"

"For drunkenness," Kotelnikov corrected him sullenly. "You keep your yarns to yourself. Your tongue's as filthy as the mop they wash the deck with, Khrulev!"

Husein half-opened Basov's cabin door. The chief engineer was sitting at the table, his head in his hands.

"Toothache?" asked Husein, closing the door cautiously.

"No, my teeth are all right," answered Basov, stretching. "What makes you think that? I just can't get to sleep. I didn't sleep last night and I can't now either."

Husein sat down on the edge of a chair and opened out the telegram, but for some reason folded it again.

"In the dumps, then?" he inquired sympathetically. "I noticed it long ago. What's the matter?"

"One gets all sorts of ideas," answered the engineer in a weary voice. He raised his head and gave a short laugh, whether at himself or at Husein's question it was hard to say. "Got a wife ashore," he added unexpectedly.

"Young?" Husein's teeth flashed.

"What do you think? I'm not so old myself, am I? By the way, there's no need to be so formal when we're off duty."

Husein settled more comfortably on his chair and cocked one leg over the other in satisfaction.

"And that's what you're fretting about?" he said, lightheartedly. "When the navigation season's over you'll have a spell at home. No children? They'll come, too."

"It's not all that simple, Mustapha."

"Why, don't you get on together?"

"No. They sent me here and it didn't suit her."

Husein's smile disappeared.

"Ugh! What a life! And here's my story," he burst out, unable to restrain himself.

"I made the acquaintance of a girl, old chap. She's a wonder, a real pearl of a girl, I tell you. Just finishing the institute. But how can you keep up an acquaintance when you can only see her twice a month? Sometimes we call in port at night, sometimes early in the morning, when she's got no time. I don't ask her to come to the pier—we might be late or I might not be able to leave the tanker. And then the lads are sharp-tongued on the pier—they'll try to make up to her: Bored, aren't you, lady; couldn't we keep you company, and so forth. They wouldn't think twice of hurting her feelings. We meet on the boulevard and have the most marvellous chats together. She wants to know all about our life aboard and why we don't fulfil our plan. She seems to think a lot of me, she's expecting something great. You're fiery and tenacious, she says, and so fearless."

"A sensible girl," said Basov. "What did you answer?"

"A lot of rot, of course. Told her just to be patient, we'd be famous, too. And now it seems I don't stand a chance with her. There are lots of chaps on shore. Fiery ones, and tenacious ones, it's only a matter of choice. Perhaps she's already met somebody the time I've been at sea. She's capable of doing a serious job herself too. She was a foreman at practice work. The seasonal workers have a great opinion of me, really, she says. It made me feel down-hearted listening to her. We are not bound on the same course in life, Alexander Ivanovich."

"According to you, all seamen must remain bachelors for life," said Basov with a smile. "That's nonsense. Kotelnikov, for example, has a wife and child, the boatswain has kids going to school. And you should see what fine children they are!"

"What about yourself? You should practise what you preach!"

Basov rose and started walking about the cabin.

"I was only kidding, Mustapha," he said guiltily. "I've got no wife. I'm single. You asked about my teeth and I thought it funny. It was a silly joke. Excuse me."

"So you took me in," said Husein with a drawl, wetting his hand-made cigarette with his tongue. "O. K. Joke to your heart's content." He opened out the telegram. "Here, read the *Agamali*'s answer."

He waited patiently till the engineer had finished reading.

"Twenty-five thousand tons above plan," said Basov, "it's not to be trifled with. But I think we'll be up to the mark, if, of course, we mobilize all resources."

"What resources?"

"Speed at sea and in loading. Perhaps there are others too."

Husein started thinking.

"Couldn't we increase the *Derbent*'s load capacity?" he asked.

"No, Mustapha, the ship isn't made of rubber."

"None of your jokes... How much fuel do we take on in port? A supply for four trips?"

"Yes. But what's fuel got to do with it?"

"If we only ship fuel for one trip, we can take three hundred tons more useful cargo."

"Hell," cried Basov. "You're right! I never thought of that. Why do we take a four-trip supply?"

"I don't know. It's a rule. In case there's another deluge, I should think."

"It's not right anyhow. We should take cargo, not ballast. Why didn't anybody think of it before?" Basov stopped. "Couldn't we get rid of something else?"

"In the anchor-room there are a lot of chains, spare anchors and other junk," Husein said thoughtfully. "Then there's the engine-room stores and workshop. If we collect all the scrap iron and old stuff there is on the ship, it'll come to about fifty tons."

"A total of three hundred and fifty tons more per trip?"

"You see," Husein said, beaming, "and you said we couldn't increase the load capacity!"

## IV

When the second engine had been regulated, the *Derbent* covered the distance to Astrakhan roads in thirty hours. But there a hitch occurred. On the tanker's arrival, the tug brought up only two lighters, the third being unserviceable.

In the wireless-cabin, Volodya Makarov strained his vocal chords in vain, calling the port dispatcher. "We've sent to Astrakhan for spare ones," came the monotonous, indifferent answer, plunging the operator into fits of powerless rage.

The filled lighters were heading off to the north. The loading pipe on the *Derbent* had been stretched out and hung over the deck like a huge rusty trunk. Gulls were soaring and screeching over the tanker, snatching tiny silvery fishes from one another. The sea, pale green by the ship's sides, became a deeper blue towards the horizon, merging with the enamel of the sky. The seamen on watch were dejectedly pacing the deck, looking towards the north where the other lighters were to come from.

Kasatsky, the navigation officer, bored with waiting, ran to look for the captain.

"You just imagine," he said as he appeared in the saloon, "we saved five hours this time. We should show ourselves in our best colours to the shipping line, really we should."

Yevgeny Stepanovich was sitting at the table stirring his tea. In the shining, bulging side of the ship's tea-pot, he could see his face, bloated beyond recognition, with monstrous crimson swellings instead of cheeks. While talking to the mate, he kept casting side glances at the tea-pot, unable to take his eyes off the fantastic mask.

Kasatsky went on:

"It wouldn't be bad to send a telegram to the management, something like this: On the basis of our emulation and shock work. . ."

"Enough!" Yevgeny Stepanovich interrupted him in disgust, and the face in the tea-pot tossed about and became covered with a net of wrinkles. "Stop making up false documents. Shame on you!"

"But my dear man, it's nothing but the pure truth," Kasatsky replied, smiling. "Why shouldn't we turn it to some advantage? How long have we been having nervous fits because we were in bad books? And now all you can say is: Enough! Anyhow, have it your own way."

"I don't want to fool anybody, and I've had enough of those telegrams." The captain got more excited at every word, like a man who has at last plucked up courage to voice his own opinion. "You must understand that all these shattering reports are nothing but lies. The emulation has only just started, and you and I have nothing at all to do with it. Don't forget that!"

As usual in his rare moments of anger, Yevgeny Stepanovich impatiently anticipated some retort that would give him the advantage and prove how just his indignation was. But Kasatsky was silent, his face showed fear and meek bewilderment.

"It never occurred to me that you could interpret such petty things that way," he said, grieved. "Perhaps I overdid it a little, trying to show the situation in the best light. In the shipping line they are very disturbed about the poor beginning of the navigation season. They have already dismissed one of the captains, I hear. And frankly, I should not like to have any other commander."

"Dismissed him, did you say?" asked Yevgeny Stepanovich.

"It grieves me to think that you could be.... Such an honest old campaigner, a respected man! I tell you honestly, I have a special feeling of consideration for you."

"But can't I see that, my dear fellow!" the captain murmured. "Believe me, I very much appreciate your attitude, but I am worried by all these showy messages. It seems to me we have sent too many of them lately. To say the honest truth, aren't we to blame for a lot ourselves? We get stuck on the shallows while loading, for example. Really, who's to blame. And do you remember the story about the ballast water? Really, you know..."

Kasatsky instantly calmed down and took a seat at the table.

"Yes, I agree," he said impatiently, "who does not slip up now and again? But it seems we are coming to a turning point now. The chief engineer did not let the off-duty men go ashore and overhauled the engines. He had no right to deprive the men of their rest, but we'll have to close our eyes to that."

"He reported it to me."

"Yes, probably with a wolfish look, as much as to say: I despise you, but I must talk to you. Don't pay any attention to him, he's a very queer chap. I, for my part, always give him to understand that I'm not a chip of the past, as he thinks I am, but just like anybody else here. Ha-ha! And that, of course, is quite true. To me, my dear Yevgeny Stepanovich, this emulation business has been a sort of revelation. A wonderful universal method of processing any human material. All the long-range guns of human moral were brought into play, even such eternal ones as 'glory' and 'valour.' There's something old-fashioned in the very word 'challenge,' but something beautiful and forceful too. Indeed, it now seems that a new expression of intelligence has appeared on the men's faces. Briefly—I'm all for it."

Yevgeny Stepanovich listened in silence. He was already overcome by that vague, passive frame of mind that he had during conversations with the first mate. All he could do was to follow the unexpected turns in his interlocutor's thoughts, turns in the endless labyrinth of which he seemed to get dazed.

"So you think a change has set in?" he asked meditatively.

"There's no doubt about it. And we've got to do all we can to develop this success. A lot depends on the shore organizations. The dispatchers have their favourites—like the *Agamali*. A model ship gets priority in everything. Therefore we must get the *Derbent* the reputation of a model ship. If we sent the management a telegram on the lines I said..."

"Well, I have no objections. Let's do so," Yevgeny Stepanovich agreed. He felt sorry for having been so hasty and wanted to make a concession quickly, so as to wipe out his guilt towards the mate.

"We'll make it brief and dignified," said Kasatsky, taking out his message pad: " 'On the basis of social emulation and shock work, we have succeeded in increasing speed.' That will be sincere and discreet enough. Don't you think so?"

He finished writing the telegram and handed it to Kutasov. He walked up and down and then stopped in front of the port-hole, swaying on his heels. The captain's brow wrinkled as he read the telegram.

"Good," he said at last. "It will be quite dignified like that."

"There's another thing," said Kasatsky with a yawn. "Somebody suggested we should do away with the four-trip fuel supply for the diesel engines. Basov thinks that if we take off the ship the superfluous fuel and junk of all kinds, we can increase its freight capacity by three hundred and fifty tons. That's a good idea. I just wanted to warn you not to take it into your head to oppose it."

"Excuse me," said Yevgeny Stepanovich, astonished. "You want to do away with the fuel reserve?"

"Leave a supply for a single trip, Yevgeny Stepanovich. . ."

"But really?"

"There you are, I knew it," said Kasatsky, laughing. "It would be more to the point to ask why we carry a four-trip supply."

"Just in case—There are plenty of reasons—They all do."

Kasatsky yawned.

"Reserve fuel for one trip is quite enough even in stormy weather," he said softly, "and three hundred and fifty tons a trip—that's three thousand a month, and about twenty thousand above plan in a season. That's clear enough."

"But isn't it dangerous?"

"Of course it is! You risk getting a premium and thanks from Godoyan. Well, agreed?"

"All right!"

"Basov says we can do considerably more than the plan if we mobilize all latent resources," said the mate pensively. "He seems to be right. In any case, he's dug up one resource already. That vulgar crank will probably make a career for himself, you'll see."

# V

The last lighter came two hours late. The tug towed it alongside the *Derbent*, churning up the water with its screw, gave a piercing hoot and was quiet. On the deck of the lighter, sullen sleepy men in sheepskin coats were moving sluggishly about, laying out the filling pipe. The sailors were watching them over the side of the tanker.

"There in the roads they are nothing but bureaucrats, paper-scratching rats," Volodya Makarov said nervously. "They don't care a damn that we've lost two hours. We'll never get anywhere this way. We must shake them up somehow..."

"We'll put in a complaint to the manager of the Caspian Shipping Line," Kotelnikov said judiciously. "He'll smarten them up."

Husein looked at the speakers, his brows twitching feverishly. He was intolerably irritated by the sluggish movements of the men of the lighter and their apathetic faces.

"D'you always go about like that?" he shouted down. "Ahoy! You on the ironclad!"

"Don't bully them," Kotelnikov advised. "They'll only dilly-dally out of spite."

But Husein was not to be calmed. "Tell your bungling chiefs we'll put a complaint in!" he threatened. "We'll find a way of putting things right."

"Why blame us?" came the answer from below. "We have no say in the matter."

Husein walked away. It was useless cutting down the time in port and saving minutes when the result of their efforts could be reduced to nil by a dispatcher in the roads. The crew had the success of their emulation at heart, but that success depended on the dispatcher, on those thick-skinned lighter-men, and on the pier workers. Husein tried not to look at what was going on on the lighter and to contain the dull irritation that was seething in him, and which was all the worse because, in point of fact, there was nobody he could be angry with.

He became somewhat calmer as they left the roads: the *Derbent* was doing twelve knots. Then his watch came, and it was a relatively quiet one—the engines lost no revs, the fuel was flowing properly. All the same, an importunate thought sometimes goaded him: perhaps it was all in vain?

He had dinner after his watch and went to sleep. But waking up, he saw through the port-hole a thick milky-white fog.

Fog always filled Husein with bitter melancholy and stirred up in his heart grievances that seemed to have already worn off. He went out on deck; the lights on the masts were blurred, as if wrapped in some white silky material. Voices and steps had a hollow sound. Volodya came up to him.

"Listen to what our commanders have done," he said in a hoarse voice. "What stupidity! And then this fog! We're sure to be late now!"

Husein was astonished neither by Volodya's sad face nor by what he said. Could anything good happen in such a fog? He inhaled a breath of the thick air, and the sweetly taste of it made him spit overboard.

"Just imagine, they sent a telegram: 'On the basis of emulation and shock work...' Speculating, the rascals!"

"To hell with them!" said Husein indifferently. "This fog is like a wall. There, we've lost speed, I can tell by the sound of the engines."

"It makes me sick to think what they are speculating on," said Volodya. "Well, see you later."

Husein remained alone. Everything around him was moving slowly and noiselessly. Grey patches of fog were creeping over the deck, clinging to the hatches, mounting the rungs of the ladders, and they made everything smell damp, musty and stuffy, like exhaust gas.

The *Derbent*'s horn gave a short hoarse blast and was answered by a shrill screech from a ship coming in the opposite direction, its green light blinking in the fog. Husein crouched down with his arms round his knees.

"It's rotten," he said softly in a voice that sounded weak and hollow. "They're disgracing our emulation with their telegrams, the rotters that they are! And those on shore are just the same." He impatiently turned over in his mind all that had happened in the last few days, in the hope of finding something still worse that would fill the cup and justify him falling into desperation.

"The fog will delay us a lot," he thought, "and Zhenya will not come to the boulevard. What with the fog and the late hour, no, she'll certainly not come. How long is it since we saw each other. I bet she's forgotten all about me. And there's Basov with his great ideas. What can he hope for with a band like that on shore, all shielding one another so that you don't know who's to blame! Messages, false reports. . . . But perhaps Basov doesn't hope for anything? Perhaps he's just like that Astrakhan dispatcher, just like Kasatsky and Alyavdin, only much craftier? We're nearing port. There's the island, we'll see the lights now. What about a sip of beer?"

He went to the side of the ship and putting his hands on the rail he looked towards the harbour lights swimming in the fog. He stood there, chilled in the damp air, until the gangway rattled down. Then he ran down on to the pier and went off without a look back, swinging his arms with relief as though leaving the tanker for ever.

The men on watch were fussing about the deck, shouting to one another in the fog. They had no time to bother about Husein. An hour later, he was seen by sailors from the *Derbent* who had dropped into a bar to warm themselves. Among them was Yakubov, the fitter, the one Husein had taught to use the crane, a quiet, unobtrusive chap, who had given up smoking for the only reason that whenever he bought cigarettes he gave them all to the others. He was astonished to see Husein and tried to go over to him and take him back to the ship. But Khrulev held him fast by the sleeve.

"Just you keep away. Our shock-worker'll soon show what he's worth," he whispered mockingly. "Sit still, I tell you!"

Sprawling on his chair with a whole battery of empty beer bottles in front of him, Husein looked round with mad burning eyes, to catch the evasive glances of his neighbours. His extinguished cigarette-end stuck to his lower lip, which was hanging and covered with beer froth. The waiters had been hovering anxiously round the table for a long time. Opposite him sat his chance drinking companion,— a small weak and terrified chap in shabby clothes. He was screwing up his small drunken eyes with an expression of submission, waiting for an opportunity to slip away.

Suddenly Husein rose and swept the bottles from the table. He staggered over the pieces of coloured glass towards the door where he was met by an army of waiters in white, menacingly waving their serviettes. He pushed one of them with the flat of his hand. The chap groaned as he bumped his head against the door frame. Husein rushed out into the street. Whistles sounded behind him. He made off at a run. In the bar Khrulev rocked with laughter, slapping his hands on his knees, while Yakubov offered the waiters money, asking them not to make a scandal.

Husein no longer hummed in the soft high voice he had at sea before sunset. Short-breathed from drinking, gasping, he bellowed like a ship's horn and shook his fist in the air.

Passers-by turned off into the roadway. Under the lamp-light before the entrance to a cinema, a few youths shouted at the top of their voices:

"Beachcomber! Loafer! Soaker!"

At the cross-roads, Husein stretched out his arms to stop a girl who was running away, terrified.

"Caught, Marusya!" Then seeing her young face pale with fear, he said with a sad, forlorn smile: "What are you afraid of? D'you think I'll do you any harm? Ah, you darling!"

His violence suddenly disappeared, giving place to a weak, submissive melancholy. He dropped on a bench on the boulevard and tore open the neck of his shirt. The trees seemed to be drifting slowly from left to right, their trunks swimming in the thick fog.

"Of course you'll not make good now," he said to himself, moving his tongue with difficulty. "Now they'll try you again just like that—other time. Basov will be the judge, that's sure. Of co-ur-se! Well, O.K., get on with the trial! As you like! I've no objection." He raised his head and listened to the boom of a horn. "That's the *Derbent*! Eh, what a voice! They'll weigh anchor and sail away—without me. And that's that."

His left fist smarted and felt clammy as though he had crushed some sticky living thing. He raised his hand to his eyes: it was dark with blood.

"Where have I been? Bottles. . ."

His head was aching, and a sickly taste was rising to his mouth. The horn blew again in the distance, and Husein felt his feet go cold.

"What am I sitting here for? Still sitting, sitting." He counted the instants and painfully stretched his legs. "If I get up now, I might make it—No, I'm done for!"

At last, he rose from the bench and staggered on his long legs trying to keep down the fits of nausea.

"I must get there," he said aloud, "and go to Basov—Slip through without anybody noticing. He knows what's wrong with me."


Two men stood under an awning near a little provision stall. The waves were swishing against the stones by the mooring.

"You say he ran out on to the boulevard?" Basov asked in a worried, irritated voice. "And you couldn't stop him? Fine chaps you are!"

"We didn't have time. He was raving mad," Yakubov pleaded. "The waiters themselves wouldn't stand up to him. You should have seen the way he shoved one of them! He's so strong!"

"See you don't breathe a word about it," Basov reminded him. "Isn't that him coming? Look!"

Someone passed the pumping station, casting a dark square shadow on the asphalt. He went stealthily, at the same time stumbling and dragging his feet. His heavy throaty breathing could be heard from afar. Seeing the men under the awning, he stopped.

"Alexander Ivanovich!" he called in a low voice. "You won't let me on board? I understand!"

"You go to my cabin," said Basov sharply. "Try and walk straight. Go ahead."

They went along the pier one behind the other. Yakubov tactfully kept a little behind, pretending to tie his boot-lace. He felt sorry for Husein. The black silhouettes of the men on watch could be seen on deck by the gangway. The light of a cigarette twirled and flickered.

Husein drew himself erect and walked up the gang-way. Halfway up he lost his balance and groaned as he gripped the rail with his cut hand. There was laughter on deck.

"Dead drunk!" somebody said. "See that, boys?"

Arriving on deck, Basov stopped.

"Khrulev," he called, "come here!"

A sailor came forward with his hand behind his back.
"Yes?"

"It says in the rules that for smoking during loading a man is dismissed from work and brought before court. It's not your first time."

"I've put it out," Khrulev hastily spat on his cigarette, bending down to hide his face. "You're down on some chaps and you shield others when they're drunk," he added in a shaky voice. "That's not right!"

"What should I shield him for?" Basov asked unmoved.

"Tomorrow I shall put in a report, and both of you will get what you deserve. Understand?"

"But I've already put it out. . ."

"And he's already sober. . ."

"It'll be the last time. Word of honour!"

The corridor was empty. The only sounds that could be heard were voices down in the officers' saloon. Basov went to his cabin. Husein was sitting by the table, holding his head in his hands. He was rocking slightly as though suffering from some terrible pain. His shirt was covered with something dirty and sticky, and clung to his body; tufts of wet hair stood out at the back of his neck.

"Did anybody see you?" Basov asked. "There's blood on your face. Where did that come from?"

Husein raised his head and gulped.

"I'm a rotter, Sasha," he said in a low, sober voice. "I've spoilt my life and dishonoured the ship. Why have you brought me here?"

His frame shook, his mouth became distorted, and he brushed the tears over his face with his hand. Basov sighed and sat down on his berth.

"Listen, stop whimpering," he said impatiently. "You've got blood all over you and besides—you have been spewing, haven't you? Go to the tap and wash."

He rose, opened his clothes press and took out a clean shirt. Husein put his head under the tap, and rubbed his face with his hands, snorting loud and shivering. Streams of water ran down his bare arms and pattered on the floor. Embarrassed, he drew his elbows in to his sides and opened one eye.

"Take off that shirt," Basov ordered him, "put one of mine on for the time being. Ugh, what a cad you are! I'm surprised at you! Trying your drunken panics. What for, I should like to know? At a time when discipline is so necessary. Here's a towel. Do you call yourself a friend? A rotter, that's what you are!"

"Yes, I know I am," said Husein.

He dried his face and changed his shirt. Then he sat down on the chair and put his hands on his knees. The clean shirt made him feel better. Timidly and by degrees his face brightened.

"It all sort of piled up, you understand," he said in a hoarse voice. "Those officials in the roads, and then our own, fine chaps they are, with their telegrams as though we started emulation just to get praise. And then the fog."

"Somebody cast a spell on you, eh? You're just a rotten good-for-nothing. You nearly disgraced your ship. It was only luck, you know, that it ended all right."

"It's the last time, Sasha. It'll never happen again. You won't tell anybody, will you?"

"I don't know." Basov became thoughtful. "I'll tell Bredis of course. But he's a decent chap. Everything will be all right, I think."

Husein sighed and looked out of the window.

"We're already pulling out," he said, relieved. "We're off!"

## THE STAKHANOV TRIP

### I

THEY WERE having political instruction in the mess-room on the *Derbent*. All the members of the engine crew, the electricians and the sailors who were not on watch, had assembled there. Kasatsky had come too. He sat aloof, motionless, his features stern and tense. The crew had taken seats around a long table. At the end of it sat Bredis.

Basov had been delayed in the engine-room. It was quiet in the mess-room when he entered, a crumpled sheet of newspaper was being passed from hand to hand. Basov caught a glimpse of a large photograph on the first page—a broad-brimmed miner's helmet, a long oval face.

"We're reading an old newspaper today," Bredis said, turning to Basov. "We missed it because of my illness," he added guiltily.

"One thousand two hundred per cent of the norm!" said Volodya Makarov. "Grand, isn't it?"

"What I don't understand is how he did it," Husein muttered querulously. "Is he a giant or something?"

"Doesn't look like one on the photo."

"You're probably stronger than him yourself."

"Read it out, Volodya."

Basov stood by the wall, studying the men's faces as was his habit. That did not stop him from listening to what was being read; on the contrary, it even helped him.

"On the thirtieth of August, Alexei Stakhanov's brigade, organized on new lines, gave a hundred and fifty-two tons per mechanical pick in a single shift."

It was an old paper, Basov had read it long ago. Gazaryan, the motor-man, was listening with his mouth open. On his face you could see astonishment and a trace of that mysterious expression that little children have when listening to fairy tales. For him it was a wonder that had happened far away over hill and dale. Kotelnikov was looking at his comrades and biting his nails pensively. He had read all about Stakhanov and now he was enjoying the effect the remarkable episode produced on the others. Husein kept on frowning, the vein over his brow quivering like a rubber band, the brown skin on his forehead creased. He was wondering, of course, whether one could organize things along new lines on the *Derbent* too.

Khrulev was gazing drowsily at the ceiling, at the grey wreaths of tobacco smoke, the peeling paint and the lamp in its dusty wire net. He was probably busy with his own thoughts—the trip had only just started, they would not put into harbour for a long time, he would have to go on watch shortly, the night watch, a real dog watch.

Kasatsky, the first mate, sitting all alone, was listening attentively. Although he was not looking round, he was watching everybody. Who could fathom Kasatsky?

Basov knew by heart the short story of Stakhanov, the coal-cutter: technical instruction in the Irmino colliery alternating with emergency jobs, the attempts to organize the work and distribute the men in a new way, the detailed analysis of the processes of labour, taking every movement and every second into account.

It had probably not been an easy task. Basov thought of Neuman, the chief engineer, and the turner Eybat, Nemirovsky's manual and the regulating of the diesel engines. Backward engineers and bureaucratic-minded administrators had stood in Stakhanov's way too. Perhaps they had tried to browbeat him with quotations from books.

Alexei Stakhanov had had a long and hard battle with administrative officials who clung obstinately to antiquated technical standards.

Yes, that was the way it had been. Frightened administrators had snarled at him, foremen had scoffed at him. "An unfledged greenhorn" they had called him. They had dug up old books and old standards. Seven tons of coal a shift—that was the limit. What was that troublesome man getting at with his brigade? The thing was to find plausible pretexts for ostracizing him.

It didn't work, thought Basov, agitated. He fancied that it was the vague feeling of future victory that had kept him from despair when they had forced him to leave the works.

Bredis neatly folded the newspaper.

"The Stakhanov movement," he said slowly, "is first and foremost a movement for the all-out exploitation of technique. It's a movement that started from below, the administration had nothing to do with it. Stakhanovites are workmen who have mastered technique and have accumulated enough knowledge to push production forward. Capitalists cannot dream of such workers, that's clear. Only in our country can such workers exist."

Stepan Kotelnikov cocked his clever, rather ape-like face to one side and said:

"We haven't got many Stakhanovites, but we already have men who have mastered technique. If they can organize their work on Stakhanovite lines, we'll have abundance in our country and we won't have to count every little crumb. Every Stakhanov worker produces far more than he himself can consume. That means that the other workers, who have not reorganized their work, are living to a certain extent on the Stakhanovites. But what honest worker will agree to live on another man? So it's everybody's duty to work like Stakhanov, according to his ability, naturally."

"That's right," said Volodya, "that's what it comes to."

Smiling, Kasatsky rose and went to the table. His handsome eyes were shining.

"There's remarkable truth in what Comrade Kotelnikov said," he remarked, turning, to the political assistant. "The Stakhanov movement is only in its beginning, but it started in the masses, and it will no doubt spread over the whole country. Well said, Kotelnikov!"

"The lads are coming on, they've got their wits about them," Bredis remarked good-naturedly. "It's done them good to study political economy."

The political instruction came to an end. A few men grouped themselves round the radio operator who was drawing something with swift, sweeping strokes. On the paper appeared a string of trucks and a small figure in a broad-brimmed helmet. The drawing was done very quickly, like a cartoon on the screen. Then, under Volodya's hand appeared tiny lighters and above them the figure 25,000. The hull of a ship, outlined in a few strokes seemed to be sailing in over the edge of the paper, its bows fending the curling breakers.

## II

During dinner-time, Karpushin, the sailor on watch, appeared in the mess-room doorway.

"The *Agamali*'s coming," he announced in an excited voice. "And sailing so fine, comrades!"

Some of the men threw down their spoons and forks. Others ate up in haste, burning themselves with the hot borshch. All the members of the *Derbent*'s crew who were not on watch assembled on the fore-and-half bridge or the spar-deck. The ships sailing towards each other and the distance between them quickly dwindling, the *Agamali* seemed to be going at the speed of a gun-boat. Alyavdin joined the sailors watching the approaching ship from the bridge. He tried to put on an unconcerned, bored appearance, but his eyes were alight with excitement.

"You should get in touch with them, Volodya," he said to the radio operator. "It'd be interesting to know what speed they're doing."

"Wouldn't it be awkward?" asked Volodya doubtfully.

"Why should it? We're emulating them, aren't we?"

The ships came alevel and the men on the bridge could see the deck and spar-deck of the *Agamali*, with the crew standing motionless along the rail. Suddenly, the flag at her stern fluttered and slid down the staff. A murmur of approval came from the crowd on the bridge.

"Look, they've dipped their flag," Karpushin said triumphantly, "they're beginning to consider us as men! We must answer them."

He looked at Alyavdin. The latter nodded. Karpushin ran to the stern. Caps were waved on the *Agamali*, which was already receding in a cloud of grey smoke. Volodya came out of the wireless-cabin and went up to Alyavdin.

"Twelve knots," he said, disappointed. "That's their former speed laden. I should've thought they'd do more now. They seem to be taking it easy!"

"Yesterday we did twelve and a half," said Alyavdin tensely. "Now we're doing thirteen light. Upon my word, it looks as though we'll be at the head of the navigation!"

"We don't know yet. We must make use of all latent possibilities."

"What possibilities?"

Volodya played with the end of his belt with a condescending air.

"You weren't at political instruction? A pity! We spoke about Stakhanovites. Latent possibilities—that's what a machine can do when it's in skilful hands. Take the *Derbent*'s engines. When they were released from the works they gave a hundred revs and the load on the cylinders was uneven. After being regulated by the crew, they gave a hundred and twelve, and only the fifth port cylinder is a little under-loaded. Basov said we're not getting all we can out of the engines and their capacity can still be increased. That's what you call a latent possibility. Basov says..."

"Don't jabber like that! Listen, Volodya..."

"What?"

"I've read a little about Stakhanov too, and I should like to have a word with Alexander Ivanovich about something."

"Then why don't you go and talk to him?"

"Isn't he angry with me for objecting to that twenty-five thousand above plan? What do you think?"

"Rot. He's not that kind of chap."

"Listen, Volodya.' The navigator was noticeably excited but was trying hard not to show it. "Look, you chaps are doing your best to get things going and you've already succeeded to a certain extent. But you know nothing about navigation, and there are latent possibilities in the very steering of the ship. An idea's occurred to me. On the trip to Astrakhan roads we pass Zhiloy Island, leaving it wide to the left. That's making a big detour, the straight road lies to the other side of the island. There are shallows there, and with a twenty-foot displacement you just can't make it. Now when we go back light, in calm weather and without any ballast, our displacement is no more than six foot. Yet we go on the outside and make that detour all the same. We waste at least forty minutes."

"What's the depth of the channel?"

"Seven foot at the shallowest. It's quite navigable for us when we're light and not in ballast. We'd save forty minutes. There's a latent possibility for you," the navigator ended triumphantly.

"Then why does nobody sail that way?" wondered Volodya. "It's so simple."

"I don't know. Got the wind up, I suppose. I want to talk to Basov. If he agrees, we'll manage the captain."

Alyavdin offered Volodya a cigarette and ran to study the chart. Volodya liked the idea, but he made a show of indifference. He was puzzled, and even a little vexed. It would have been easier to understand had the suggestion come from Basov, Bredis or one of the motor-men. He had no great liking for Alyavdin. All he knew about him seemed hostile to the collective that had been forged thanks to the emulation. Alyavdin always held himself aloof or was somehow vulgarly familiar. But to save nearly an hour just by a change of course! Volodya could hardly wait to tell the Y.C.L. chaps the news.

That evening, the crew was listening to the wireless in the mess. Kotelnikov, Protsenko and Husein were there. They heard Volodya out without any excitement. They obviously shared his instinctive dislike of the second mate.

"When we started, he stood there with his hands in his pockets," Husein said bitterly. "But now that we've got it going without him, he sets to and rolls his sleeves up. He's only trying to cut a figure, but for us it's a matter of honour. To hell with him!"

"But the proposal's a businesslike one," Kotelnikov remarked half-heartedly.

"Suppose it is, we would have found it without him!"

"All he does is to play his old gramophone," mocked Protsenko, "while we have to work. Let him go to the devil!"

Basov came and took a chair near the others. Overcoming his sleeplessness, he had had a few hours' sleep and if he was not exactly merry, he was at least even-humoured and calm. He listened to the music coming from the loudspeaker, and whistled softly trying to pick up the tune.

"Hey, Volodya, you wonder-working radio Sparks! We've no accordion, or we could have a tune now!"

Volodya smiled, but then lowered his voice to a whisper and told about Alyavdin's proposal. The Y.C.L. members cast glances at the chief engineer, who was drawing contentedly at his cigarette and listening without effort or tension.

"So Alyavdin suggests we should sail through the channel?" he said at the end. "I don't feel so sure about that. I don't think it's even seven foot deep."

"I tell you, it's all nonsense," Volodya put in, relieved. He was pleased that everything was cleared up now and that the proposal made by Alyavdin, whom he considered to be hostile to the ship's collective, had turned out to be nothing but bluff. "He's just talking rubbish."

"He wanted to show off but it didn't work," Husein observed. "We should send him packing."

"Who?" asked Basov.

"The second mate. Let him mind his own business!"

"Are you out of your senses?" Basov exclaimed in amazement. "The chap makes a sensible proposal and you start growling. We must discuss it!"

The Young Communists became silent, Volodya shifted in his seat, looking round in confusion.

"But you said so yourself."

"It's just that I don't know enough about navigation. Alyavdin's a navigator, he should know better. We'll consult the captain, examine the course, and think it over. But I can't make out why it displeases you so much." He looked round good-naturedly as before, but seeing discontented faces around him, he stopped short, his smile disappeared, and his look became harder.

"You've got no flair," Husein muttered angrily. "Don't

you see what kind of a bird he is? He made fun of us when we undertook the job and said that twenty-five thousand above plan was nonsense. And now he wants to produce an effect and outstrip the others with his stunt. Petty, I call it."

"Hey, this is nothing but back-biting," Basov said frowning. "We're all on the same side here. I know Alyavdin as well as you do. He's a navigator, and as long as he's on this ship, nobody's got the right to stop him from taking part in the work of the collective. If he gets up to any tricks, we'll either put him in his place or chuck him out. But he wants to help us now, and if we give him the cold shoulder we'll be doing ourselves harm."

"It's not right, boys," said Kotelnikov with knitted brows, "we're beginning to shut ourselves up again, as though we were the only decent chaps here. We've spoken about this before. You yourself, Volodya, said we don't work enough with the others. Why should we repeat our mistakes..."

"But I can't bear the fellow. He somehow doesn't belong to us."

"My opinion is that we've either to dismiss him from the tanker or win him round and make use of him. We can't have chaps who don't fit in. It's always the same," Basov continued in a milder tone, "you get on with the job yourselves, and they get in your way, make fun of you and do all they can to prove that you're attempting the absurd. But if you're on the right road and stick to your aim, the others will gradually agree with you and want to help you. Half the job is to win people over. Perhaps the most important half—You just have a talk with the political assistant. Making speeches is not my line." He broke off with a smile.

"All right," mumbled Husein grudgingly. "If he helps us, we'll be thankful to him. Right, Volodya?"

"That's right."

Before the last watch Basov went up to the navigator's bridge to examine the course on the chart.

The sea was calm. Blurred reflections of the stars rocked on the crests of the broad smooth rollers. The rail of the bridge was warm, a little damp from the dew, and slightly vibrating. Had it not been for that gentle throbbing in the bowels of the ship, you would have thought she was standing still and the sea was flowing, like a river, in the direction in which the wind was blowing and the waves rolling.

Basov started singing in an undertone and looked down. A woman's dress showed up white on the spar-deck near one of the boats. Laughter and a voice feigning anger could be heard.

"Don't be naughty!"

"Who's that she's with?" wondered Basov, recalling the merry, rosy face of Vera, the stewardess, her tiny nose and the fair brows on her childlike porcelain forehead. There had been quarrels and gossip among the crew about her that spring until Bredis had put the men to shame at a meeting. She was friendly alike to all, but never stayed long on deck with anybody.

"So Vera's found somebody as well." Basov thought with a pang. "She's probably deeply in love. Well, after all, it's natural. Even ugly chaps—I'm the only one—" He switched to another line of thought. "It's fine for them to be in each other's arms on a night like this unseen by anybody. It was like that with me too, but it was probably not the real thing. That's why it ended so suddenly, as though it snapped. What have I to be sorry about?"

He went to the chart-house and tried to concentrate on the new course suggested by Alyavdin. But Musya's bare arms appeared as clear as in a dream. He could almost feel their weight on his shoulders. Her face lit up the darkness before him.

"It's as though I had always loved you, commander!"

He looked up at the dark sky sprinkled with starry sand and clenched his teeth. He must busy himself with something at once. He went along the bridge and round the wheel-house. By the emergency compass, bending over the dial, was Karpushin, one of the sailors. He was writing something down and was so absorbed that he did not even hear the steps.

"Studying the compass?" asked Basov, giving his voice that sociable tone which he knew disposed people to serious talk. "I've been thinking of studying navigation for a long time myself, but I don't seem to find the time. It's a difficult job."

Karpushin gave a start and turned round with an embarrassed smile, but he regained his calm as soon as he recognized Basov.

"No, I'm observing our course," he rattled off mysteriously. "But please don't speak loud, he mustn't hear."

"Who?"

"The helmsman on watch."

"You're observing the course?"

"I'll explain in a minute," the sailor said hurriedly, "I just want to jot this down. That's all. Look, the ship had a yaw of three degrees. He was lighting a cigarette—the helmsman, I mean. I've already filled four pages. There are still bigger deviations too, five degrees and more. If we trace the ship's course on the chart, we'll get a zigzag. This is the second day I've been watching our course."

"Do those deviations reduce our speed a lot?" asked Basov getting interested.

"Sh-sh! He'll hear. I should think they do! You've increased the power of the engine, but it's senseless as long as the helmsmen make a mess of their job. I noticed it on my own watch, when I was at the helm. And then at the political instruction they spoke about Alexei Stakhanov and latent possibilities. The way I look at it, keeping our course without any deviations is a latent possibility. Today I did the job at the helm properly and kept the yaws as small as possible—half a degree, no more. Now I'm noting the other helmsmen's work, and tomorrow I'll show them how they steer the ship. It's a disgrace!"

"Are all your notes in order?" Basov asked quickly.

"Quite. I've even noted the time of each deviation."

"Then we'll draw a diagram of their work and get the crew together to discuss it. You're right, there's a great latent possibility there."

"Is there?" asked the sailor with a flush of delight. "We'll smarten them up, Alexander Ivanovich!" He cast a side glance at the compass and opened his note-book. "There's another deviation. Two and a half degrees: Just look!"

"I see," Basov said with a grin. "But I'm only disturbing you with my questions. I'll get along."

That short conversation seemed to have freshened up his consciousness and restored his equanimity disturbed by the spectacle of other people's happiness.

"There's another discovery." He thought with pleasant surprise of the conversation with that sailor. "And so simple, so easy to understand for anybody who knows that a straight line is shorter than a crooked one. Captains, navigators, and motor-men all knew about these deviations from the course. And it's a helmsman at the wheel that makes the discovery!"

### III

The plan of the *Derbent*'s first Stakhanovite trip was approved at a general meeting of the crew. Strictly speaking there was no meeting at all. There was neither presidium nor speaker. The men came in from their watches, then went out. The air in the mess-cabin was thick with tobacco smoke and Bredis did not even attempt to restore order. He frowned a little when the noise grew and the voices swelled into a disorderly, excited hum. He sat there without looking round or even stirring, apparently plunged in thought. Only the short remarks he interposed at rare intervals showed that he was listening with great attention and could understand everything in spite of the hubbub. This meeting, as all others, did not go off without clashes. Karpushin laid out on the table a sheet of paper with a crooked line drawn in pencil. Flushed with awkwardness and embarrassment, he related his observations at the emergency compass. Those around him started laughing and talking all at once. Kotelnikov frowned and looked for the helmsmen among the crowd.

"Do you know what it's like?" he started in a serious tone. "It's like Pyotr and Ivan dragging a log. Pyotr exerts himself, strains every muscle, and Ivan puffs and pants. It's not nice of you, comrades helmsmen, as a matter of fact it's downright rotten of you!"

"It's a pack of lies, comrades," boomed sullen voices. "He sleeps at the helm himself! The ship has yaws when he's on duty too!"

"It's not!"

"He deserves a pasting for this!" somebody said in a cautious voice.

Husein's face twitched and his heavy body shot up from the bench.

"Who said that?" he thundered, the blood rushing to his face. "Come on, show yourself!"

"Easy, boys," said Bredis, still not moving. "Remember where you are. Karpushin is talking sense. The helmsmen must pull themselves together and not spoil the achievements of the crew. We'll check on them to begin with."

"Right. Keep a check on 'em!"

"Aye, aye! Keep a check on the helmsmen!"

"Carry on. . ."

Alyavdin, the second mate, was sprawling on a chair with his usual bored and scornful look; his head was thrown back and his eyes were screwed up on account of the smoke. But he kept on watching the door. The captain now came in, now went out on to the bridge. Basov was delayed in the engine-room. Alyavdin started to get uneasy. Had they really forgotten about his suggestion?

The captain came back, sat down by Bredis, grunted, and wearily closed his eyes. Kasatsky appeared in the doorway, cast a sharp inquisitive glance over the meeting, and smiled, apparently at his own thoughts. Basov was the last to come. He was grimy and tired-looking. The smoke-black on his eyelids made his eyes look hollow, and his whole appearance was gloomy and menacing. But he smiled and went straight to Alyavdin.

"Sit down, there's plenty of room," said Alyavdin, moving up on his chair. "I was afraid you wouldn't come."

His voice did not show its usual assurance and he immediately felt vexed with himself. "He'll think I'm grovelling," he thought, "you've got to be just as slipshod and coarse with him as he is himself. That's the secret of his authority."

Basov sat on the edge of the chair and absent-mindedly put his arm over the back of it.

"We've got everything ready to overhaul the fuel pump," he said with a glance sidewards. "That's all that was left."

Alyavdin put on an attentive air, vexed with himself at not being able to find an answer but at the same time gratified at being next to the chief engineer and talking to him before everybody.

"What about the new course?" Basov called out, turning towards Bredis. "You three have studied it, why don't you say something?"

Captain Kutasov stirred nervously.

"To tell you the truth, we did not come to any conclusion. The channel seems deep enough to afford passage with a seven-foot displacement, that is, light; but on the other hand, so little is known about that course. What do you think, Oleg Sergeyevich?"

"I was not one of the three," Kasatsky replied with a smile, "but I have already told you my opinion. It is navigable."

"I know it is, but it's a great responsibility," said Yevgeny Stepanovich hesitatingly. "Others show caution, why should we take risks. If the others are afraid, it means it's dangerous. It is, isn't it?"

"Well, that's saying a lot. It's true there is a small risk."

"You see, there is a risk. How can we?"

"Only fishes can swim without any risk, Yevgeny Stepanovich," said Kasatsky with a mealy smile. "Perhaps we could ask the captain of the *Agamali* to plot a course for us?"

There was an awkward silence. Many of the men lowered their heads and bit their lips to hide a smile. Basov hemmed and frowned at the first mate. Kasatsky himself seemed surprised at what he had said; he looked round with innocent, amused perplexity.

"I mean we should take the risk if it is reasonable and seems expedient," he continued unruffled. "We'll save about an hour in the channel. That's about a hundred thousand tôn-miles a trip. Then we must consider that we are opening the way for others. In a word, I'm in favour."

"You studied the chart too, Yevgeny Stepanovich," observed Bredis. "You had no objections as far as I remember."

The captain became pensive and propped his cheek on his pudgy hand. He was in a difficulty as usual because they were trying to persuade him and he wanted to get it over and agree with them. Yet he was afraid of the responsibility, which he was not, after all, obliged to take upon himself.

"All right, leave it at that," he said at last in a firm, resolute voice, like one who has let himself be persuaded and wants to hide his weakness. "I'll take the ship through the channel myself. After all, there doesn't seem to be much risk," he added in a half-inquiring tone, as though waiting for the others to agree and put him at his ease.

Alyavdin's face had so far kept on changing, sometimes expressing gloomy spitefulness, sometimes brightening up. He now beamed, unable to contain his joy, and forgetting his intention of being slipshod and coarse with Basov, he whispered to him:

"That's a real rationalization proposal, isn't it?"

While the tanker lay at berth in the next port about a hundred tons of useless weight was taken off it: old anchor chains and anchors, heavy engine spares intended for the winter overhaul. The fuel reserve was reduced to one trip's supply. That allowed the loading of an extra three hundred tons of useful cargo.

In the engine-room they put the fuel pumps right and cleaned the injectors. Mustapha Husein, grimy and dishevelled, popped out on deck and called the wireless operator.

"You can do me a service," he said, embarrassed. "You see, I'll not be able to get away today. So will you ring up somebody for me."

"I get you. No time for fun today," Volodya grinned. "You look like a cannibal out of a children's story book. And what's the somebody's name?"

Husein gave him a slip of paper.

"I'll tell her you're not in the mood. Perhaps she'll go out with me, who knows?" he said pushing his cap back.

"You won't play the cad, will you, Volodya?" Husein asked, looking doubtfully at his messenger. "See you don't, or I'll tear your guts out!"

Before their arrival, a telegram had been sent to arrange preparations for their Stakhanovite trip. The pier workers and the pumping-station men had been informed. The station worked well: the oil was pumped on at full pressure, the pipes rang, the towering hull of the *Derbent* slowly sank lower in the water.

The captain and the mates were watching the loading from the navigation bridge. The animated, somewhat solemn bustle of the preparations had taken possession of Yevgeny Stepanovich. While at sea he had read the latest newspapers, and in his mind was the figure of Stakhanov, wreathed in lightning glory. Yet he still felt a vague apprehension. It came suddenly and seized on his heart by surprise. So much was happening on the ship that was quite new, and all that newness went against his inclination for the customary, familiar way of doing things.

At the meeting they had persuaded him to sail along the channel. He had agreed because the risk did not seem considerable and because everybody around him was discussing Stakhanov's daring rationalization. But when he went up on the bridge, he remembered the disaster of the *Kavkaz* stranded on the shallows near Biryuchaya Kosa and his assurance vanished. Rusty chains and coils of cable were being dragged over the deck. Out of the engine-room stores they were carrying heavy cylindrical objects the use of which only the chief engineer knew. While Basov stood on deck hurrying the workmen, Yevgeny Stepanovich calmly reckoned in his head how much all that heavy stuff could weigh. But the engineer disappeared into the engine-room, and suddenly Yevgeny Stepanovich felt uneasy—after all, nobody had ever done that before. Just suppose the spare parts were needed at sea, or there was not enough fuel in a storm!

Yevgeny Stepanovich would have liked to have a talk with the mate; he had even started a conversation several times, but Kasatsky's answers had been laconic, he was evidently depressed about something. His face had gone paler, the senescent puffiness of his cheeks—Yevgeny Stepanovich had not noticed it before—was now quite pronounced. And besides, Kasatsky smelt of vodka, his eyes were sombre and had a wicked gleam.

"What's the matter with you?" Yevgeny Stepanovich whispered when they were alone for a minute. "You look ill. Has anything happened?"

"I've got a headache."

"It's drink. You should give it up, really you should!"

"Leave me alone. Do you want me to go to the cinema or something like that? Listen. All the chaps here are very young. Or is it just my fancy? I mean those there on deck."

"They are not all that young. Basov's about thirty. There he is."

"No, he's only a youngster. A capable youngster, that's all!"

"I don't understand you."

"You don't need to either. You're an old man."

"You should go and lie down. What's the matter with you?"

"Oh, it's nothing. Look at Alyavdin."

The second mate ran up on to the bridge and stopped to catch breath. He looked at his watch and smiled happily.

"We've taken on seven thousand tons in three hours," he reported, beaming. "Grand, Yevgeny Stepanovich. The pier never worked like this before. I ran to the pumping station, to thank them, and they laughed. 'We're working for Stakhanovites today,' they said. 'Show yourselves at sea, that'll be thanks enough for us!' But it's time for us to draw off, Yevgeny Stepanovich, this is a shallow mooring."

"All right, cast off," the captain agreed. "What do you think, Oleg Sergeyevich?"

"I don't know. You ought to know."

"Draw away," the captain decided, suddenly brightening up. "Go, my friend, and let off about ten metres from the capstan. So everything's going well, you say?"

"Remarkably well, Yevgeny Stepanovich!"

The men on the pier took in the pipes. Drawn over to the side, they hung over the pier, pouring out black streams of heavy oil. The *Derbent*'s electric windlass thundered. The ship glided slowly along the pier into deep water and stopped. This time they only set one pipe up to pump in the last thousand tons of cargo. It was getting dark. Husein went out on deck and sat down on one of the rungs of a ladder. He hummed softly as he wiped his face and bare chest with a cloth, breathing in the fresh sea breeze.

The sailors came up the gangway back from the town, among them Volodya Makarov. He went up to Husein and saluted with a click of his heels.

"Orders carried out," he said with comic pomp. "I was told to give you her best regards. She spoke of you with great affection. I was moved to tears."

"Stow the funny stuff," said Husein with a frown. "What did she say?"

"Really though. You could see she was longing terribly for you. When I told her you were busy, her voice broke. Tell me, what's she like?"

"You wouldn't understand. Ah, hell! How rotten, Volodya!"

"What's rotten? When I told her we were going on a Stakhanovite trip, she seemed to cheer up and asked all sorts of questions. By the way, I think she liked my voice. They chased me out of the telephone booth in the end. A splendid piece she is!"

"A lot you know about it!"

The workmen on the pier closed the valve of the pipe-line and started hauling on the tackle to raise the pipe. Loading was over. The metallic voice of the *Derbent* thundered deafeningly, drowning for an instant all other noises. Then the blast broke off and the echo answered in a short gruff bark.

"We've finished the loading in three hours seventeen minutes," said Volodya, looking at his wrist watch. "Grand chaps those pier workers. We've never filled up so quickly before. Well, motor-men, just give us knots now!"

Husein jumped up and stretched with a merry smile.

"We've got the fuel pump in order now. We'll give you at least thirteen knots this trip. Does that suit you? We'll put up a speed today, Volodya! You'll see."

### IV

About midnight Kasatsky came out of his cabin. Treading with affected firmness on the damp boards, he went along the spar-deck and leaned against one of the davits, his pointed chin sticking up. Far away in the sky, the thin crescent of the new moon was shining in the pearl-grey clouds. The trembling glow of the harbour lights was slowly sinking into the sea.

Kasatsky grunted, shrugged his shoulders with a yawn, and went tapping with his heels past the man on watch. The latter stepped aside as the mate neared him. Kasatsky went on up the ladder on to the bridge, past the wheel-house and down. There he stood again before the same question-mark-shaped davit with the pulley at the end, the wet canvas glimmering in the light of the moon, the lights at the mastheads, and lights along the edge of the sea.

"Prison-house!" said Kasatsky aloud. He started at the sound of his own voice. "Your exercise is over. Would you mind going back to your cabin?"

The corridor ceiling lights were dim with dust, the door-plates loomed white. A bell rang down below. From Alyav-din's cabin came the mellow wail of the gramophone. The mate swayed on his heels and rattled a bunch of keys.

"Dancing are you?" he muttered between his teeth. "Dancing, you idiots. But it's a prison-house you're in all the same."

He went back to the man on watch.

"Khrulev?" The sailor smartened himself up; his silhouette was blurred in the darkness.

"Come nearer. Well, how are things with you?" Kasatsky asked, yawning. "Bored, poor chap, are you?"

"Naturally, it's boring. A night watch is a real dog's watch."

Khrulev kept treading from one foot on to the other, trying to see the mate's face.

"Well, are you satisfied with your work?" Kasatsky asked carelessly. "A lot has changed on board. We'll get premiums. Are you glad?"

"Of course I'm glad."

"So you're satisfied?"

"If you want to put it that way."

Their faces were vague white patches in the dark, their voices seemed to be probing each other.

"You know we've got famous men on board now. How do you like that? By the papers you would think that Tatar

149

Husein was the only one to be fulfilling the plan, and the others were nothing but muck."

"You're telling me. Bloody hard on us."

"As for you, my man, you'll never be famous. You're not cut for it. With the little wireless operator it's another matter."

"Well, we'll see! Yesterday one of the engines went wrong and the light went out. There's not much I miss!"

"That's the stuff. You've got a head on your shoulders! You must know everything that takes place on board. Today it's an engine, tomorrow it'll be something else. Then we'll be able to put everything in its right place."

"But suppose we have a breakdown out at sea?"

"Sh-sh! What are you talking about? Who's on watch down there?"

"The boatswain. He's half deaf."

"Good. There are no flies on you. You understand that everything depends on me now? The captain just doesn't count."

"He's an old dodderer," the sailor sneered edging closer. "I notice everything, you can be sure of that."

"Good fellow! I'll have a talk with you when the time comes," said Kasatsky, looking at the distant lights in the sea. He turned back and went exactly the same way again.

A door half opened and a round head covered with sparse silvery bristles peeped out. It remained motionless, the glasses of spectacles flashing.

"Yevgeny Stepanovich!" Kasatsky exclaimed joyfully. "Really, are you still awake? And I, my dear fellow, am in such pains. Here's where it hurts"—he put his hand to his chest. "A horrible gnawing worm. It will eat me away in the end. But why are you not asleep yet?"

The captain squeezed between the door and the frame and ran his hand over his head.

"I am reading the *Song of the Stormy Petrel*," he said with a softening smile. "Do you remember it, my friend: He who is born to crawl, cannot fly. What pride in those words for those who can fly, what bitterness for those who can't!"

Kasatsky burst out laughing

"My dear fellow, that's all rubbish. . . Still, I'm glad you're awake." He rocked on his heels and protruded his lips with drunken familiarity. The captain stepped back, twitching his nostrils.

"You're drunk," he said sadly. "When will you put a stop to this? Straighten your cap."

"Drunk? Of course I'm drunk. What else would you like me to do in this prison-house? The only thing is to swill down vodka and to study the classics. Come along to my cabin, Yevgeny Stepanovich, just for a minute. I have such terrifying dreams. You won't refuse me that favour, that tiny little civility? What boredom! Now I'll open my cell. Yes, my cell! We're in a prison-house, you know! There's no need to look round, there's nobody here, we're all alone. One can see by your face that you're in a prison-house. You so virtuous, so unhappy, and you can't get away from here! Except, of course, into the water!"

The captain followed the mate into the cabin. On the little table there was an inkstand and an ingenious antique clock with shining cog-wheels turning jerkily, and a little grimacing porcelain clown swinging on a trapeze. The lamp-shade cast a green light, the floor was covered with a soft carpet. There was a smell of alcohol, perfume and honeyed tobacco. It was cosy, warm, pretty. But Kasatsky had a hideous grin and spoke of melancholy, sleeplessness and terrifying dreams.

"There's nobody on this ship I can talk to but you. You're the only one I want to confide in. Is there any sense in Bredis, for example, sympathizing with me, giving me a sermon and telling me I'm a chip of a dying class. It's horrid to be a chip, a useless thing, and besides, it can cut your hand, eh? Ha-ha-ha! Throw the chip out, so that it won't be in the way! Out with it at once!"

Kasatsky rounded his eyes and started stamping his feet in a kind of half joking, half sincere rage. Every muscle of his distorted face was quivering. Then he mopped his brow and smiled a sweet, tired smile, like a man on the stage after a difficult turn.

"But I refuse to be thrown out, that's the trouble!" he continued, in a mysterious low voice. *"Mein Kaffee schmeckt mir noch sehr gut!*\* as the old German ladies say. What do you want me to do?"

Yevgeny Stepanovich let himself drop into an arm-chair, folded his arms on his stomach and sighed.

"What drivel you're talking," he said in an irresolute voice. "Who wants to throw you out? And anyhow, why do you drink if you don't know what to do with yourself afterwards? You look shocking."

Kasatsky paced the cabin.

"Tell me, don't you sometimes feel awfully, awfully old? Not senile. No, old. Like the mossy stones in the Persian wall in our town. You've seen dozens of generations live and die, and you have suffered with them for every one of their blunders, and stupidities. Continents have been discovered, pyramids have been built, laws have been promulgated. And those continents have been populated and cultivated, and wearisome tourists gape at fragments of statues. On the sites of old cemeteries and battle-fields, slaughter-houses and public conveniences have been built. People are in a hurry to live, as if they had to achieve something never dreamt of before. Try to destroy their conviction. They will just shove you out of their way and go on without a look back. But it's not them I am talking about. What about you? What's your position? You are old, and everything has long been boring to you. What can you do about it? Run away into the taiga, where the wolves are bound to devour you? Or pretend that you believe in the sun of to-day and march in step with those who want to carve life anew? They will give you a place in their ranks, general respect and butter on your bread. But it's all very difficult

---

\* I still enjoy my coffee (German).—*Tr.*

and tiring. And the worst of it is, it's not toy swords the people around you fight with. They fight to the death, and those who fall are honoured as heroes. If you don't want to give yourself away you must go under fire. But the only reason why you pretend is that you want to save your life, which, the devil knows why is after all the most precious thing you have. And so you play your comedy, you go crimson in the face and croak with exertion, like a clown lifting fake weights. Sooner or later they'll find out that your weights are paper ones and they'll pitch you off the stage in disgrace, thereby depriving you of your bread and butter, which is what you were doing it all for. The game is not worth the candle, as they say. And then you know beforehand that it's bound to happen, sooner or later..."

Yevgeny Stepanovich cast a bored look at the clock. He no longer felt sleepy, but a kind of numbness, a leaden apathy seemed to weigh him down in the arm-chair.

"I don't know what you are driving at," he said in a dull voice, staring irritatedly at the mate's face. "It's like an allegory. Is it yourself you're talking about?"

"An allegory! That's exactly what it is!" Kasatsky repeated the word with delight. "That's just the word for our situation. We are so cautious, even with each other, that we resort to allegories. Ah, how clever of us, scoundrels of the past! But what do you think of it all?"

"I think you're just drunk. A sane man would shudder at such thoughts. They give one the creeps."

"Indeed?"

"Yes. We don't dare to talk of the past like that. All those sculptors, generals, and even alchemists were right in their way. They were infinitely above you, because they believed and sought. Without them we should never have known what we do know."

"But they decayed!" shouted Kasatsky. "What did they torment themselves for? Did they bring happiness and peace to anybody? Were they happy themselves? Nonsense!"

"Ah, you can't understand anything, not a thing!"

"Just you think a little, Yevgeny Stepanovich. In a hundred years not a nail of your coffin will be left—but to hell with the past! Was it the past I was talking about just now? You understood me, I hope?"

"Yes and no. All that I understood is that you hate those down below. You hate them for being young and for being ready to sacrifice themselves, for being happy, and listening to music. Their happiness is beyond your reach, so is their belief in the future. There's no place for you in that future. You are too—alien. But your hypocrisy is appalling, Kasatsky. The way you behaved at the meeting! You even insulted me, but I am not angry. Sometimes I'm disgusted with myself. But you, how can you live with thoughts like those! Some day people will point at you and shout: He's a hypocrite."

Yevgeny Stepanovich pronounced the last words almost in a whisper. His face had grown pale, perspiration beaded his forehead. Kasatsky was swaying on his heels and grinning. He seemed to wince at every word the other said, as though it stung him.

"I'm not afraid of anything, not of the devil himself," he snapped coarsely. "They've not got brains enough to see through me. And you won't give me away, my dear fellow, because there are strong ties between us. I am nearer to you and you can understand me better than Basov, the chief engineer. Don't deny it!"

Kasatsky paced from one corner of the room to the other, smartly turning in each. His shadow now contracted into a thick patch at his feet, now stretched out and leapt up the wall.

"I don't care a damn for their judgment," he muttered indistinctly. "They can't penetrate into the convolutions of my brain. But if they only knew..."

He went to the table and slowly unscrewed the cap of a black thermos flask. He shuddered as the transparent fluid gurgled into the glass, drank it off at one draught and then put his hand over his lips. He broke off a piece of bread and popped it into his mouth.

"Listen, stop that, will you!" Yevgeny Stepanovich weakly protested. "Or I'll go away, this very minute. Enough!"

The smell of alcohol in the cabin became stronger. Down below the gramophone groaned for the last time and died away. Kasatsky stood rooted by the table, his long fingers thrust in his hair.

"Well. I want to tell you something. Don't think I'm pricked with remorse or afraid of my own thoughts. I'm not! I want you to know about this. But only you. I am sure that in the main we have the same thoughts, even if you do quote the classics. Well, just imagine that I very nearly sacrificed myself one day. You don't believe me? But I mean it. Anyhow, it was a long time ago, in nineteen hundred and six. You see, I even give you dates, so it's the honest truth, and not an allegory. A shocking time, that was. Worthy shopkeepers, gambling-house owners and adventurers belonging to the Society of Michael the Archangel were beating up workers and students in the streets. Broken-hearted people—those who no longer believed in anything—committed suicide in their houses. Liberal barristers and dentists who formerly held moderate political views kept their blinds drawn, and when they had to go out they did so only with a mysterious, doleful expression on their faces. A foul, shocking time! Do you remember it? Probably you were sitting tight too? Well, well, I'm only joking, of course! But I was caught by the storm in real earnest. It pitched and tossed me so that I only managed to hold on at the very brink of the precipice. Clung on by my little finger nail. I don't know what it was that prompted me to get mixed up in the fight. Thirst for adventure? The romance of conspiracy, secret meetings, weapons in my pocket and in the garret? Or perhaps just the spirit of the times—it's a mighty factor with impressionable people. Probably a little of everything.

"At that time I had just finished the naval school and was serving at the Kronstadt forts. The situation was alarming there that summer. The cruiser *Gromoboy* had just returned from the Far East. After the Tsushima defeat the sailors were raging like devils: they would go about in bands, gather at street corners, and shake their fists at the officers. I knew a few out of the underground organization. Most of them were just common people, sailors, sappers, mechanics from the workshops. They apparently did not trust me much. And I fancied those merry fearless people held meetings just for the excitement of it, to relieve their boredom. They would talk, threaten, and then all agree that it was too early for action. I really liked it. I imagined myself to be a conspirator and kept weapons hidden, but down in my heart I felt sure that nothing would happen, and that it would be better that way anyhow. However, it would not have been against the grain to throw out the admirals, seize the ships, and sail on Petersburg with red flags. That would have been a good outing....

"One of them rather alarmed me—a torpedo-man whom they nicknamed Turok.* He seemed to be the soul of the organization: a huge pock-faced chap with tiny gimlet eyes. Once Senya, an orderly, arrived at a meeting with his head bandaged. It appears an officer had thrown boiling-hot tea in his face. Turok listened to his story, as pale as death, 'Call me a rotter if they see the end of this summer,' he shouted. 'We'll cut the whole cursed stock of them out with the roots. Senya, let's have a look at you.' They undid his bandages: his face was all red and blistered. What a row they kicked up! It turned my heart. All that was nothing like the exciting game that had attracted me.

"To my misfortune the chap felt some kind of special sympathy for me. He used to say to me, with an almost loving smile: 'You are out of their camp, but you've come over to us now. That's why I love you like a son.' His affection jarred on me, but what was I to do. Perhaps I would have broken with the organization then, but it tortured my self-respect, my petty youthful self-love, to think they might

* The Turk —*Tr*.

imagine I had got scared. Thus the summer went by. Strictly speaking, I was happy. My new position, my gold-braided tunic, my dirk, the novelty of all these things had not worn off. Coffee-houses with music in the broad street, the array of smart women, the Gipsies from the Strelnya. What beauty! Night trips on cutters in the bay, the white night over the Markizova Luzha, the pearly sunrise. Carefree light-heartedness, dizziness from wine, visions of desperate deeds ahead. How could one reflect in the middle of all that or really get to know oneself? Hurrying home one evening, I found a note on my table: 'The devils have cast out the monks. Come to the bazaar.' I understood that something important had happened, but somehow I did not believe there was any danger. I remember shaving and spraying my cap with perfume before going out. After the meeting I wanted to spend a while on the boulevard or in a coffee-house. It always added zest to it, to go straight from the meeting to a café. In ten minutes I was in another world. Of course I kept it a secret, and I was horrified myself at that unnatural mixture, but I liked it.

"I arrived. Turok met me in the corridor, embraced and kissed me three times. 'Comrade,' he whispered, 'there's a revolt on the ships in Sveaborg. They've thrown the officers overboard and trampled the tsar's flag underfoot, they're sailing on Kronstadt. We've had a telegram.' The place was full of people, the whole organization was there. It was as hot as in a steam bath. The unbuttoned tunics, the faces red with excitement, the voices hoarse with shouting, and a kind of desperate and absurd enthusiasm. I heard the orderly, Senya, so quiet as a rule, shouting: 'Brothers, our sufferings are over now! Drown the dragons!' And Turok answered in a tone of affection: 'We won't leave them to breed, you can rely on that, Senya, my boy!' Then he said to me with a triumphant smile: 'It's come at last!'

"I was sitting in a corner, waiting for some more cautious chap to come to his senses and stop it all with the thought that it was too early for action. Then it would have been as usual, happy and entertaining, with no horror about it. But it turned out different. 'Tomorrow we shall rise,' said Turok, 'and support our brothers. If anybody is too fond of his skin, let him go and not be in the way of the others. It's a serious business, brothers. Well, I put it to the vote: who's in favour?'

"Nobody went away and nobody stopped the torpedoman. They all raised their hands in silence. I looked at the others and raised mine too. For a minute I had no will of my own. Then they discussed the plan of the rising. It seems I took part in the discussion and gave advice. Turok said to me: 'By four bells tomorrow the gun-crews must be led out of the forts. Try and put the guns out of action!' I agreed.

"I felt like someone who's put a noose round his neck to feel what it's like to be hanged. He knows he's only got to stand on his tiptoes and he'll be able to breathe freely again. But suddenly he slips, the noose tightens, and he hangs in real earnest.

"I tried to remember what I had to do next day. Shooting practice, riding with Mako, the young Chinese girl, a fête at the Yenisei Regiment. But something had come over me, and I could not remember the faces or the names of the officers of the Yenisei Regiment. They had become blurred and confused. It was as though my soul was paralyzed, and half of it had suddenly turned into stone. But I had no difficulty in imagining what would happen to me at the forts. The commander would probably shoot me dead as soon as I opened my mouth. Turok seemed to guess my thoughts. He came and sat down beside me: 'Ah, my dear friend, there'll be many of us missing tomorrow! Don't think of that!' No, not if I could help it! I went out into the street. What the devil was that? Music on the boulevard—*Toréador!* Do you understand?"

Kasatsky laughed a crisp nervous laugh and tapped on the captain's knee. Yevgeny Stepanovich started.

"Hurry up and get it over," he muttered angrily. "How did you manage to save your life? Did you run away after the mutiny or what?"

"H'm, not quite. I'm telling you my feelings, Yevgeny Stepanovich, not facts. Do you think I turned yellow? Got scared to death and started praying? Well, I didn't! I tell you, I was quite calm just then. I stood and listened, and the cursed music reached my ears. I could picture them all, dancing. The sky was clear, a pale green—the next day would be windy and sunny. But what did that matter to me, I thought, when the next day I would almost certainly be killed? There at the meeting they were kissing each other, rejoicing over something, anticipating something. Could it be death? Of course not! Or were they sure they would survive? No, they couldn't be. So it was what would follow their death that they were rejoicing over. Suppose we manage to seize the forts, the ships, and the arsenals, I said to myself, suppose we arrest the officers, break through to Petersburg and arm the people. My imagination could go no further. By then I would no longer be living. Why should I rejoice at what I should never live to see? I was a living man. Only the day before I had had a future so great I could not compass it. But all that would be left of me at the celebration would be a dead shadow."

Kasatsky met the captain's persistent gaze and looked away.

"I have lived a long time, Yevgeny Stepanovich, my hair is grey. But I wouldn't say I'm fed up with life. What good would it have done me to be in a sack at the bottom of Markizova Luzha? Probably everybody would have forgotten about me by the next day. Perhaps some kind soul would have squeezed an article about the dead hero into the underground newspaper. Ugh! A dead hero sounds just as absurd as, say, a charming corpse. Do you want to be a charming corpse, my dear fellow? That has no charm for me, I prefer the prison-house. But why are you looking like that? Don't you agree with me?"

"You've not finished your story," said Yevgeny Stepanovich in a trembling voice. "Carry on, please."

Kasatsky cracked his fingers and turned away.

"I don't understand what you want.—Oh, to hell with it! You want facts? Well, here they are. They mutinied at the appointed hour and stabbed the guards. They got hold of stacks of rifles and tried to break through to the fort; they were met with machine-gun fire. They rushed at the arsenal and were surrounded by soldiers from the Yenisei Regiment. They had no more cartridges. The shooting started. There were not many of them left. By evening everything was over. What else do you want to know? Sorry, I don't remember the details. The ships did not come from Sveaborg anyhow. Whether it was a mistake or a provocation, I don't know. Everything quietened down astonishingly soon. They took corpses away on cutters, they washed the streets."

"Oleg Sergeyevich, what about that Turok?" the captain asked in a hardly audible voice. "Will you tell me what happened to him?"

Kasatsky rose and paced up and down, shivering from the effect of drink.

"Why must you ask about him? You're really inquisitive, you know. What d'you mean by it?" He stopped and looked away, with something between a smile and a grimace on his face. "They hanged him. Do you want the details? Sorry, I don't remember."

Yevgeny Stepanovich sat motionless. He was breathing heavily, his face was deeply flushed.

"You've not said everything, Kasatsky," he said, with the impetuosity of an irresolute man plucking up courage to speak the truth. "Enough! You need not say any more. I heard about that horrid business. There was treachery in it, and you know it. You..."

"You fiend!" snarled the mate, his whole body trembling. "So that's what you've been imagining! No, you really have gone out of your mind. Listen..."

"What on earth did you tell me all this for?" exclaimed Yevgeny Stepanovich, gripping the arms of the chair in an effort to rise. "What demon was it that brought you and me together! I have no sympathy for you. Your thoughts, your very presence makes me sick. Ah, why can't I unmask you—and myself too!"

"My dear chap, what is the use of tormenting yourself?" said Kasatsky, stretching out his hands with an ingratiating smile. "So you have a skeleton in the cupboard too? I knew it! I did indeed! We are bound by strong ties, deep down in our souls! But for God's sake, not a word about it! The time has not yet come for us to die. Why, even here we have good times. Very good ones, even. Now we'll play at this emulation game. I'll arrange it. I'll arrange every-thing, Yevgeny Stepanovich. Only not a word.... And if you should try..."

He did not finish his sentence. He rushed after the cap-tain. The expression on his face was changing in quick succession from ingratiating friendliness to menacing scowls. But the captain suddenly became limp and looked embarrassed. There was no trace of his former outbursts of wrath.

"I myself have memories like those, perhaps worse," he said in a sad voice. "I can't forget either, I try to find some excuse for myself, just like you. But we must not talk about this. Do you hear? Never again. As for telling anybody. No, I won't! Never."

**V**

The news of the Stakhanov trip spread to every corner of the harbour. The *Derbent* put out to sea and nothing was heard of her till morning. At 6 a.m. she answered radio calls when the head of the operational department of the shipping line inquired about her speed. It was an unpre-cedented speed that Tarumov, the wireless operator, entered in the log-book. Fourteen knots. That was too much, there must be some mistake. The management rang up asking for a quick reply. Tarumov decided to check up and called the *Derbent* a second time. He missed the time for the weather broadcast and let a heap of unforwarded telegrams pile up on the table. He kept tapping away until at last the hoarse hum of the *Derbent* answered: "All well. Speed fourteen and a half knots." And then, after a short pause came a loud sharp rapping like an oath: Ninety-nine. Tarumov roared with laughter and pulled off his earphones. In the international radio amateurs' code, that figure meant: "Go to hell!" Either joy was making Volodya Makarov cheeky or he was really angry at the frequent calls.

"You understand, Musya," said Tarumov, "they've beaten all previous speeds. The *Agamali* does twelve knots laden, and that's considered good going. But the *Derbent* beats all records."

"Let's wait and see. They've not yet arrived in the roads. Of course that's a grand speed, but they've got to keep it up," Beletskaya answered composedly. "They've always been lagging behind so far," she added.

Soon there was a telephone call from the editor of *Bolshevik Kaspia* inquiring about the *Derbent*'s speed. Musya answered in matter-of-fact voice:

"Fourteen and a half knots according to the latest reports. You don't believe it? In that case you'll have to come to the wireless-station to make sure for yourself. Yes, yes, congratulations. If only they are not held up in the roads. We'll ring you up when there's more news."

At eight o'clock Beletskaya and Tarumov were relieved. As usual they went arm in arm as far as the cross-roads. Neither of them spoke, but used to each other as they were, the silence did not weigh on them. Suddenly Musya asked:

"It'll probably be in the papers about the *Derbent*. Don't you think so?"

"Bound to be."

"With photos?"

"Whose?"

"Theirs, the Stakhanovites?"

"Why, there are forty-five of them. They'll probably take photos of the best, not all."

"It'll be interesting to see what they look like. Listen, Arsen."

"What?"

"I read that some of the administrators were badgering Alexei Stakhanov last year. Were they really?"

"Of course they were. But why do you ask?"

"Well, it's strange, somehow. Good-bye, Arsen."

"Good-bye. What's come over you today? Your eyes have got so big. See you don't get run over by a tram."

Towards morning Tarumov called the *Derbent* again. The tanker had not lost speed during the night. She had covered the distance to Astrakhan roads in thirty-one hours. A string of lighters was waiting for her by the Tyulen Bank. Early in the morning the wind became cooler and there was a swell. The last lighter had difficulty in coming alongside. In spite of this, the unloading was done in three hours. The tanker set off on the return trip, and a heavy swell chased after her from the north, threatening to reduce her speed.

The other shift had day duty at the wireless-station. Tarumov came on in the evening and looked at the log-book. There was no mention of the *Derbent*. She was expected after midday, but the operator heard her calling as early as 8 a.m.

"Zhiloy Island abeam. Arrive in two hours. Inform loading pier."

"How can that be," the duty-man wondered. "If they have Zhiloy Island on the beam they've at least three hours' sailing. Perhaps the wireless operator's got mixed up?"

"Ring up the dispatcher's office," Tarumov grinned. "Nobody's got anything mixed up, it's quite true!"

"But it can't be. I used to be a sailor myself. I ought to know!"

"You don't know their new route, though. They're sailing round the other side of the island, up the channel. It's much shorter."

"But it's too shallow there."

"Its eight foot deep. They're sailing light and without any ballast. Besides, they've got rid of all useless weight to lessen their draught. They've worked everything out, don't you fear."

"Hey, what chaps! No wonder everybody in the port is talking about them. They'll hear of them in Makhach-Kala, Astrakhan and Krasnovodsk now.

"I know one of them, Makarov, the radio operator. Just an ordinary chap, only a boy. Quite a merry sort."

"And I know their captain. Nothing out of the ordinary either. A nice old man. Always very courteous. Very quiet."

Musya listened, biting her lips. She had been quiet all morning, and nobody had taken any notice of her. Suddenly she said to Tarumov with affected indifference:

"There'll prebably be a lot of people on the pior. What about going to have a look?"

"Why not?" said Tarumov, "I'll go with you."

"I'd like so much to go for a walk." And she hastened to add: "It's such a lovely wind!"

They went along the road to the petrol dock. Musya pressed her shoulder to him and played with his fingers without saying a word.

Tarumov was thinking aloud

"What is the Stakhanov method? Rationalization, rational organization of labour, making full use of all the machinery. I should think you can apply it wherever you have mechanisms. Why not apply it in radio communications too? I tap out a hundred odd signs a minute and waste no time calling up. But there's more to it than that. If you tune your set and get rid of all unwanted noises.... What do you think, Musya?"

They went round the corner of the workshops and were blinded by the dazzling radiance of the sea.

In the middle of the bay, a steel giant was slowly turning, its rustly yellow sides towering above the water. At its stern was a wake of seething foam.

"Is that her?" Musya asked, standing still.

"Yes, that's our Stakhanovite. Come, let's hurry."

"No, wait."

Some men went past them towards the pier, talking with great animation and waving their brief-cases. Tarumov caught fragments of the conversation: "A hundred and twenty per cent of the assignment for the trip..."

Musya freed her hand and stared at the pier.

"You can see fine from here," she said, "I'm not going any farther."

He looked at her with astonishment and a kind of hope, remembering that Basov was on the *Derbent*. So it seemed Musya did not want to see him.

Tarumov took out his watch. "Exactly ten," he said, "they've done the trip in sixty-three hours. I'll run to see them berthing. You stay here, Musya."

He waved and ran downhill to the pier. Beietskaya remained alone.

## VI

In October the *Derbent* shipped a hundred thousand tons of heavy oil to Astrakhan roads.

In the second week, she outstripped the *Agamali* and topped the list of the Astrakhan line tankers. But in the third week the *Agamali* successfully carried out her first Stakhanov trip and came close up to the *Derbent* threatening to regain first place.

Emulation had by this time become part of the life aboard. Big premium money, articles in the newspapers, and radio messages from one ship to the other were commonplace things. There were no more emergency jobs in the engine-room, running repairs were carried out without any trouble. Even the crew's conferences assumed a peaceful character: new suggestions were discussed in calm and called forth no mistrust.

One morning towards the end of October during political instruction, Bredis was seized with a fit of coughing; he turned pale and buried his face in his hands. The sailors jumped up and fussed helplessly round him. Bredis raised his head and looked bewildered at his hands: they were covered with blood.

"The instruction's over, you may go," Kotelnikov announced gloomily.

But nobody went away, they all crowded round the sick man, peering into his face. Husein offered him a handkerchief and looked desperately round running his fingers through his hair.

"A stupid business," murmured the political assistant. "Why are you looking at me like that, Mustapha. We'll still put up a fight together, my lad. Call Basov."

They took him to his cabin and put him to bed. He stretched out his thin body in his berth, fixed his gaze on the ceiling and lay silent.

Basov arrived. He ordered water to be brought and sat down on the sick man's berth.

"We'll be in port in two hours," he said, "I'll call up first aid."

"No need to."

"As you like. Then I'll take you myself on the tram. You've got yourself in this state, Herman."

"Oh, enough of that!" The political assistant turned over with difficulty, gasping for breath. "I knew this would happen, Sasha, only I didn't think it would be so soon. However, everything in its own time. There are only two months left till the end of the navigation. It's not very long. And in spring the political administration will find somebody. But still, these two months—I should like to see the navigation through."

"Don't be a fool. Do you want to die at sea then? We aren't doctors, Herman. We'll soon wear you out, if we haven't done so already. Tomorrow everybody'll have forgotten again that you are ill, that you must be spared. It's not a sanatorium here."

Basov warmed the sick man's cold hands in his own, squeezing them as though to soften the unavoidable harshness of his argument.

"It's not such a simple matter to leave the tanker," the political assistant said. "The Regional Party Committee won't be able to find anybody to replace me so quickly."

Basov did not answer.

"Why don't you say something?" Bredis said with a grin. 'You'll have to take the political side over for a time. That's as clear as the sun in the sky." Then he hastily added: "Nobody can force you, of course, you've the right to refuse. In that case everything will have to remain as it is."

"A fine political worker I'll make! Are you making fun of me?"

"No use talking about it then. I'll lie up here for a while. And really, why should I go ashore? The most important thing for consumptives is pure air. And there's enough of that at sea. Make some tea please, Sasha."

Basov fussed about for a long time with the tea-pot, making a lot of noise with the lid. The colour mounted to his face. His very ears were on fire.

"We'll have time to go to the District Committee while the ship's in harbour," he said at last, as though the matter was quite settled. "If they have no objection to me for the time being, you should stay in town."

They were silent for a while. Bredis sipped the tea, wrinkling his nose and smiling guiltily.

"You feel like cursing me now, don't you?" he said. "But you're a good comrade. I really don't want to die, you know, Sasha."

"I should think not!"

"If only everything goes well on board. I sometimes think things are not so good as they seem. The commanders for example—The fact is, I've been reading the log the last few days. All the telegrams the captain's been sending—they were dictated to him. Do you know who by?"

"Yes."

"H-m. I've been keeping my eye on him for a long time, but I can't find anything concrete. There isn't anything, is there?"

"No."

"Keep your eyes open, Sasha. But then how can you; you've got enough to do with the engines. D'you know what? I'll stay on for another trip, shall I? Perhaps I'll get better."

"Nonsense! Do you think you and I are irreplaceable? What use will it be if you die here on board?"

"All right. I'll rely on the active members of the crew. Did you notice how the last political instruction periods went off? Not many of the men remained silent. If only I wasn't ill. Who's that outside, Sasha?"

"The lads They're worried about you Suppose you have a sleep, Herman?"

"Fine chaps. Hearts of gold. All right, I'll have a sleep and go ashore today. I'm so anxious to get better—and come back."

When the ship berthed, Bredis left the tanker. He walked along the pier, a tall, awkward figure with narrow drooping shoulders. The wind ruffled his fair hair and made his long overcoat beat against his legs, as though mocking at his weakness. The men crowded behind him, jostling each other to support him, and from the side of the tanker those on duty waved their caps as they watched him go.

They did not forget him on the *Derbent*. They often thought of him in off-duty hours in the mess-room. They missed him and inquired about him when in port. But serious events which were soon to happen on the tanker absorbed their attention. Later, recalling events of the past season, and trying to reconstruct their logical sequence, the men would say: "That was while Bredis was still political assistant, that's when it was!"

## THE GALE

I

At dawn, before sailing, the captain received the unexpected order to proceed to Krasnovodsk. Volodya brought him the telegram and stood at the chart-house door, shivering and rubbing his eyes with his fist.

"How do you like that?" said the captain with vexation, pushing the paper aside. "Leave everything and go the devil knows where. What have they got in Krasnovodsk? Light oil, they say."

A gust of wind snatched up the paper, bellied out Volodya's shirt and set the skirt of the captain's sheepskin coat flapping. It was getting light quickly.

"They've not got the slightest idea of the set-up here," the captain grumbled. "We have electric motors and all sorts of things on deck. The chief engineer said a spark from one of those motors is enough to cause an explosion. And tell me, who'll have to answer for it?"

"They asked us to confirm agreement," Volodya reminded him. "May I do so?"

"Wait a while, my boy. As I was saying: who'll have to answer for it? The captain, of course! All they do is to work out plans and write orders, and the captain's got to carry them out. Suppose I refuse? Indeed, we can't change the type of cargo without a special inspection of the ship. Let them appoint a commission and make a report, and then we'll even ship petrol if they like."

"So I must tell them we refuse?" asked Volodya, turning towards the door. The icy wind chilled him through and he did not want to be kept standing there. He knew by experience how hard it was to stop the captain when he started talking of responsibility and the management ashore. "I'll tell them all right, Yevgeny Stepanovich.'

"Wait, where are you going?" said the captain, all in a flurry, fussing around looking for the dispatch. "We can't refuse just like that. They'll accuse us of upsetting the plan. Where's Kasatsky?"

"He's asleep in his cabin."

"Wake him up—No, there's no need to. You'd better call the chief engineer. We'll think it over."

The sun appeared at the surface of the sea, tinging the lower edges of the jagged clouds with crimson. The ship's white superstructure became tinted with pink, fiery streamers began to meander over the water, and the electric light in the wheel-house dwindled and faded into a tiny white blur.

From the north came ragged clouds like puffs of grey smoke, the forerunners of a heavy grey storm-cloud. And from the north too, like a reflection of the movement in the sky, came scurrying little waves with glittering crests of foam. Grey wreaths of smoke rose from the *Derbent*'s funnel, only to be snatched up by the wind, rolled together and dashed on the deck.

"There's a north wind rising," said Yevgeny Stepanovich, wrapping himself warmer in his sheepskin coat. "A real autumn north wind. And the barometer's falling."

The wind lashed him in the face as he stood on the bridge and poked icy fingers down his collar, and tickled his back.

Below, the canvas cover of a life-boat bellied out by the wind was flapping with a low hollow noise. The helmsman looked round on hearing the captain's steps and took a firmer hold of the wheel.

"The navigation season will soon be over now," Yevgeny Stepanovich thought as he went down the companion-way. "How long is it? November, December—no, only half of December. How many days are there in November?"

He met the chief engineer coming out. The latter touched the peak of his cap. His face was red with the wind and seemed swollen and angry. He looked away without a word, as though reluctant to start a conversation. His chin, sunk in the raised collar of his jacket, gave him a sullen look.

"He doesn't like me," Yevgeny Stepanovich thought sadly, "Kasatsky is right. Why did I call him? I should have waked Kasatsky. What can I talk to him about?"

"It's a good thing you're not asleep," he said aloud in a friendly voice. "Do you see what's coming? Now you can expect a strong gale. And besides we have to change our course. Have you heard?"

"The radio operator told me," answered Basov. He turned round as if looking for the operator, and not seeing him he looked at the sea again.

Yevgeny Stepanovich felt offended, yet something prompted him to go on with the conversation, for he wanted to dispel Basov's distrust.

"Really, I don't know what to do now," he said, touching the engineer's hand lightly as though he wanted to draw him nearer. "On the one hand, we know Krasnovodsk oil is light and should be shipped only on petrol tankers. And we have motors on deck and the men smoke everywhere in spite of orders. On the other hand, if we refuse, we'll upset the shipments plan. And I don't want to do that. (Stupid, he thought to himself, you'd think he was trying to persuade me to upset the plan and I was refusing. And I seem to be trying to ingratiate him. How vile! Am I really?) I did not want to give an answer without consulting you," he continued. "Although, of course, I'm sure you will agree with me. (Yes, definitely, ingratiating him.) We know we're all responsible not only for our own tasks, but for the shipments as a whole. To put it briefly, I think we should confirm agreement and make for Krasnovodsk."

Basov remained silent, his eyes cast down as though plunged in thought, and Yevgeny Stepanovich got agitated: suppose the engineer said it was not his business or did not answer at all? The position would be terribly awkward. Basov suddenly looked round, as if wanting to make sure that nobody was anywhere near. Yevgeny Stepanovich mechanically did the same.

"Last year the oil-tanker *Partisan* burnt out," Basov said in a low voice. "Don't you remember how it happened? They were carrying Krasnovodsk oil too. Somebody smoked on deck or dropped a wrench, I don't know which. There must have been a crack in the hatch and gas leaked through it. There was an explosion, the seams of the deck burst and the hatches were blown open. Luckily, it happened during the day and the crew were able to launch the life-boats. A few got burns, of course, though not severe ones. But the ship was a total loss."

"And why did the men get burns?" Yevgeny Stepanovich asked in a faltering voice. He had already forgotten all about the insulting indifference of the engineer and his own humiliation. Every word Basov said went straight to his heart.

"Why they got burns? When the deck was blown open the oil flowed on to the sea. Oil burns very well on water."

"Then why are they sending us?" Yevgeny Stepanovich flared up. "Why, it's a crime, isn't it? We can't agree to it under any circumstances! What do you think? You say a man dropped a wrench. Can't one of our chaps—er—drop one too?"

"I don't know."

"There you are. Oh, what the hell must we do! Look, you're a Communist," Yevgeny Stepanovich lowered his voice. "Tell me honestly: isn't this order ignoble, isn't it a crime?"

"Well, I'm not a specialist, but I can't see where the crime is. That light oil must be shipped and there are not enough petrol tankers. The *Derbent*'s deck lets no gas through and the hatches are air-tight. Besides, the escape-vent is very good. So there's no direct danger, but it's up to us to do away with any chance risks. Even Krasno-vodsk oil does not take fire of itself." Basov smiled in his collar as he said the last words.

"But can't we refuse all the same? Let them appoint a commission and give an official decision."

"We can't refuse. You said yourself that would upset the shipments plan. I only mentioned the *Partisan* to show that we must be more careful when we are loaded and keep an eye on the men. Or else you never know..."

A gust of wind blew in from the north and covered the bay with dark rippling patches. Yevgeny Stepanovich cupped his hand round his ear:

"What did you say?" he asked.

But Basov only shivered, stuck his hands deeper into the sleeves of his pea-jacket, and on his wind-chapped lips the captain read: "Cold!"

II

Husein rolled over in his berth and knocked his head against the iron wall of the cabin. He woke up and felt cold. He opened his eyes and turned towards the port-hole. Dim grey light trickled in and tiny drops of water were dancing in it. Husein remembered that he had been lying in exactly the same position looking at the port-hole before going to sleep. It had been like looking through a telescope at a large pale-blue star on the dark-blue velvet background of the sky. There had been but a light occasional splashing of the sea below.

Now everything outside seemed full of a swelling hollow noise like a gigantic gloved fist striking regular blows on the bulkheads. Water was ceaselessly gurgling down from somewhere. Husein sometimes felt surprisingly light, as though he was falling into a pit. Sometimes he felt heavy, and seemed to press against his berth as he was pitched up to the right. At the same time, the ceiling tilted, the corners of the cabin rocked, and a tin which had fallen on the floor, rolled from one side to the other. Now it stopped as though it had hidden in a corner, and just rocked to and fro, sometimes it rolled quickly from one end of the cabin to the other with a metallic clang, when it bumped against the legs of the table.

Husein jumped up, lurched, and caught hold of the side of the berth. He stood for a moment stretching, his arms extended, just in case. Voices and the sound of steps could be heard on the other side of the partition: and Husein stood still to listen, with his sweater over his head. At last he pulled it on and put on his jacket. He pulled his cap down as tight as he could so that the wind would not blow it off.

In the corridor he came across Dogaylo warming his back by the hot walls of the galley. His oilskins were dark with water and a mesh of wet grey hair stuck to his forehead. He looked embarrassed, as if he had been caught doing something wrong.

"What's the matter with you?" Husein asked in a friendly voice. "Trying to get dry, are you? It's no use, you'll only get wet again. Hey, what a roll! We didn't take on any ballast, eh?"

"Yes we did," Dogaylo drawled plaintively, blinking, "but see what's going on. Come out on the bridge!"

Husein went to the exit, but near the door a violent icy wind struck him in the chest and he was thrown against the wall. He put his hands out again so as not to bump against the door-post.

He stopped on the bridge, deafened by the howling wind which took his breath away and brought tears to his eyes. Dimly through his tears he saw a huge white and green wave rise above the bulwark, crash down on the deck and sweep over it in a gurgling stream. Then a second one rose, shaking its shaggy crest. The *Derbent* crushed it under its hull, rolled over, and shook the water off like a gigantic sea-bird.

Two figures in wet oilskins came towards Husein from the spar-deck. They were holding on to the railings, their legs wide apart. In one of them Husein recognized Kotelnikov, in the other—Khrulev.

"Where's the bo'sun?" shouted Kotelnikov, coming nearer. Husein looked attentively at his face, trying to make out the question. "Where is he? The slacker!"

"Leave him alone, he's got himself all in a sweat," Husein answered, shouting as loud as he could and pointing towards the corridor. "Well, suppose I take his place. What's doing?"

"The waves are washing over the motor, they've torn the cover away," Kotelnikov shouted. "But that's the deck-hands' job, not yours."

But it excited Husein, and he wanted a bit of exercise before going on watch. They didn't have a gale like that every day, why should he stay in the cabin? By now he had got used to the deafening howl of the wind, his face was on fire. He went towards the bridge and Kotelnikov followed him, holding on to his shoulder. Khrulev came mincing behind, casting looks of fear at the water swirling on the deck below. They went over to the port side of the spar-deck, where the wind was not so violent.

"Looks as though we'll be late," said Husein. "What do you think, Stepa?"

"So you've woke up, have you, old chap? We're bound for Krasnovodsk, and from there to Makhach-Kala. Nobody'll overtake us now."

"Well, isn't that grand!" said Husein. "But what about our emulation? The *Agamali*'s still on the old line, isn't she?"

"Makes no difference. We'll count the ton-miles. We'll manage all right that way."

Husein nodded. In that case it did not matter whether they went to Krasnovodsk or anywhere else. He felt fine with his chest open to the wind. He was impatient to see what had happened to the motor, but Kotelnikov hung back. His face suddenly turned green, and he made a movement with his neck and mouth as though trying to swallow something that had got stuck in his throat. He hung over the railing, breathing heavily.

"He's been spewing since morning, I see," sniggered Khrulev. "All his grub's overboard by now. Some sailor!"

Kotelnikov was spitting out thick, viscous stuff, moaning and swearing. His disorderly hair was streaming in the wind.

"Go ahead," he shouted at Husein angrily. "What are you standing there for? Hell!"

The sailors on watch were standing in a group on the fore-and-aft and Kasatsky was explaining something to them, pointing down to the cargo deck. There Husein saw the ill-fated electric motor, completely uncovered, glistening with water. The waves were not lashing the fore-deck so wildly. Only seldom did a white crest unfurl over the bulwark and send bubbling streams rushing over the dark shining steel deck, where they were swirled around the hatches.

"That must be done in two moves," Kasatsky was angrily shouting. "One—get the canvas there and throw it over the motor, two—pull it tight and fasten the cord. If I had top boots I'd show you myself. Two will be enough though. You, Fomushkin and Khrulev."

The spare canvas was lying close by on the bridge, the cords already passed through the rings. Husein bent down and caught hold of the edge.

"Ah! The giant's turned up!" Kasatsky said with a smile. "He'll show you how to work!"

Husein gathered the canvas together and unravelled the cord.

"All right, I'll try. I'll take Khrulev with me. We'll be able to cover it between us."

"That's right," Kasatsky said hastily. He even put his hand to the canvas as though he intended to help. "I tell you, there's nothing to it!"

"Two of us isn't enough," muttered Khrulev, looking around miserably, "we need another chap."

"Another ten!" said Husein, with a roar of laughter. "Have you got a rupture or something!"

They dragged the canvas to the ladder leading to the deck. Husein went down three steps and slung it over his shoulder. Volodya Makarov popped up from somewhere and shouted angrily to Husein:

"Can't they do it themselves! Leave them alone, Husein!"

"I'm helping my comrades," Husein smiled back in reply. "Why not help when you're asked?"

Foamy streams of water swirled under his feet, the railing of the ladder was swaying. He could see Khrulev's pale face floundering near him, the eyes goggling and the teeth biting into the lower lip. Then the deck appeared all shining.

"Hold me fast if anything happens, Mustapha, won't you?" Khrulev pleaded in a terrified voice. "Everything is reeling in front of me!"

"I'll hold you up all right," came Husein's mocking answer. "By the leg, or a little higher up. Ha-ha!"

They ran along the wet deck and threw the canvas over the motor. Husein crouched down to pass the ends of the cord through the slides of the motor.

"Hurry up!" muttered Khrulev, pulling at the cord. "Hurry up, Mustapha!"

Then he suddenly dashed away. Husein only heard a stamping of feet and a shout. He did not raise his head at once, he first tied the knot tight. Then he saw a towering bottle-green wave with a milk-white seething crest rise high above the side of the ship, swirling and swishing threateningly. Husein pressed his whole body to the motor, clutching his arms round the shaft. In the last instant he saw quite clearly his hands and his finger-nails, which were white with the strain of clinging to the shaft, and the coarse fabric of the canvas with its reddish oil stains.

Then it was as if the icy sky had crashed down on him: he felt a sickening boom in his head, and something caught him, dragged him along, twisted his arms, and dashed him to the deck. Stunned, almost unconscious, he concentrated all his strength in his hands and did not unclench them until the water had rushed over him and washed away, leaving nothing but bubbling foam on the deck. Then he managed to rise and immediately started running, without any feeling in his body. Up above everybody was shouting something but their shouts seemed as faint as the humming of a gnat.

The second wave struck at his legs after he had gripped the rail of the ladder. Slipping, he fell on his knees, but rose again immediately and started going up the steps. He did not stagger till he reached the bridge. Then he leaned over the rail and spat out a long stream of salt water.

Before him he saw the terrified face of Volodya and the cold laughing eyes of Kasatsky. He heard Khrulev saying to somebody:

"I shouted to him, but he stayed there like a statue. Just wouldn't move!"

"Very imprudent," Kasatsky observed sternly. "You can easily get washed overboard like that."

Husein looked down and saw the wet canvas, tightly drawn over the motor. He was feeling awfully cold and his teeth seemed to be chattering away somehow all by themselves. Volodya put his arms round his waist and pressed him lightly on the back. Then, turning to those standing round, he said in a biting tone:

"If it had not been for him you would still have been there this evening discussing how to do it. Ugh, what a pack!"

Basov had spent the night watch in the engine-room. He was feeling very sleepy. But in the morning the gale broke out and he did not get a chance to sleep. He suddenly noticed that the water coming out of the cylinder jackets was hot. Basov felt it and scalded his fingers. It turned out that there were intervals when the pumps were unable to pump in water from the sea because of the heavy rolling of the ship. The circulation had to be put right.

Towards midday, the gale became fiercer, the waves pitched the ship so hard that at times the screws were out of the water. The needles of the indicators jerked, and the roar of the engines constantly changed pitch. It was becoming dangerous to keep up the speed of the ship and yet Basov was reluctant to decrease the revs of the engines. Several times he went up on deck to have a look at the weather. Then his assistant Zadorov would remain by the engines. He was nervous and kept looking from the indicators to the door above through which Basov would be coming back. He smoked one cigarette after another. But the wind kept rising, driving southwards green mountains of water peaked with jagged foamy crests. Now and again heavy slanting rain came lashing down. Low clouds blotted out the horizon. There was a ring from the bridge: Basov went to the speaking tube and heard the captain's voice asking: "How is it down there?"

"Everything is in order, but the swell is laying the screws bare. We'll have to slow down."

"Do you think so? All right. Slow down the engines."

"Aye, aye! Slow down the engines!"

Basov waited for the ring-off, but after a short silence an irresolute voice came out of the tube:

"Wait please.... Perhaps we could hold on a while."

Basov clapped the receiver on the rest, went to the instrument panel, and turned both wheels. Zadorov was drowsing, squatting on his heels and swaying like a dervish. The ship heeled over and he fell on his side. He got up, rubbed his bruised thigh and started swearing sleepily. It was stuffier than usual in the engine-room, or at least it seemed so to Basov. He felt an irresistible inclination to sleep. At one time he almost dozed off, standing at the control panel with his eyes open. He fancied he was at home and Musya, putting her arms on his shoulders, was gently and lovingly rocking him—now drawing him to her, now pushing him away. That was quite understandable, because she was angry with him for some reason. But she had not known what to say to him when he had suddenly appeared. Somebody was hammering on a metal lid and making sounds as though kneading dough. Musya shook her head reproachfully. "The third watch," she said angrily, "the third watch. Sasha, that's not right." He gave a start and opened his eyes.

"The third watch is being relieved, I tell you," Husein was shouting, smiling, "and you still standing there! You're working yourself to death! Oh, the devil take you—I had an accident. Do you hear?"

"An accident?" Basov repeated blinking. "H'm—And what's the weather like? Will the storm soon be over?"

"The weather? It's been blowing up to eleven points, they just said so in the weather broadcast. A real witches' sabbath! And I had an accident. Only you'll get wild with me, I know you will."

Mustapha was very animated. His cap had been carried away by the waves and he had a kerchief borrowed from Vera tied round his head. He told how the wave had washed over him on the deck, rolling his eyes to make his account more terrifying, but it was obvious that the memory had no terror for him. Then he looked at the indicators and went to check the lubrication of the engines and feel the temperature of the exhaust water. Basov stood by the control panel and watched him for a time, then he dozed off. Musya came out of a dark corner again. She seemed to give out a terrific heat. She lowered her eyelashes and bowed her head as though ashamed of having come to him first. He was terrified she might go away again into the dark and he took her by the hand. "Are you glad I'm with you?" she asked. "Then I'll stay. Do you want me to?" He thought that was just what he wanted and he nodded. But she suddenly burst out crying and said angrily: "Last year the petrol tanker *Partisan* burnt out. You're a Communist. Tell me: they're sending you to Krasnovodsk. Isn't that a crime?" He wanted to answer her, but she had stopped crying and was drawing him to her by the hand. In her eyes he saw the old familiar expression, melancholy and plaintive, like that of a sick dog.

"I think it would be better for you to go away," he said, freeing his hand. Then he opened his eyes.

Yakubov the fitter was standing in front of him, holding out a plate with bread and rissoles. Basov looked at his watch—it was dinner-time. He suddenly felt very hungry.

"How did you guess?" he asked, embarrassed, beginning to eat. "I didn't know myself that I was hungry. That's a good chap!"

Yakubov did not go away. He stood there smiling as he watched Basov eating, and his eyes were devoted and kind and rather amused. There was a noise outside like beating on a tambourine. The black shadows of the engines were swaying and water was gurgling under the steel plating. Above something like heavy rain seemed to be falling. Yakubov looked round anxiously. But seeing Basov go on eating he immediately regained his calm.

"Well, thank you," said Basov, handing back the plate. "Anything new on deck?"

"Same as before. Wind eleven points, they say. The water's got into the lower corridor and the anchor-room, because we had no time to make the doors watertight. The deck-hands are run off their feet. Kotelnikov is still sea-sick. He's green in the face and says his heart is bursting. I brought him a sweet to suck, but he won't take it. Some chaps, of course, can't bear a storm. As for me, it doesn't bother me. I even like it. It's a wonderful storm. A bit terrifying, all the same. You feel so small, you know."

' Terrifying?" asked Basov with a sleepy smile. "It's not that bad."

He leaned against the control panel again and dropped his head. As he fell off to sleep, a short pleasant thought crossed his mind: How comfortable!

This time his sleep was light and restless. All the time he was conscious that he was asleep and that he was in the engine-room. When Musya again appeared he got vexed. "This is no good," he thought. "I must put a stop to it." He made an effort to wake up, but he could not.

Musya was not alone. There were engineers and technicians from the ship-yards hanging round her; they were smiling with affected politeness and helping her to put on her shoes, which she kept taking off and throwing away. None of them took any notice of Basov. They probably did not even see him because he stood motionless. Neuman was among them, and the disgusting thing about it was that he was making more fuss over her than all the others. He would bend over quite near to Musya and look into her eyes with sickening obsequiousness.

Musya behaved as she always did with visitors, she was self-assured and insolent. She laughed loud and breathed in short quick gasps. But Basov could see that she was by no means gay: she knew quite well that he was there and was only pretending not to see him. Somebody mentioned his name, but she only directed a fleeting glance at him and shook her head. "Oh, I don't know where he is," she said. "I've not seen him for a long time!" She did not like lying and it was hard for her to smile when she did. Basov could see that quite well. It hurt him just as much as if he had been insulted himself. Then he suddenly remembered the whole thing was only a dream and he opened his eyes.

Volodya was coming down the ladder, gesticulating to him. Basov could see by the look on his face that something had happened.

"Just a minute," shouted Volodya, gasping, "can't you come up on deck with me? I seem to have made a mess of..."

"Why, what's happened?" Basov asked rubbing his eyes. "Be calm, Volodya!"

"I am calm, really I am," Volodya claimed. "But I've got myself into an awful mess. Kotelnikov is really ill, he's lying there and rolling his eyes all the time. They all seem to have lost their heads, and I'm the only one—"

"Look here, what *is* the matter now?" Basov inquired angrily. "If it's only a trifle I'm not coming."

Volodya took hold of his sleeve and pulled him towards the ladder.

"Come, do! First of all the aerial snapped. You know, a big wave came, the superstructure of the ship shook, the masts went just like that"—he parted two fingers—"and my aerial gave a twang and snapped. And I've got to keep in touch with Krasnovodsk and all the rest of it. If anything happens we'll just go to the bottom and nobody'll know. So I tried to find a way out, and fixed up a wire, but there were no insulators. I started to call Krasnovodsk, they couldn't hear me. So I increased the tension to get more power, and I must have overdone it. There was a crack, a smell of burning, and that was the end of it. I took the motor to pieces and found the insulator was burnt through. Now I can't think of anything else I could do."

"So you come to me, as though I was an electrician," said Basov, following Volodya all the same. "What do you expect me to do?"

On the bridge he hunched up his shoulders and turned his back to the wind. It had got very dark. Storm-clouds were banking up just overhead, constantly changing shape. The white crests of the waves flashed in the half darkness. Seething streams of water rushed over the cargo deck, and the lights at the mast-heads described wide circles somewhere above, almost in the clouds.

In the wireless cabin, Protsenko, the junior electrician, was sprawling on a chair in a cloud of smoke, calmly gumming a hand-rolled cigarette. Parts of the dismantled motor and pieces of burnt wire lay on the floor. Iron bolts rolled here and there with the tossing of the ship.

"Just look what a fine mess our radio operator has made!" said Protsenko, kicking a bolt that was rolling about on the floor. "Can you imagine it! Ugh!"

"Get out of here!" shouted Volodya, with tears in his voice. "You always get on my nerves the way you jabber when something's gone wrong!"

He turned and looked shyly into Basov's face.

"What must I do now, Alexander Ivanovich?"

"I don't know," said Basov. "What's that thing there that you've gone and spoilt? The dynamo?"

"Yes," said Volodya in a dejected voice. He suddenly realized that the chief engineer knew nothing about wireless and could not help him. He immediately went away from him and squatted down, miserably fingering the motor.

"So this is what fed your wireless?" inquired Basov. "Well, can't it be replaced by something else? Accumulators, for example?"

"Accumulators are eighty volts, and the motor one thousand two hundred. It's just ridiculous," said Volodya shrugging his shoulders. "Do you know what," he added in a distressed tone, "you go, they're waiting for you. I'll manage somehow by myself."

"Let them wait. One thousand two hundred? Yes, of course. You said yourself you'd changed the tension. So your transmitter can work on less? Say six hundred volts?"

"Perhaps so, I don't know."

"Well, we must try. We've got accumulators. How many, Protsenko?"

"Eight or nine. No, eight."

"Well, eight times eighty volts is six hundred and forty. Protsenko, take some of the deck-hands and bring the accumulators here."

Volodya looked up at Basov with his mouth open. Prot·senko crushed his cigarette with his heel and went out.

"So you want to feed the transmitter with those accumulators?" asked Volodya in amazement. "It won't work."

Basov whistled as he examined the shining wireless valves through the grating of the transmitter.

"A wonderful thing," he said in a tone of curiosity. "It is indeed— Why won't it work then?"

"Well, nobody does it like that. Whoever heard of such a thing. First of all the accumulators won't last long enough."

"But we don't need them for long—just for one trip until the dynamo's repaired. Don't look so miserable, Volodya."

Basov no longer felt sleepy. He examined the transmitter from all sides and then looked out into the corridor.

"What are they dawdling over?" he asked impatiently. "Go and shake them up, Volodya!"

The operator went slowly to the door.

"There won't be enough room for them here either," he said gloomily. "Some idea you've got there!"

"Go on, hurry up," said Basov.

While they were bringing the accumulators he had time to open the back of the set and have a look inside. He saw valves, thick wire spirals and the shining condensers (he cautiously felt them) and decided that after the gale he would get Volodya to explain all that to him.

The accumulators were bulky and heavy, there was hardly room for them on the floor of the small wireless-cabin, and when the ship pitched the acid splashed out over the floor.

"They've messed the whole cabin up," Volodya growled, "and the acid has eaten holes in their clothes. It's all no use."

Protsenko squatted down to connect the wires, sticking out his tongue with the exertion. Suddenly he got an electric shock which made him jump and bite his tongue. He got angry.

"What are you standing there for?" he snarled at Volodya. "Give a hand, you son of a bitch!"

The operator was about to sit down by the accumulators, but he rose again.

"Alexander Ivanovich, it won't work."

"What's the matter now?" asked Basov, turning round.

"Why, we've got no aerial. I fixed the wire direct to the stays because we had no insulators. So you see, all our efforts are useless."

"Can't we put something else instead of the insulators?" asked Basov. He screwed up his eyes and looked tensely at the operator.

"We've replaced half of it as it is," he was going to mumble, but his eyes met Basov's, which had become harder, and he said nothing.

"Hell!" growled Basov, impatiently, "he's gone quite mopish! Come, let's go and look for something, Protsenko."

"Perhaps Narzan* bottles would do?" Protsenko suggested dubiously. "Glass is a good insulator, isn't it?"

"So it is! Bring some bottles."

Volodya suddenly went as red as a lobster and started bustling about; then he shot out into the corridor. Basov watched him go with a frown, and Protsenko winked slyly and got out his tobacco-pouch.

The operator came back with a pile of empty bottles, and set to work without even a look at anybody. He strung the bottles together, working with such a will that beads of sweat stood out on his temples and forehead; then he coiled up the wire and went out quickly, the bottles rattling around him.

"Let's go and see," Basov suggested, "he's in a mood to climb to the very mast-head now. He might fall, for all we know!"

Sailors in oilskins were standing on the bridge under the light looking up at the radio operator who was clinging to the spiral ladder, dangling over the deck with each lurch of the ship. He was clutching convulsively at the stays,

_____
* Narzan—mineral water from the Caucasus.—*Tr.*

trying to tie on the heavy string of bottles. Protsenko took the end of the wire, climbed on to the roof of the cabin, and fastened it to the lead-in. Then he sat on the roof with his legs over the side and started looking up too.

"Be careful, Volodya!" Basov shouted. "Tie it with an overhand knot. Hey, you'll fall!"

In the golden column of light shed by the lamp, streams of water now and then washed over the deck and flowed overboard. The wind now came in vicious squalls, blowing spray in the men's faces, now dropped powerlessly, whirling fine watery powder round their legs. The ship lunged cautiously, shaking off the foam, and then slowly straightened up.

"The wind's falling, boys," somebody near Basov said. "If only we could get warm!"

The voice was damp and hoarse and spoke with a weary drawl. Basov suddenly felt that he too was dead tired, and that if he had nothing to keep him busy he would just fall into a sleep as heavy as death. But Volodya had already come down. He went to the light sucking a scraped finger.

"I've put it high enough," he said, catching breath, "you can probably see it from here. Look!"

They went back into the cabin. The operator put on his headphones, pressed down the switch and started tapping.

"There's current all right," he said with hasty excitement, and he turned to Basov as though vexed at the engineer not saying anything and not showing any pleasure. "Do you hear? It works, I tell you."

"Good," said Basov. "Now call Krasnovodsk."

He listened to the tapping of the key and the first doubt

came to his mind. He imagined some kind of quivering green threads, stretching out in all directions from the wireless cabin. They soared over the sea like streamers but fell into the water before reaching the shore. "We must establish contact all the same," he thought obstinately. The green threads disappeared.

For a long time Volodya tapped away; his elbow was trembling, the tuft of hair on his head was bobbing up and down. Then he turned the knob of the receiver and his face took on that sharp, concentrated expression he always had when he was taking a message in Morse. The loudspeaker hissed, whistled and pattered loud like a shower of small beads on glass.

Protsenko came with resounding steps, stopped sharp at the entrance, and then noiselessly pushed the door ajar. The loudspeaker became silent.

"That's that!" cried Volodya, beaming. "They say we're hard to hear. If only they knew what we're working on. Shall I tell them, just for fun? They wouldn't believe me!"

"And you said it wouldn't work!" Protsenko said teasingly. "A lot you know!"

Basov went out on to the spar-deck. His feet were as heavy as lead. He gulped in the cold air and raising his head saw through a gap in the clouds a clear-swept strip of starry sky. The wind had already spent its unbridled violence and was blowing in gusts. Sometimes a calm set in and the hum of the engines and the paces of the sailor on watch on the helmsman's bridge could be distinctly heard.

"If only I could turn in!" thought Basov. "Undress and get under the blankets! No, it would take too long to take my clothes off. Just my boots, that's enough." Black spots were swimming before his eyes, and he felt himself reeling and gently sinking. Now he must get some sleep, really, he must. Just a look at the engines. . . .

Somebody rushed along the spar-deck and bumped into him in the darkness.

"Alexander Ivanovich, I've been looking for you everywhere!" said Kozov, the motor-man, holding on to a button on Basov's jacket. "There's something wrong with the auxiliary motor. The fuel regulator's out of order. The motor's revving like mad. It'll be flying to pieces any minute. Zadorov's raving—he keeps growling at me and threatening to have me up for trial, as though it was my fault. Please come, Alexander Ivanovich."

"You say the regulator's broken?" asked Basov on the way. "But why didn't the engineer stop the motor? It's sheer panic! All right. Waken up the electricians and the senior motor-man of the second watch. Look smart!"

"Mustapha's only just come off watch, Alexander Ivanovich!"

"Do as I tell you! Tell the electricians to switch over to the emergency lighting. Throttle down the motor. Wake up Husein, and Yakubov, the fitter, too. And don't you get excited. We'll put it right in no time."

"Aye, aye!"

"Rotten organization," thought Basov, going down to the engine-room. "The duty engineer is afraid of the engines, gets nervous and shouts at the motor-men, and the motor-men run about the ship looking for the chief engineer. Rotten organization, and rotten commanders too. The fact is, I'm a bad organizer; that's why they can't do without me!"

He no longer felt tired, a dull irritation against the duty engineer, against the motor-men and against himself was seething in him, making him coarse and harsh and rousing in his subordinates a feeling of fear and hostility.

At the door of the engine-room stood Mustapha Husein, naked down to the waist with a woman's kerchief on his head; he was stretching, rubbing his eyes and smiling sleepily.

"Get a move on," said Basov, looking past him with an estranged expression. "You can have a sleep later. What are you waiting for when there's a break-down in the engine-room?"

"For you," said Husein still smiling. "I've already been there, stopped the motor and inspected it. The regulator's broken, just as I thought. We'll start putting it right now. What's the idea of flying at me like that? What a vicious chap you are!"

"But when did you manage all that?" Basov stammered, reddening. "You say they've begun to put it right? Well, well!"

"They called me long ago. And do you know what? You should turn in. You can't go on for forty-eight hours without a sleep. Look, you're flying at people as it is."

"Don't take any notice of that," Basov said, with a smile of confusion. "It's this blasted gale!"

"I'm not offended. But you go to bed just the same and don't interfere. Superfluous chaps are only in the way, you said so yourself."

"Ho-ho! So you're kicking me out, are you? Right you are, I'll go. But you won't make a mess of it, will you, Mustapha?"

"Don't you worry."

"Well, good night, Mustapha!"

"Good night!"

"This time I really must go to bed," Basov thought as he went over the bridge. "They weren't waiting for me after all, and they can quite well do without me. The organization's not so bad either. They'd already stopped the motor, found out what was wrong and got everything ready to put it right. I could hardly have done it so quickly myself. There are some very good ones among them, like Husein; and all together they're much better than each one taken separately, because they complete one another. How could I have such rotten ideas about them when I came here? How could I form an opinion anyhow? No, it was just sleeplessness and the gale. The gale!"

## CHECHEN ISLAND

### I

IT HAD a strange deceptive smell, that Krasnovodsk oil. When they laid pipes and started pumping the dark hissing liquid into the tanks, Dogaylo stuck his nose out and said:

"Like fruit drops or some other kind of sweets. Sniff to your heart's content!"

And the sailors did sniff. It was as though a tray of hot confectionery had been brought on deck. But afterwards there was an unpleasant sort of tickling in the nose. Dogaylo pinched his nose and said, "Phew! What a stink though!"

But towards the end there was no more of that either. It was as though ordinary crude oil was being pumped through the pipe-line. Only Fomushkin, who had been standing by one of the hatches, complained of a pain in the temples, and Dogaylo went anxiously away to the side of the ship and did not say another word.

In Krasnovodsk the captain received another order from the shipping line—to take in tow the tanker *Uzbekistan* which had been disabled in the gale. It was an unpleasant, ticklish job, but all the same Yevgeny Stepanovich was in a good frame of mind. He had weathered the gale on the open sea with its alarm and unbearable tension. Everything was fine. So Yevgeny Stepanovich felt an afflux of friendliness towards everybody.

"Look," he said to Kasatsky, "just you look: how charming! The little white town and the red cliffs above it. And the golden sand-banks all around the blue bay! What amazing beauty!"

Kasatsky looked tired and ill; he had brown pouches under his eyes. His tunic had stains of tobacco-ash on it and was all creased, as though he had been sleeping with it on.

"The town is white, that is true," he answered derisively, "and the cliffs are certainly red, there's no doubt about that. But you seem to be in a very joyful, pink mood now. How is that?"

He turned his head slowly and riveted his bulging eyes on the captain's tie.

"Anyhow, it's a good thing that you are feeling merry. But I am used to looking ahead, you know. The north wind is no longer blowing, everybody's glad. But I'm not. That is to say, I'm satisfied, of course, but not in the same way as you. As soon as gladness raises its shrill stupid voice within me, I begin to think over things. And it turns out that no matter how much you sing, something unpleasant is bound to happen at the end and you'll have to play 'Parting'."

"But after that it will be all right again. Won't it?"

"I don't know. Perhaps it will. I'm fed up with the abstract themes. Look, there's the *Uzbekistan* at pier over there. We must have a look at her before we take her in tow. Let's go."

"Ah, that towing business! We can't refuse either! She

has been disabled, but her tanks are already full of oil and it must be shipped.

"We'll have to tow the old hulk, there's no getting out of it."

"You seem to be glad—"

"No, it's just that I've brought you back to reality and proved that there are still unpleasant things. Give me your arm, you merry man!"

They went down to the cargo deck and towards the gangway. Yevgeny Stepanovich sniffed and stopped.

"What is that smell?" he asked in surprise. "Is it the oil?"

"Have you only just noticed it? Yes it is, Krasnovodsk oil. What are you frowning for? It has a peculiar smell, but not an unpleasant one."

They walked leisurely along the shore. Kasatsky talked about the interesting qualities of Krasnovodsk oil—the aromatic substances and benzines it contains and the low temperature at which it takes fire. Yevgeny Stepanovich thought that Kasatsky knew much that other mates did not know, but somehow he did not like to show his knowledge and even read the newspapers all by himself, locked in his cabin.

On the *Uzbekistan* they were welcomed by a good-natured, stout, ginger-headed man who introduced himself as the mate. They went to the fore-deck together, had a look at the towing gear and agreed how to secure the tow cable.

"We never have any luck," the fat man said with a complacent smile. "The winter overhaul was badly done and now we don't have a trip but something breaks down. Yesterday a shaft got jammed but we took on the cargo just the same. We can't go back light! But there again, between you and me, it's not right because our deck is not in order."

"Really?" asked Kasatsky, with apparent apathy. "But that happens often enough."

"They welded it in one place, but obviously not well enough. There's a smell of gas. And we have no gas vents either. It's against the law."

"We must go back," said Kasatsky in a hurry. "It's time, Yevgeny Stepanovich."

The ginger-headed mate yawned and went back to his cabin. There was washing hanging out on deck and coils of cable lying about. Yevgeny Stepanovich shook his head. "They've made a pigsty of their ship, the swine!"

For some reason, Kasatsky did not go straight to the gangway, but turned off in the opposite direction along the deck. Yevgeny Stepanovich submissively picked his way after him. The nearer they came to the after-deck, the stronger the sweetish smell became. The captain felt a tickling in his nose.

"Aren't their hatches battened down?" he asked, sniffing. "What the devil! This is really against the law!"

Kasatsky went round the superstructure and on to the gangway without stopping.

"Have you got that paper with you?" he asked quickly.

"Which paper?"

"The radiogram you got from the shipping line today about taking the *Uzbekistan* in tow! Let me see it."

He looked at the form, folded it and twitched his nostrils.

"We'll file this," he muttered, worriedly, "just for the sake of order, you know."

"Really, I'll refuse to take her in tow!" said Yevgeny Stepanovich, with a start. "I'll go and send a telegram at once."

"Steady. What's come over you? There's a smell of gas on deck. What about it? They've got permission from the inspection board to carry on service. If you refuse they'll accuse you of upsetting the plan."

"Do you think so?"

"I'm sure they will."

"Ah, what a dog's life a captain has!" Yevgeny Stepanovich sighed. "Curse the minute I agreed to leave the office!"

During the loading, a chap in a seaman's cap came to the gangway of the *Derbent*. He looked about fifteen years old but he had an air of importance and affected gravity. He had a note-book in his hand and was obviously very inquisitive, for he kept standing on his tiptoes, trying to see what was happening on board the tanker.

"Good afternoon," he politely greeted Dogaylo. "How do you do?"

"What, do you know me?" asked the bo'sun in good-natured amazement. "Where've you come from?"

"No, I don't know you yet," answered the other. "But you're taking us in tow, that's why I came to make your acquaintance. How do you do!" he nodded to the sailors who had gathered by the side of the ship. "I'm wireless operator on the *Uzbekistan*, my name is Valerian."

He ran up the gangway and held out his hand to the bo'sun.

"Well, how do you do, Valerian!" said Dogaylo, laughing. "Things are in a bad way with you. We're going to tow you."

Kotelnikov, Husein and Makarov came out of the mess-cabin. Glancing at the newcomer, Volodya shouted:

"Why, it's Valerian!"

He ran up, seized the youngster by the shoulders and whirled him round in front of him.

"Valerian, where did you pop up from? How did you get here? On the *Uzbekistan*, are you? He was in the same promotion as me,"—he turned to his comrades—"the youngest of all. They didn't even want to admit him. True, isn't it, Valerian? Come on now, tell the truth. But look at him now: goes to sea and isn't scared! And he's only a kid!"

"It's very interesting," said Valerian with dignity. "I already told you I am a wireless operator. And I manage fine too! How did you weather the storm? I was on duty at the wireless all the time, without any relief! Because

some ship could have been wrecked, and I would have heard it and saved—that is, we would have saved them. A very important duty, that is, you know. Did you read the order from the People's Commissar about preventing accidents? Well, that was why I remained at my station without any relief!"

He was trying to speak with an air of indifference, but he was obviously excited at talking to so many grown-ups, especially strangers. His voice now sank to a gruff bass, now rose to a squeaky boyish treble.

"My wireless is very powerful," he went on with enthusiasm, "and I've already carried out a lot of interesting experiments (I'm an old wireless amateur, you know). Now, I'm thinking of sending an article to *Radiofront*.* You see, I tried to keep up communication with the Black Sea ships, and I succeeded too, but only in the evening and for short periods. Science affords an explanation for that. Unfortunately I had to stop my experiments because the control station heard me and sent me a reprimand. Just try and argue with officials!"

"Ah, what a grand kid!" said Husein in rapture. "And what was the reprimand for?"

"For hooliganism on the air. But that's nothing, it's a fine life at sea all the same. We've got a large library, about thirty volumes or even more. Besides, I'm a Young Correspondent. I write about oil shipments and the Stakhanov movement. To tell you the truth, I had a reason for coming here, I even brought my note-book to take down your impressions. What are you laughing at, Volodya? I

* Radio amateurs' magazine —*Tr.*

should like to speak to one of your Stakhanovites. How did you manage to set up your records?"

A fair crowd had already gathered, and for a moment he felt embarrassed. But seeing the merry, good-natured faces, he opened his note-book with an air of importance. Husein hooked him under the arm and they walked along the deck, followed by the inquisitive crowd.

"So the whole thing was a question of the engines and saving time in loading? Just a minute, I'll write that down. It's a kind of invention, isn't it? No? Well, perhaps it was stupid of me to say that. Stop laughing, Volodya! I forgot to tell you I'm a designer too. I make little gliders out of wood and paste-board. It's very interesting. Unfortunately, there's nowhere to fly them—our deck's not big enough and they all flew overboard and got lost. And I built an electric motor too, quite a small one. It weighs no more than a few grammes and works on a pocket battery. And it's made entirely out of Soviet material, mind you!"

Volodya roared with laughter. He took the visitor in his arms and lifted him up.

"Out of Soviet material!" he repeated, spluttering with merriment. "Ah, how you can prattle!"

"Enough, Volodya, don't be so childish," said Valerian, frowning and freeing himself. "Let me have a talk with the chaps. Do you hear, Volodya!"

He straightened his shirt and turned to Husein.

"You'll give me all the details about your Stakhanovite trips when we get to Makhach-Kala, won't you? I'm sure we could adapt a lot from them for our work. On the *Uzbekistan*, we stick to the old methods. The chief engineer is asleep half the time. I think he's got sleeping sickness and doesn't know it. There is such a disease, you know. A gnat bites you and there you are! Laughing again, Volodya! And by the way, things are in an awful state with us. The engine broke down yesterday and he didn't even notice it. And let me tell you confidentially—" he put on a mysterious expression, and Volodya leaned closer to him, a smile ready on his face,—"there's a crack in our deck and gas leaks out. Word of honour! In port they stopped it up, but not properly, because there's still a smell. And we have no gas vents. So you see!"

He said it all in one breath. Volodya still smiled mechanically, but a silence set in.

"How long has it been like that?" Husein asked. "Do you remember?"

"A fairly long time. In port the captain got an engineer to come—I've forgotten where from—"

"From the inspection board, probably?"

"That's right. He said it had to be stopped somehow till the end of the navigation season, then he turned round and off he went. And they just did it anyhow!"

"So the inspection board allowed you to carry on shipping with a deck like that? Without any gas vents? Impossible!"

"But I remember quite well. He just turned round and went away."

Kotelnikov bit his nails and frowned.

"We must do something, boys," he said in a low voice. "They can't put out to sea like that. That's clear."

"But what will you do?"

"We'll get in touch with the shipping line and tell them about it. It can't be left like that."

"It's too late," said Volodya, "they'll have finished loading just now. I say, Valerian, have you any electric motors on deck?"

"Yes, there's a windlass on deck. Where else could it be?"

"Perhaps there's still time?" asked Husein, looking around in alarm. "Perhaps we should waken Basov?"

"It's too late, Mustapha, Basov's not a wonder-worker. And nobody'll believe us anyhow. Once the inspection board has given permission—"

"None of your chaps smoke on deck eh, Valerian? Or do they?"

"No, it's sort of forbidden." Valerian looked at the three of them one after the other, blinking guiltily. He was sorry that the conversation, which had started so well, had taken that turn.

"Well, boys," said Kotelnikov, "it's too late to do anything now, but in Makhach-Kala we'll get the Party organization on to this question. What is your political assistant thinking of, comrade Young Correspondent?"

"I don't know. He's not been with us long." Valerian was silent for a while, and then he suddenly smiled in an appealing boyish way. "Do let's talk of something else."

Everybody liked the young operator from the *Uzbekistan*, and they waved their hats to him as he went along the berth to the shore. Dogaylo even had a fit of emotion as he watched him go.

"I had a son—he died," he said sadly. "A nice clever lad like him, he was. He'd be thirty or more now—"

### III

The day went by as uneventful as any other at sea, split up into four-hour watches. Out at sea the swell had not yet calmed down completely. The reflection of the sun tossed on the slope of the waves. The tow cable creaked at the stern, and farther behind loomed the high bows of the *Uzbekistan*, her mast standing out in black against the blue background of the sky. The men of the *Derbent* had soon got used to her, as if they had had her in tow for ages and there were no men and no inflammable cargo on board, but only the masts, the rusty hull and the white superstructure. In the evening, when it got dark and the lights went on in the cabins, she vanished altogether. There was just the creaking cable disappearing into the darkness with a garland of lights at the end and waving chains of trembling lights deep down in the sea. Invisible waves came and broke the chains asunder, but they joined together, only to be broken once more and so on, over and over again.

Kasatsky stood on watch in the dead of night lost in contemplation of those glimmering chains. He leaned his elbows on the rail of the bridge, drew his sheepskin coat closer round him, and remained still. Far behind the stern, the golden chains were wriggling like snakes. He watched them, unable to take his eyes off them, although the sight somehow jarred upon him. He was glad when he heard voices below, and he bent as far over the rail as he could to listen.

"There must be an island here. Which one is it?"

"Chechen Island."

"Chechen? Blimey! You seem to know the whole sea!"

"Why not? I've been sailing it ever since I was a youngster!"

It was a rather hoarse, mocking voice that was asking the questions, the bo'sun's squeaking tenor was giving the answers.

"Must be Khrulev," Kasatsky guessed.

"Uncle Khariton?"

"Yes?"

"Where were you yesterday evening when we were putting the canvas on the deck motor? We looked for you everywhere."

"I don't remember, lad. I must have been doing something. I don't remember."

"That's a bare-faced lie! Husein said you were in the galley. Lying quiet there, were you?"

"It's him that tells lies. He's an ill-bred cub, he has no feeling for others."

"I agree with you there. But still?"

"If anybody wants to get drowned, it's his business. I'm an old man."

"There you are! And I had to buckle to! He was nearly washed overboard yesterday, that Husein." The last thought was added like a pleasant reminiscence.

Kasatsky listened, his features frozen in a smile, his thin white ear peeping out of his woolly collar. But the conversation ended there.

"Well," said Kasatsky in a low, satisfied voice. "We've passed Chechen Island. I'll have to take our bearings." He went into the chart-house, blinking in the light, and stretched himself, arching his back like a cat after a feed. As he bent over the chart, he heard a loud, booming noise somewhere outside, like a hammer striking a steel plate. At the same instant Khrulev let out a scream on the bridge and flung the door of the chart-house open.

"What's the matter with you?" asked Kasatsky, turning round. "Has something stung you?"

He saw Khrulev, his face livid and his mouth agape, and he sprang to the door. Beyond the stern, where the chains of light had been shining before rose a swaying plume of crimson smoke and through it the masts and rigging of the *Uzbekistan* could be seen lit up in pink. Kasatsky was already running to the companion-way but he suddenly stopped dead, biting his fingers. Khrulev's white face, blind with fear, appeared again and his hoarse voice shouted.

"He-e-e-lp!"

"Shut up!" yelled Kasatsky. "Shut up and carry out my orders!"

He stamped his feet, and seizing the sailor by the neck of his shirt, drew him towards him.

"Do me the pleasure of calming down and listening. The tow cable must be cut. Drop it overboard at once! Understand! Look smart!"

"I need an axe," muttered Khrulev cowering. Then he said: "Aye, aye! Cut the tow cable!"

Kasatsky pushed the sailor away and rushed down the ladder. Khrulev hurried after him breathing heavily and whimpering: "In a second! We're done for!"

"Where's the axe?" Kasatsky asked, without slowing down. "Do you hear me?"

"There's one in the fire box," said Khrulev groaning. "I'll bring it now. Oh, quick, quick!"

The air trembled with the hollow roar of an explosion, and behind the stern rose another black fiery plume of smoke, dotted with glowing sparks. The ship's bell on the *Uzbekistan* clanged madly and then suddenly stopped. Dogaylo ran out on deck. He was dragging a life-buoy, bumping blindly into things and staggering. He bumped against a hatch and gave a loud shout, "Ugh!"

Khrulev jumped down to him and seized his hand.

"Uncle Khariton, give us an axe, quickly! Oh, we're done for!"

"An axe?" Dogaylo stuttered, dumbfounded. "What do you want an axe for now? It's a life-buoy you need!"

"Give me an axe at once, you old bastard!" roared Khrulev. "Or I'll knock you stiff."

Dogaylo stepped back and dropped the life-buoy. Both the men disappeared out of the trembling beam of light coming from the stern. A minute later, Khrulev rushed into the light again with an axe over his shoulder. He ran up astern with surprising speed, his mouth wide open gulping in air. On deck Dogaylo was looking for his lost life-buoy, uttering low groans and crossing himself. At last he found it and started to put it on over his head, listening to the strokes of the axe coming from the stern. The ship lurched as it was cut loose from the *Uzbekistan* and he staggered and fell sitting on the deck, frowning. Kasatsky ran into the light and bumped into him.

"That's that! We're saved!" he said with a trembling forced smile. "Throw that useless thing away, you old fool, and waken the captain up."

Just then Husein came out of the engine-room and stopped on the fore-and-aft bridge, listening.

"The tow cable's snapped!" he shouted, seeing the men on deck. "We must stop the ship, Comrade First Mate!"

"Go back to where you came from!" shouted Kasatsky. "Everything's in order. Go back!"

But Husein suddenly ran on. The pink reflection of the fire shone in his eyes.

"Where's the captain?" he shouted, looking wildly round. "Hey, you there! Can't you see there's a fire!"

"Go back!" cried Kasatsky. "I'll have you up for trial for not obeying orders in an emergency!"

But Husein was no longer looking at the deck nor listening to the mate. He stood still for a few seconds, thinking. Then he rushed to the spar-deck, up the ladder to the navigation bridge, and disappeared.

"He wants to sound the alarm," Khrulev guessed. "He'll waken everybody up, Oleg Sergeyevich. They'll make us go back!"

For a moment everything grew dark and the patches of light on the black sea went out. But immediately a golden cloud of sparks shot up behind the stern and the sky flared up a fiery crimson.

And as though burnt by the glowing blaze, the *Derbent* roared deafeningly in the dark.

Basov was lying on his berth with his clothes on, his bare feet stretched out and his chin sticking up, as though felled by a bullet. Between his loosely-closed eyelids something irritated his eyes, and he thought that morning had come, that the pink sun was rising, and that just by his ear something was roaring with a long drawn-out roar, making the cabin walls tremble. Half waking, he turned over on his side to avoid the red rays of the sun that were tickling his pupils between his eyelashes. The blast broke off suddenly, and in the ensuing silence Basov heard shouts. Still he did not move, but lazily wondered why he felt so sleepy when morning had already come, and why they had not wakened him for his watch as he had asked them. He heard the door fly open and somebody rush in, bumping into a chair in his haste. Then, opening his eyes, he realized that it was not the sun that was shining. He saw Husein's face bending over him, trying to frighten him, he thought.

"What time is it?" he asked, with a sleepy smile, groping for the switch. "What did you say, Mustapha?"

"I tell you there's a fire on the *Uzbekistan!*" said Husein, shaking him by the shoulder. "Get up quickly!"

Basov switched on the light and sat up on his berth.

"There's not!" he shouted at the top of his voice. "It's impossible!"

When the light went on, he was dumbfounded not by Husein's words, but by the expression on his face, the same old expression of vacant and oppressed despair that it used to have during the first shameful trips.

"Look what the rotters have done!" exclaimed Husein in a hollow voice. "Everything's lost now. Done for!"

"Keep calm, Mustapha." Basov pulled on his boots and rushed out into the corridor, buttoning his jacket as he went. "Who's that shouting?" he asked, listening attentively.

"The lads have assembled on the spar-deck. They insist on turning back."

They went along the corridor on to the cargo deck. Basov stopped and raised his hands to his temples.

"What's that?" he asked in a whisper. "What's going on, Mustapha?"

Far astern was a towering cloud of smoke, the centre of it burning with a blinding ruddy glow like a red-hot coal, sending up sheaves of golden sparks.

"They've cut the tow cable and are sailing away," said Husein despairingly. "I sounded the horn but Kasatsky chased me away. Listen, do something! There's still time. Are we really going to sail away like this, Sasha?"

He peered into the engineer's face, but he suddenly realized that Basov was just as powerless as he was. He had to take orders from the captain, he was not free to turn the ship back. And if he insisted they would threaten to bring him to trial or chase him away just as they had done with him, Husein.

But Basov suddenly recovered his calm and looked back, as though measuring the distance to the burning ship. He turned about unexpectedly and strode in silence to the ladder. Husein followed him, in silence too, his mind a blank.

On the spar-deck, the men were looking round with fear, not able to recognize one another in the flickering light of the fire. Their voices now swelled and shouted all together, drowning one another, now sank to a whisper so that every word said aloud could be distinctly heard. Then the men would all look at the one who had spoken, as though waiting for an order.

Kasatsky's tall form could be seen on the helmsman's bridge, near the ladder. He was standing motionless, except for an occasional turn of the head when the noise below got louder.

Next to him, the heavy stooping figure of the captain was leaning over the rail. He was stirring continually, making all sorts of small useless movements. He twitched his shoulders as if he felt cold and started buttoning up his tunic, but suddenly left off and turned his head, looking now at the burning ship, now down at the spar-deck, groaning and twisting his fingers.

On the spar-deck, Yakubov, flushed with excitement, was wiping his wet face with his handkerchief; his eyes seemed swollen with welled-up tears.

"Let them come down here!" he shouted, beside himself with rage. "Let them explain why we are sailing away! Chairman of the ship's committee, make them explain!"

"Enough talking!" shouted Kotelnikov with a look of hate at the bridge. "We must force them to turn back."

"Here with the captain!" shouted somebody.

"The captain is here."

"Where?"

"There! Crumpled up on the rail!"

A short silence set in. The men crowded by the ladder looking at the blurred figure on the bridge, forgetting the fire for a while in their morbid curiosity.

"And that youngster's burning, probably," came the plaintive voice of Dogaylo in the silence. "The radio operator. He's burning alive, boys! Burning!"

"Turn back!" Kotelnikov shouted furiously, his eyes flashing. At once a wild shout broke out on the spar-deck.

"Here with the captain!"

"The captain!"

"We must save those men! Do you hear?"

"Arrest them!"

"Where's the political assistant?"

"Are you out of your mind? The engineer took his place long ago. We've not had a political assistant for a long time!"

"What are they doing, the scoundrels! Launch the boats! What are they doing, comrades?"

"What are you talking about?" yelled Khrulev, edging through the crowd. "Do you want to get burnt to death? The wind is blowing sparks about. Haven't we just the same cargo? You lot of sheep!" He started pushing the men aside in a bossy way, and as he went past Yakubov he said with a menace in his voice: "You keep quiet. You know what you can get for breaking discipline. Watch your step!"

Suddenly he saw Basov coming round the corner. He stepped hurriedly aside, squeezing somebody against the bulwarks with his back. A silence immediately set in, the men stopped crowding together and made way for Basov, who went straight to the captain's bridge. Behind him loomed the bulky figure of Husein. Volodya Makarov, pale and gasping with excitement, ran to meet him.

"Valerian is still there, I can hear his signals," he cried like a man half out of his mind, seizing Basov's hand. "I can't listen to it. Are we cowards?"

Basov pushed the operator aside and ran up on the bridge. A few men immediately rushed after him and the whole crowd pressed towards the ladder.

"What's the meaning of this?" shouted Kasatsky. "Be so good as to go back. Yevgeny Stepanovich, stop this disgrace, I can't work."

He stepped back from the ladder to let Basov pass, but immediately ran ahead of him and barred the way into the chart-house. The two suddenly stopped and faced each other breathing heavily like two wrestlers ready to grapple.

"Was it you that cut the cable?" asked Basov in a low voice. "Why are you sailing away?"

"That's not your business," Kasatsky answered in the same low voice. "The captain's in charge here."

A ring of men quickly closed around them, all of them breathing in short heavy gasps.

"I'll punch his face," Basov thought, mechanically drawing his hands up for a blow and riveting his eyes on the white bridge of the mate's nose.

Husein's face appeared over Basov's shoulder, his teeth bared with rage. Behind him were others that could not be recognized in the weak light of the glow.

"Hit him, Mustapha!" came Yakubov's hoarse voice from behind. "Don't be afraid, swipe out at him. Here's a chisel!"

The crowd suddenly pressed together with a dull hum, as though caught in the swelling storm of excitement. They pushed on from behind, forcing Basov against the mate's chest. Basov regained control over himself and lowered his hands.

"Be calm, lads!" he shouted out, elbowing himself free. "All unnecessary men off the bridge! We're going back to pick up the men of the *Uzbekistan*. To your stations!"

He felt the hot wall of bodies give way behind him and shouted as loud as he could, his voice breaking:

"Stand by for orders! Clear the bridge. Second mate and donkey-man report to me. Prepare to launch the boats. Keep calm, lads!"

"You have no right!" Kasatsky's voice was heard above the others. "It's the captain that gives orders here! And you raised your hand at me. Everybody saw you!"

The men who had approached the ladder stopped irresolutely. Basov approached the immobile form of the captain, who was crumpled up by the rail.

"Yevgeny Stepanovich," he said in an insistent voice. "We must turn back. There are men burning there. Come, compose yourself. Listen!"

The captain took his hands away from his face and looked eagerly round as though in the hope that the fiery sky, the blast of the horn, and the shouts had only been a fancy of his. He saw the pink reflection in the window of the wheel-house and clutched his collar with trembling fingers.

"I don't know, my friend. I don't know anything!" he said in a miserable voice. "My God, my God! What do you want!"

"You don't know?" came a mad roar from Husein, who was pushing the men aside to get a better view of the captain. "You don't know? You must know, if you're a commander and not just some old. . . ."

He rushed to the wheel-house without finishing his sentence. A few men hurried after him, while the others pressed resolutely on again towards the ladder.

"You're ruining yourself, Yevgeny Stepanovich," Basov said, trying to hold up the captain. "We'll both be brought up for trial if those men die. Come, lean on me."

In the wheel-house Husein pushed the helmsman aside; the latter, staggering against the wall, muttered:

"Chuck it! Chuck it, I tell you. You'll answer for this."

"I'll answer all right, old chap," said Husein, sticking out his elbows as he turned the wheel. "Dont you bother, I'll answer!"

Basov dragged the captain to the wheel-house, holding him up by the arm.

"So you say we must turn back?" asked Yevgeny Stepanovich. "Somehow, my dear friend, I've not got my ideas about me. Do everything that's necessary until I come to myself again. You see I am really ill."

The golden cloud rolled past the stern and floated in a huge arc on the port side. The sea on the beam was sparkling with fiery patches.

"Ah," sighed Yevgeny Stepanovich closing his eyes. "I feel bad: I'm going to die. Let me go."

He pressed his hand to his chest and sat down on one of the steps. His heart was thumping madly; his whole body seemed to be crumbling away, shattered by a disgusting shivering. At that minute he hated his sweating, trembling body and his broken voice. Somebody dashed past and accidentally brushed the captain's face with the skirt of his jacket. The captain turned his face away and thought that it was useless to cling on to life and that the best thing now would be to cease existing altogether. But the next instant he noticed through his closed eye-lids the flickering red light getting nearer and nearer, and brighter and brighter. He almost choked with anguish.

"Alexander Ivanovich!" he called in a low voice. "We have Krasnovodsk oil in the tanks you know! Oh, my God!"

"Open the water cocks everywhere!" Basov shouted, pushing the sailors towards the ladder. "Second mate, watch the course. Hey, bo'sun! Stand by the acid batteries! In case of fire act according to instructions. Open the water cocks!"

Alyavdin was now standing near the helmsman, with a tense, pale face. He was obviously excited, but was trying to be calm and efficient. He was satisfied, all the same, at the test he was being put to.

"To port a little!" he cried, encouraged by the sound of his own voice. "A little more! Hold her!"

The fiery glow had described a half circle, and the sheets of foam round the ship had turned a pinkish colour. At the place towards which the ship was headed, a yellow column of smoke divided the glaring crimson sky in two, swaying like a tree in the wind, with fiery roots creeping over the water at its foot.

"There's no danger at all, I assure you," said Basov going up to the captain. "You seem to have recovered. We'll have to lower the boats now." He added the last words as he turned away, and it was not clear whether he was asking for permission or giving an order.

"It'll soon be over now," the captain thought. "We shall approach on the lee side—He's doing everything right, and they're all obeying him, even Alyavdin. Provided he doesn't lose his head!"

On the starboard bow the burning ship came into view, belching smoke over the water. Its bow, unscathed by the fire, was raised. Tongues of fire were licking the water all around, darting up to the black crest of the waves.

"The oil is burning on the water," Yevgeny Stepanovich said to himself. "It's flowed overboard and caught fire." The horn barked defeaningly, and he fancied it rent the fiery sky with its blast. Then all was quiet, and he could hear voices calling to one another below, the water gurgling, and Basov shouting into the speaking tube:

"Slow down! Start the emergency engine. Good."

A long foul puff of scorching wind blew over the ship and a powerful monotonous roar could be heard, like a furnace stoked to red-hot with the wind howling in the ash-pit.

"To port, further!" Yevgeny Stepanovich shouted unexpectedly, crossing himself with stealthy haste. "Hold her!"

## IV

On the spar-deck the sailors were pulling the canvas covers off the life-boats. One was brightly lit up by the glow of the fire, and below it, by the side of the ship, the seething foam was pink. The second was on the other side of the spar-deck, and the noisy waves below it were invisible in the dark.

Husein was the first to jump into the boat that was lit up, and standing in it, he unfastened the oars. After him came the middle-aged sailor Fomushkin. He had until then been fidgeting nervously near the side of the ship and helping to uncover the boats.

"It's safer here in the boat," he muttered. "Farther away from the oil."

He sat down at the rudder, clutching the gunwales with both hands, and cast a guilty look at Husein, as though ashamed of his fear.

"Off we go!" cried Husein. "Soviet sailors don't abandon their comrades! Understand?"

He was animated, almost merry, now. While the sailors were working the davits, he kept looking at the burning ship as though impatient to get a closer view of it.

Volodya Makarov came running up out of breath, gesticulating to the sailors who were lowering the boat.

"Wait! I'll go with them!" he cried. "Wait!"

"Lower the boat!" bawled Husein, standing upright and balancing with his hands. "What are you stopping for? Off we go!"

"How can you, Mustapha?" stuttered Volodya. "Basov's going, and you and Kotelnikov. We've lived together and now—"

"You've got to keep in touch with the shore. Go to your wireless! Don't you believe in discipline!"

The boat glided down along the side of the tanker, and Husein, pushing off with one of his oars, turned her nose into the waves.

"How can you?" Volodya repeated sadly. "I'm the only one not to go!"

The boat plunged between the black rollers, shipping water. Husein's oars rose in broad sweeps over the water, he himself now bending forward, now leaning back as though going to lie on the bottom. The hull of the *Derbent* receded into the darkness, ablaze in the glow of the fire, and from under its stern the second boat glided out, a pale pink and as frail as the skin of an orange.

"There's Basov coming," said Husein, plying his oars. "Soviet sailors don't abandon their comrades!" He repeated the sentence with pleasure and thought Basov would like it too. "I'm right, aren't I, brother?"

The boat flew up on a high wave and was brightly lit up on the crest. The first gust of smoke blew towards it.

Fomushkin coughed and twisted his mouth convulsively in an attempt to smile.

"Keep her towards the fire!" shouted Husein, turning round. "Where are you steering to?"

"There's nobody there," muttered the other, turning to look at the blazing ship, "the water's on fire! Look!"

Broad strips of light were flickering around them and the water glittered as it dripped off the oars. Husein kept looking over his shoulder, trying to see what was happening on the *Uzbekistan*. He saw pointed tongues of fire rearing over the communication bridge and the empty windows of the upper cabins belching clouds of sparks. Over the bulwark, blazing torrents of oil were flowing as out of a boiling cauldron, spreading over the water in fiery streams, dimly visible through the pall of smoke.

"There's nobody there!" Fomushkin obstinately repeated. "Let's go back, Mustapha!"

"Look here," shouted Husein menacingly. "Not another word from you!"

Pink puffs of smoke came blowing towards the boat, and through them something like a buoy could be seen. The buoy came nearer, tossing on the waves. It seemed to be wriggling strangely, like a living thing with tentacles all round. Husein dropped the oars and went to the bow of the boat. He saw two men clinging to a life-buoy with their heads turned to the approaching boat.

"Give me your hand," Husein shouted to one of the men looking up at him out of the water. "Come on, comrade!"

The hand was slippery and cold. Husein cautiously caught the limp body under the armpits and dragged it over the gunwale.

"Lie down, brother, have a rest," said Husein, drawing the life-buoy nearer. "Well, come on, the next!"

The second was almost naked, and his slippery body kept slithering out of Husein's hands. One eye was closed tight, the other now opened in a senseless stare, now closed its trembling lids. He dropped on the bottom of the boat, drew up his knees and lay huddled together.

"Friends," he said, taking a deep breath, "we thought we'd had it."

"You can tell us later," said Husein, taking the oars. "Where are your boats?"

"I saw one of them. It was launched," the rescued man said, between fits of shivering, "but it had no oars. I think it overturned when I jumped out. God, it's cold!"

The second of the *Derbent*'s boats came racing up behind, pitching on the waves with rowlocks creaking.

"The wind's changed," shouted Basov, who was sitting at the rudder. "Don't waste time, Mustapha!"

"We've got two," Mustapha replied, bending over the oars and looking at the first men they had saved like an angler who has landed a good catch.

Fomushkin, who had been sitting motionless all the time, suddenly jumped up. He frowned with impatience and took off his coat. He stepped over the thwart and raised the naked man by the shoulders.

"Here, put it on," he insisted, "I don't need it."

"Damn it!" said Husein. "And I've got nothing at all."

He looked at his bare chest and his shirt with its rolled-up sleeves, regretting he had nothing he could give.

A thick shroud of smoke was advancing on them. It curled round the sides of the boat and swirled like water under the strokes of the oars. Somewhere quite near, pale tongues of fire flared up and streams of scorching air blew on Husein's face. He started coughing and wiped the welling tears away with his eyelashes.

"That's oil burning," Fomushkin wailed, looking back. "It's spreading, we won't get out of this, Mustapha."

"Shut up!" Husein ordered. "There's somebody hailing us." He jumped on to the thwart and listened.

Through the monotonous roar of the fire came a weary drawn-out cry like that of an exhausted man who has given up hope of being heard.

"Coming!" Husein yelled. "Hey! Shout up!"

This time several voices shouted in answer, but the shouts were deadened as by a wall. The sharp bow of a boat appeared out of the smoke and glided slowly past. The sailor sitting at the oars doubled up shaken with a fit of coughing. Basov left the rudder and jumped over to him. Tears were streaming down his cheeks and he kept licking his parched lips and breathing in the pungent smoke.

"Row!" he said in a strange hollow voice. "Row or I'll...!"

The sailor raised his red face. His eyes stared like a terrified horse's. He began to row. The wind scattered the smoke and blew over the sea black flakes of soot. Suddenly, on the clear-swept patch of sea, they all saw an overturned boat rocking on the waves. Several men were lying across it. Others were struggling to crawl up its slippery sides, but a wave came and dashed them back into the water. Patches of oil were smouldering and smoking all around, and a dense stream of fire was spreading slowly from the opposite side.

Fomushkin left hold of the rudder and, twisting on his seat, started looking round with half insane eyes. The boat swerved to the left.

"Look, Mustapha," he stammered indistinctly. "Look behind! It's on fire!"

The motionless silhouette of the *Derbent* stood out in the distance and red sparks were flashing like lightning along her spar-deck.

"The *Derbent*'s on fire," Fomushkin moaned, writhing like an epileptic and shaking his fist at Husein. "You'll have my life on your conscience, you bastard. Where can I go now? Nothing but sea all around. Oh!"

His eyes rolled monstrously in the dark, and he sobbed loudly, choking with smoke. Husein clenched his teeth and scrambled over the thwarts to him. The boat rocked.

"Shut up!" he bellowed. "Or I'll tear you to pieces! I'll throw you overboard! Shut up!"

He raised his fist but did not strike. Then he grabbed the sailor by the collar and dragged him from his seat. The red lights on the *Derbent* flashed once, then again, and went out.

"Look, you fool," shouted Husein, choking, "it's the reflection of the windows and you start blubbering. You shit!"

He pulled the rudder out of its socket and sat down at the oars. Basov's boat was already near the edge of the fire. It was lurching dangerously because of the men clinging to the sides in their haste to get out of the water. The overturned boat was tossing on the waves, its wet sides reflecting the fire like mirrors. Husein rowed nearer and drove his boat at full force against it. Then he immediately jumped to his feet. Clutching hands and dark heads with hair smoothed out by the water and ghastly upturned faces showed on the water.

"Easy," shouted Husein, dragging over the side a heavy body that drenched him with streams of water. "Don't all cling to one side. You'll overturn us."

He could feel on his face and his naked chest the unbearable nearness of the fire; his eyes seemed about to burst with the searing heat. But he went on pulling the slippery bodies out of the water and laying them on the other side of the boat so as not to upset it.

"I'll take you all," he said, splashing a handful of salt water on his face. "Don't clutch like that! D'you think I'll leave you here? What d'you take me for!"

His hands came up against a motionless, completely naked body and he tried to raise it, but it slipped out of his grasp. He caught it by the hair, and this time did not let it slip away. The overturned boat was already smoking. Small yellow tongues of fire were creeping out of the shroud of smoke and cautiously licking its sides. Basov's boat had turned its stern to the fire. It sailed past quite near and Husein could see Basov rowing, slowly raising his oars as though there was a heavy weight on them.

"Come back!" the engineer shouted, in the same ringing voice as before. "Your shirt's smouldering on your back. Come away, I tell you!"

But Husein was still struggling with the dead weight of the lifeless body. He raised it half out of the water and, gathering his strength, seized it under the armpits.

There was a sudden scorching gust of wind, red sparks flew about, and Husein felt an unbearable pain. Somebody near him moaned aloud between clenched teeth and started kicking against the gunwale. Husein strained every muscle and slowly overcame the weight hanging on his hands. Once he had at last pulled the body out of the water, he fell on the thwart and groped for the oars.

He could see nothing in the smoke, a fit of coughing seized him, black circles swam before his eyes. He rowed, mechanically raising and dipping the oars and throwing his body back, guessing the direction.

By degrees the smoke got thinner, the air purer. Husein breathed deep several times, cleared his throat, and spat overboard. His eyes were streaming with the heat and soot, but through his tears he could see curly coils of smoke floating in the wind, and beyond them the black and gold hulk of the burning tanker. The fire was sweeping over it like some shaggy red beast leaping over the superstructure and gnawing into the deck. Fountains of burning oil shot up under its fangs. Then the tanker rolled slowly over on its side, showing its flat bottom above the water, and out of its holds rushed a raging torrent of golden lava, which lit up in the darkness a broad circle on the sea.

On the very edge of that illuminated circle lay the *Derbent*. The white life-boats rowed towards her, packed full with men. Their bows rose and fell, the blades of their oars gleamed as they tossed on the waves. Three were in front, one was lagging behind. The middle ones slowed down to let the last one catch up with them. The oarsman was rowing with unsteady strokes, swaying on the thwart like a drunken man. Another man took his place and the lagging boat soon came level with the others. They sailed on for a while in a line side by side, but suddenly they all slowed down at once with oars poised above the water.

The burning ship's stern subsided into the water, her black bows rose wreathed in clouds of smoke which blackened the sky above. The smoke soon dispersed. Where the *Uzbekistan* had lain there was nothing more to be seen. Nothing but broad strips of oil like roads on the sea burning with dreary flames.

The rows of port-holes and the lighted windows on the upper deck of the *Derbent* stood out more clearly. The metallic blast of the horn rent the air calling in the boats.

Husein crouched on the bottom of the boat, leaning his shoulder on a small figure sitting next to him. When the hulk of the *Uzbekistan* disappeared in the sea, the small figure started sobbing and Husein grasped his hand in silence. The hand was small and slim, and Husein thought that the rescued man must be very short and thin, like a child.

"Is that you, Valerian?" he asked softly.

"Of course it's me," answered the young wireless operator in a deep bass. "Who are you?"

"Husein, a motor-man from the *Derbent*. What are you crying for? Are you burnt?"

"No, not much. I feel sorry for our tanker. Don't you?"

"Yes, I do."

The boy heaved a long trembling sigh.

"There's our boat, so it's saved. The other got overturned. I was in it. But some of our men are missing." He pressed against Husein's shoulder and whispered: "Listen. This is Uncle Kolya, our stoker, lying here. He's not moving and doesn't seem to be breathing either. I'm afraid..."

"Sh-sh..." said Husein, embracing the boy. "Uncle Kolya's dead."

Men crowded by the side of the *Derbent* lit up from behind by a powerful light on deck. Fomushkin plied his oars energetically, looking over his shoulder at the cables hanging from the davit blocks over the side of the spardeck.

"Make fast!" shouted Husein, standing up. "Ahoy! *Derbent*!"

He was breathing in short irregular gulps. He could feel something surging and scratching in his chest. His skin was on fire. His eyes were half-blinded with tears.

The boat glided upwards and by the side Huseln saw Volodya looking at him with anxiety and alarm. He gave Volodya a smile, like a man who recognizes a sympathetic friendly face bending over him after a terrible nightmare. He was about to say that he could hardly see or stand on his feet and that he was in pain, but he did not. He just ordered in a hoarse, businesslike voice:

"See to the dressing, Volodya. Some of them have burns."


V


Basov stood on deck, holding to his face torn bandages soaked in a solution of manganese. He was bored by inaction. He wanted to look into the engine-room, but Dogaylo insisted that he should hold those cool cloths to his face.

"You've got to see gangrene doesn't set in," said the bo'sun, raising a warning finger. Then he hurried to the saloon, where the burnt men were being bandaged.

There were a lot of them and they all complained that they were cold and could not breathe. Basov wandered in too, but somehow was not able to find himself a job. Some of the *Derbent*'s crew knew first aid. The electricians undressed the victims or just tore the wet rags off them. Vera did the bandaging, looking anxiously into each apathetic blackened face to make sure the bandage was not too tight.

The *Uzbekistan* navigation officer lay face down on the table. He had been wounded in the head by the explosion. He clutched at the oil-cloth and twitched his shoulders as Volodya picked scraps of hair out of the wound, frowning and casting irresolute looks at the iodine bottle.

"I just can't stand it," the navigation officer gasped, crimson in the face. "What are you fiddling about with me for, boy?"

"Just bear up a little while, please," answered Volodya with a desperate look on his face. He dipped a piece of cotton wool in iodine and passed it over the edge of the wound. The navigation officer gave a start, gnashed his teeth and swore.

"It's all over," said Volodya, with the expression of a surgeon who has just performed a complicated operation. "Vera, bandage this comrade."

Mustapha obediently held out his burnt hands to Volodya. His face had been bandaged in haste, and his inflamed watering eyes peeped out through slits between the bandages. He noticed Basov and his spirits rose.

"Smarting, er?" he asked mockingly. Then, looking at his own hands, he exclaimed: "Just look! As red as carrots!"

"Be quiet, you chump!" Volodya growled with sullen sympathy. "You'd think it was my skin peeling off, not yours."

Bits of bandages and rags littered the floor. There was a hospital smell about the place. Naked, moist human bodies shone everywhere under the bright lights. Basov stayed a while and then went out on deck. The sky above the masts was the transparent blue that precedes dawn. The stars seemed bathed in it and shone through it as through crystal clear water. But Basov still fancied he saw on the sea the reflection of the ruddy light, and at times it was as though he could not see at all. His hands and face were burning and he could not forget the sights of the night before. Everything he had done that night was so fantastic that he did not want to think about it. And he had done nothing to start it. He thought of the men who worked with him, whom he loved and was proud of.

Only a few months before he had thought they were all good for nothing, insincere, and petty. No, they had been quite different then. Those men had disappeared, he had forgotten their names, and what they looked like. Husein, Volodya, and the fitter Yakubov—those he had known for a long time. They were no worse than the fitters or Eybat the turner he had once been so proud of.

When he left the works in spring he had thought life for him was ended. But now he knew better: the following year, new higher norms would be established. Many ships had now started Stakhanovite trips, the *Agamali* was again catching up with them, threatening to take first place. What would the crew of the *Derbent* be like the following year? Basov thought that if he were now to leave the *Derbent*, his absence would make no difference. And precisely because of that, he knew that he would not leave the tanker at the end of the season.

He began to cheer up. Holding the bandage to his face, he started whistling a wild, swaggering melody. He was out of tune and from time to time he had to stop whistling to clear his throat. He went along the deck, and suddenly, reaching the anchor-room, he halted and the whistling broke off.

On the deck, covered with the flag from the stern, lay corpses. The wind had turned up the edge of the flag and showed the stiff stretched feet of the dead men. How could he have forgotten them? He himself had helped to lay them out there, it was he that had covered them with the flag. He remembered that there were two of them, and that one had been drowned before the life-boat had arrived. He had known that all the time, but now, for some reason, he had forgotten.

"It's fatigue," he thought, as though trying to find an excuse. Then he attempted to bring back the staggering feeling of irreparableness that he had when he saw the dead men for the first time.

But however he tried, he did not succeed in concentrating on sad thoughts. The swaggering tune still rang in his ears.

"What's the matter with me?" he thought. "Men have lost their lives, that's irreparable. How can I think of petty things, be glad and dream of the future? Have I become hard and lost my feeling for men just because I have learned to command them? If so, this is no place for me."

"Wrong!" came the answer. "You went into the fire for those men and made others do the same. You loved them even though you did not know them. What other feeling could have prompted you to act as you did last night? But they died, and all that became useless. Mustapha Husein nearly lost his life pulling a dead body out of the water. He does not know what fear is, he has a great warm heart. Compared with him you're dried up and dull in spite of all you know. But he is merry. While dressing his burns he thinks of the engines, and of what he'll do ashore. Would he do the dead any good by being sad?"

Basov straightened out the flag and went away. His face was burning but his heart was calm. He looked at his watch, wondering whether it was time to radio the port about their arrival. He heard the gurgling of water. They had forgotten to close the cocks on the spar-deck.

Then he met Kotelnikov, who smiled mysteriously and took him over to a lamp.

"I've got something here," he said, holding his hand behind his back. "Something interesting. Want to see it?"

He handed him a slip of paper written in careful, sloping handwriting. By the light of the lamp Basov read:

"Cannot help *Uzbekistan* because of strong wind and sparks. Send rescue ship—*Derbent*—Kutasov."

"The first mate wrote that, er?" Basov guessed. "Where did you get it?"

"Quite simple. While Mustapha was blowing the horn, Kasatsky wrote it and gave it to Volodya to send it by wireless. Of course, Volodya didn't send it. He wanted to throw it in the lavatory, but I took it off him. Why, that's a valuable document, I said, give it here! It'll come in handy at the trial." He carefully folded the paper. "They won't get out of it now! We'll make the parasites sorry. How many years do you think they'll get?"

"I don't know," said Basov. "I'm not a lawyer. But it's a pity about the old man."

"Who's it a pity about?"

"The old man, I said, the captain. It's a pity. In reality he's very unfortunate."

Kotelnikov's smile vanished.

"A pity! Well, strike me pink! What do you want to do now? Shield him? Is that what you mean?"

"You didn't understand me," said Basov, embarrassed. "Shield him? I only said the old man was wretched and—"

"Wretched did you say? Have you seen what's lying there?" Kotelnikov shouted all of a sudden, pointing in the direction of the anchor-room. "Had it not been for your old man, those charred corpses would still be living men. Listen to me: if you're thinking of shielding him—"

"It didn't even enter my mind," Basov hastened to justify himself. "It was just stupid of me to say that."

"I should think it was! It's a good job for you we're alone. The lads are angry now—Listen. That young wireless operator is asleep in my berth. Mustapha brought him in. Safe and sound, only his hair a little singed. He was whimpering at first. Felt sorry for the tanker and his note-books getting burnt! There was a lot of interesting stuff in them, he said. He's fretted himself to sleep now. He's so thin, his arms are like spindles, you should have a look."

The sky in the east was quickly getting light. Beyond the sea rose mountains like towering clouds, and behind them banked clouds like snow-clad mountains. The edge of the sun appeared and the crests of the waves became a pearly pink.

## NECESSITY

### I

When her relief came at last, Musya put on her things in haste. She had only one wish—to get away without being noticed, so as to avoid questions from her colleagues. But Liza Zvonnikova hovered round her and pleaded in a whining voice:

"Why don't you tell us, Musya darling. What a dreadful thing to happen! Come, Musya, dearie, tell us!"

"I've got a headache," Musya said hastily, putting on her beret in front of the window. "It's so terrible that one doesn't like to recall it. Tarumov'll tell you all about it."

She went to the door, but Liza caught up with her and took hold of her hands.

"But Musya, your Sasha's on board. What's happened to him? Musya, darling!"

"Have you only just remembered?" Musya let fly spitefully. "I don't know anything. Leave me alone."

She ran out into the porch and down the steps. The sun was rising behind the white houses; the wind wafted a smell of hot bread from the bakery. People were running to the tram stop, jumping hastily on to the running-board. Their faces were worried just as usual, and still a little sleepy.

Musya got a seat in the tram between a fat old woman sucking a sweet and a dark-faced man in a *papakha*.* She felt very lonely.

"They'll be arriving at Makhach-Kala now," she thought. "Sasha will be standing on deck looking at the shore. But why should he look at the shore? He's probably sleeping calm in his cabin. He's always so calm and satisfied with everything and I worry myself to death, I don't know why. Oh, enough of that. But suppose he's burnt and lying with the others?" She imagined white beds and motionless figures covered with sheets. She shuddered and looked round anxiously. The fat woman was crunching her sweet, looking in front of her with sleepy eyes, her cheeks trembling with the jolts of the tram. The man in the *papakha* was about to get out and kept looking out of the window.

"How long is it since we saw each other?" Musya thought. "May, June, July," she counted quickly on her fingers, moving her lips—"August, September, October and half November—He's never sent any news of himself, just put me out of his head, and that's all about it. Well, let him go to the devil, it's better that way. Oh, if only I were home!"

She shot a glance of hate at the fat old woman and drew her feet in. The tram crashed over a crossing, the trees on the boulevards flashed past the windows.

"How stupidly I behaved today. Tarumov probably thinks I'm just a sitting hen like Galya Goncharenko who takes her husband's photo to bed with her. Disgusting! But does it matter what he thinks? The thing is I'm so afraid and there's nothing I can do about it. I feel as if I'm going to burst into tears. Ah, I'm just crazy!"

* Caucasian fur cap.—*Tr.*

Musya got off the tram at the corner of Molokanskaya Street. Two men were standing on the pavement reading the paper. The tall one in the seaman's cap said to the other:

"It happened last night, so it will be in the papers tomorrow, not today." He looked at Musya and smiled. Then he nudged his comrade. "Splendid girls in Baku!" he said. "Real pearls!"

Musya stopped when she got to the cross-roads. The seaman was looking at her with insolent curiosity. He even seemed about to come up to her. Musya thought for a second. Then she suddenly ran as fast as she could over the road.

"I'll ask in the office whether there's any more news," she said to herself. "Nothing extraordinary about that. They all ask, I'll not be the only one. But what can they tell me there when I've just come from the wireless-station? All the same—Oh, what a fool I am!"

She got furious at the seaman who was still staring at her, at a lorry that cut across her way, and at herself.

She did not, in fact, learn anything new at the shipping line office. Some women were standing at the entrance. One of them, quite young, in a yellow blouse, had turned her face to the wall so that nobody would see her crying.

"Don't be upset," Musya said to her. "Is your husband on board?"

"No, an acquaintance."

"On which ship?"

"The *Derbent*."

"Don't cry then." said Musya. "My husband's there too, but I'm not crying. I tell you everything will be all right."

The girl wiped her eyes and smiled.

"Do you think so?"

Musya ran along Olginskaya Street. Her cheeks were on fire.

"Why did I tell her about my husband? Why did I tell a lie? I had no reason to come here. Why, he's alive and calm as usual, and probably not thinking about me. And still, that girl was crying. Oh, nonsense! It was he that signed the telegram—But that doesn't mean much. He could have signed it even if—Oh, I wish everything was over!"

She stopped at the hotel entrance and looked in the mirror on the door. Before her in the mirror stood a girl with a beret on and dark vexed eyes. Her hair half covered her burning ears.

"Well," Musya whispered hatefully, "where'll you go now? You must wait. What use is your anxiety to anyone? You should have stayed at home."

The girl in the mirror answered with a grimace and a hideous grin. Musya wandered on. She went along the Molokanskaya, turned off mechanically into her yard, and went up the stairs. Children were dragging a wooden horse noisily on the landing. Her neighbour brought wet washing out.

"Musya dear, an engineer came to see you last night," she said. "Istomin, I think his name is."

She had a knowing, sympathizing smile, as people who have long been married usually have when talking of other people's love affairs.

"Did he leave any message?" Musya asked.

"He said he'd come tomorrow. 'You're hiding her from me,' he says, 'but I'll find her just the same.' 'You've guessed right,' says I, 'look, here she is in my pocket.' What are you blushing for, Musya? I've always wished you well, I think he's a very nice man."

"There's nothing between us," said Musya dejectedly. "You're just making fun of me."

"Oh! I know. You're a secretive young lady, aren't you!"

Musya went into her room and lay on the bed, huddling up with her hand under her cheek as she always did before going to sleep. But sleep would not come, although her whole body was aching tired. She felt uncomfortable all the time and tried to find a more restful position. There were moments when her mind grew torpid and misty figures flashed before her eyes. But a sudden pang would waken her and fill her with such terrible anxiety that she wanted to get up immediately, go somewhere and do something. Yet she knew there was nothing she could do but wait.

"I must have done something wrong," she said, turning on her back and opening her eyes. "Let's go over everything and put an end to it—Sasha's on the *Derbent* and I've no news of him. That's the chief thing. But I'll soon get to know everything, and besides, it's no fault of mine. He's got different—no, he always was different to what I thought. I thought he was a bungler and a dreamer. Now the papers write about him. And Yakob Neuman has turned out to be a hinderer, they dress him down at meetings, and he tries to make out that he never had any intention of badgering Basov the Stakhanovite. But what's that got to do with me? That's a lie! You badgered him just like the others. Only nobody knows. Just like Neuman. How disgusting! Still, when that dreadful thing happened today, I was anxious for him. So I'm not so bad after all. Another lie! You never felt indifferent to him, he always meant a lot to you. But his failures scared you and you shied away from him like a horse. You got the wind up, that's it. That's clear! Anything else? Ah, yes, that Istomin! You set him as an example to Sasha because he gets on well and the management have a good opinion of him. And Sasha listened. What does that mean? He listened in silence and said nothing. Cry now, you fool!"

Musya turned over in bed, bit her lips, and did cry. She remembered how she went to meet Istomin one day at his office, at the shipping line management, to go to the theatre with him. That was about the middle of summer. Sasha had been at sea for a long time, and she used to meet Istomin nearly every day.

Godoyan's car was outside the entrance and the little driver fussed about, wiping the wind-screen. A minute later, Istomin came out with a few colleagues. He went straight to the car without noticing Musya:

"Good evening, Nikolai," he greeted the driver politely. "How are things? Is Stepan Dmitrevich at the conference?"

He took out his cigarette-case and held it to the driver. Musya noticed the affectation in his movements and the tone of his voice. Probably the driver did too, for he took a cigarette with a show of unconcern and pressed it between his greasy fingers.

"A nice little car that is," said Istomin to a middle-aged man standing by him. "If only we had one like it!" He turned round and saw Musya.

"I'm a little late," he said in quite a different tone—surer and more impressive. "I was delayed, excuse me."

Musya felt he had purposely pronounced the last sentence louder so that his colleagues standing on the pavement could hear it. Her eyes met the driver's and she blushed.

"You've come in time," she said curtly. "Well, let's go!"

Just then Godoyan came out. He put his brief-case under his arm, took off his spectacles, and squinted short-sightedly as he wiped them with his handkerchief. Istomin let go of Musya's hand, put on a serious face, and made a short, smart bow. Godoyan raised his hand to his cap and got into the car.

"Did you see that?" Istomin asked, walking by Musya's side. "He knows me and always greets me when he meets me. He does not take any notice of the others. Did you see!"

There was no wind at all that evening, and the air hung motionless over the town, burdened with the fragrance of flowers and the smell of petrol. The red and green lights of ships were gliding over the smooth surface of the bay. Musya watched them and answered Istomin's questions distractedly, feeling lonely and unwanted.

Several months had passed since then, but she suddenly remembered everything as clearly as if it had been only the day before.

"Tomorrow I'll go to the pier," she thought, calming herself a little. "But shall I? Sasha'll think I've come because of the articles in the papers. It doesn't matter, let him think what he likes! If only I can just see him once! Now that I've made up my mind, I won't think of anything else and I'll be able to sleep. A minute though! How could I make such a mistake? Was I scared by his failures? No, there must be something else. I couldn't understand the chief thing in him: the necessity for him, as he is, to go the hard way, the only way that exists for him." The old woman's face appeared before her, and the thought that she had had such difficulty in arriving at, was suddenly blurred and distorted. The old woman was sticking a sweet in her mouth and her cheeks were quivering like a bulldog's. It took Musya some time to get rid of that old woman's face. Falling off to sleep, she turned over on her side and saw another face, calm, a little phlegmatic, with little creases in the tanned skin round the eyes. She stretched her hands out desperately towards that face, afraid it would disappear.

"I've missed you so much, commander," she complained, smiling blissfully. "But are you already going away? When I've been longing for you so much? Listen, I know now that you must, it's time for you to go. You see, I'm not keeping you back, although it's so hard for me. So hard, so clear and so fine!"

The beloved face was shrouded in a mist and disappeared. It did not appear again and Musya dreamt only of an athletic competition, of her duty at the wireless-station, and of telegrams. But all the time she was sleeping the bright proud feeling of the first dream did not leave her.

## II

One by one, gingerly gripping the hand-rail with their bandaged hands, the men rescued from the *Uzbekistan* went down the gangway to the pier. There they lingered, casting warm parting glances at the sailors of the *Derbent* who were waving their caps from the tanker, those dear comrades who had come to mean so much to them. Ambulance attendants in white coats led them out through the pier barrier and the port guards cleared a passage through the crowd. On the road ambulances were hooting, loud and vicious.

Valerian Lastik was the last to leave the pier. He growled at the attendant who wanted to support him by the arm and kept trying to go back.

"Volodya, you must keep in touch with me," he shouted to Makarov, "I should so much like to stay. Why don't you look at me, Volodya?"

By the barrier he again turned round and shouted in his squeaky youthful bass:

"Tell your Stakhanovites I'll write about them. And I will always be like you..."

The gate clanged to after him, and the white coats screened him from Volodya.

"Did you hear?" Volodya asked Basov, who was standing beside him: "Tell your Stakhanovites—he's really taken a liking to us. He even blew Kotelnikov a kiss, the big baby!" Volodya laughed merrily and drew closer to Basov. "Listen to what the captain said last night: he said he and the mate had a sort of mutual pledge. They were in some dirty business in the past, I can't make out exactly what. He quakes as if he had a fever when he talks about it, and his eyes fill with tears. 'My friends, my dear friends,' he says, 'see what that fellow's done to me!' He seems to have pricks of conscience, and he's blurting it all out. Now he and the mate will be tried, and we shall get reliable chaps. If any others come to us with daggers up their sleeves we'll make short work of them. You know, I am in such a giddy mood today, you'd think it was my birthday or something. I even feel ashamed of myself."

"So long as the mood is good you needn't worry," said Basov, smiling.

"I feel ashamed just the same. There has been a disaster, men have lost their lives, and others have got such burns! Look, there's Husein having a fight with the doctor."

An old doctor from the town was trying to stop Husein, from slipping through the passage on to the deck. Husein was pushing, attempting to squeeze through sideways, and casting desperate glances around.

"Oh, you're absolutely impossible!" the doctor was saying, clasping his hands imploringly and examining Husein over his spectacles as if in doubt that the impossible creature had a human face under the bandages. "You know what you're risking, don't you? If infection sets in—"

"But they're already healed, I tell you," Husein muttered, looking at the bandages on his hands. "There's nothing for you to worry about, doctor!"

"All the same, please go ashore."

"I won't! And that's that!"

"I tell you you must! Where is your political assistant? This is just scandalous!"

Basov put his hands behind his back and strolled up to the scene of the dispute.

"You should set the others an example," he said to Husein, "and there you are making a row that can be heard all over the pier! You ought to be ashamed of yourself!"

"But I'll be still worse kicking my heels there!" Husein argued obstinately. "Listen, doctor, let me go, really!"

"But I can't let you at the engines with hands like yours," Basov explained patiently. "Try to understand, use your brains!"

"All right, I'll go then. But it's not nice of you, Alexander Ivanovich!"

"Go on, go on!"

"They're letting the public in!" Volodya Makarov shouted. "Kotelnikov, there's your wife!"

The crowd rushed through the barrier and scattered over the pier. The women came running up, stepping over the pipe-line, looking from afar at the sailors standing at the side of the tanker, trying to find their men. Basov saw a girl in a yellow blouse rush towards Husein, stretching out her arms impetuously towards him. But she didn't touch him. Her arms dropped helplessly and they stood looking at each other.

Basov turned away and went slowly to the foc'sle. By the anchor-room lay the old faded flag that had covered the dead bodies. Oil was pouring noisily out of the pipes into the hatch. Basov looked in that direction, trying to guess how long it would be before the loading was over. "I hope it won't be long," he thought, with a sudden feeling of depression. Behind his back he could hear steps approaching and receding, excited women's voices, and bits of sentences punctuated with stops to catch breath.

"I don't know how I managed to wait."

"Where is he? Call him please, comrade."

"Why didn't they inform us by wireless? I was so anxious!"

"Oh, that's nothing!" a man's voice answered.

Basov could recognize all those voices, but he went away from them to the far side of the ship and leaned over the rail. Brown patches of oil were rocking on the green waves and the broken reflection of the tanker seemed to reach the bottom of the sea.

"It's a good thing Kotelnikov's got a wife and a kid," he thought, as he looked at the trembling reflection of himself on the surface of the water. "And the girl in yellow came to see Husein too. I should have gone away somewhere when we berthed. It hurts me to watch them all, but there's nothing I can do about it. I'll go into my cabin. All I can do is to wait."

He was about to go away when he heard steps behind, and he lingered, waiting for them to go past.

"Shall I call him?" he heard Volodya's voice ask.

"No." The quick answer made Basov start and turn round. "I'll go myself."

Musya was standing two paces away from him. On her face he could see suffering and something like fear. To his own astonishment, Basov said in a ridiculously free and easy tone: "So you've come to see me! Well, well, so you've not forgotten me!"

"Just imagine, I didn't recognize you at first," Musya said in a low, rough voice. "I thought it was somebody else."

She had her fluffy shawl on, the one she had on the evening before they parted. She came nearer and suddenly flamed red to the roots of her hair and her eyes seemed to get moist. Basov took her hand and they stood there for a few seconds, not knowing what to do next.

"What do you mean: you didn't recognize me?" he asked in the same tone of affected ease, feeling a chill inside because that was not what he wanted to say. "Have I changed then?"

"You have a mark there," she said, knitting her brows and putting her hand to her cheek. "Where did you get that from?"

"That's a burn. It was very hot here last night, wasn't it, Volodya?"

Volodya Makarov nodded discreetly and looked at both of them attentively. Then he turned and went away along the deck, swinging his shoulders.

"That'll soon be better," Musya said aloud, watching the wireless operator go. "You must wash it with manganese solution. Did you think of me sometimes, commander?" she asked in a quick, threatening whisper, cocking her head to one side.

Basov squeezed her hand, and she looked up at him and smiled.

"Well, just now—" said Basov with an effort, "just as you came—"

"What do you mean: just now?"

"I was thinking of you. And as a rule I often thought of you when I had nothing to do. And now you have come, and it seems to me it's just a coincidence."

"A coincidence that I came?" Musya said, laughing. "What nonsense you talk!"

She looked round and quickly threw her arms around his neck.

234

"People keep passing here all the time. Hell!" she whispered vehemently, pressing her lips to the spot on his cheek where the skin was cracking. "And there's so much I must tell you. You've probably got at least a cabin to yourself, Stakhanovite?" She hooked her arm resolutely in his and drew him after her. "How long it is since we saw each other! I was reckoning it as I came here—six months ten days, it is. But why don't you get at least a bit angry with me? You should, for appearances at any rate! But no, you won't say anything even now!"

Basov followed her, running his fingers over hers, and he remembered that night long ago when Musya had taken him in the dark over the waste field and the shrill hoots of the tugs had shown them the way. Only now a bright sun was shining, and under their feet was the steel deck of an oil-tanker, the oil was gurgling into the hatches, reminding them of the impending separation. He still could not quite understand her, although their fingers were tightly entwined and Musya's eyes were beaming with uncontainable happiness. They found themselves in the corridor of the living quarters. There was a smell of cooking; it was quiet and half dark, only a shaft of light coming through the door, which was standing ajar. Crazy autumn flies circled in it, with wings which glittered like mica. Basov had his breath taken away by the violence with which they embraced, but as in the far-off days of their first acquaintance, it was Musya who put an end to it. She squeezed his hand to make him listen to her.

"Listen. I used to say you were queer, not like the others. Why have you not had a word of reproach for me yet? You must help me to get this off my chest. I'm always afraid my happiness will suddenly come to an end. But it won't, will it? If you don't want to hurt me, I can hurt myself. You see, I was afraid because you are so—peculiar and it was awful when you were all alone with your ventures against everybody. Just a dreamer, a schemer. You know, Sasha, some people smell of failure a mile off. I fancied that nothing was real about you, that you could only dream and were no good in the things of everyday life. I am only an ordinary average human being, commander. I didn't want to have to pity you, because I loved you. I was in the same boat as that hinderer Neuman. Don't you say I wasn't. I was. Neuman's had a dressing down from the workers but nobody knows about me, except you. And you can't be a severe judge when we've just been kissing! Well, now answer one question, only promise you'll tell me the truth."

"All right. What is it?"

"Listen. If I asked you to come ashore now for good, would you come?" Her eyes bored into his face, triumphing in advance.

"No, I wouldn't, Musya."

"You've said it all the same! Ah, you darling! I'm in love with you today, commander, as though we'd only just got to know each other. In half an hour we shall part because we must. You won't leave the ship for my sake, and I won't ask you to, even though I've been longing for you so."

"I don't know. Ah, Musya! If only I could take leave—"

"Shut up, silly!" She stamped with vexation. "You've not understood a thing. I knew you wouldn't! You can only think in a straight line, and you don't know what you're worth. Perhaps you thought I'd forgotten you. Yes, I can see you did. But I'll tell you how I felt when you were in trouble at sea. I could hear the tapping in the loudspeaker and I knew it was about you, you and your comrades and I couldn't understand anything. I wanted to cry, but I couldn't because I'm too proud. But it's all over now, you're with me and I feel fine."

They embraced, standing at the half-open door, and the draught blew their hair together and made the end of Musya's shawl flutter.

"Let's go to your cabin," she murmured blissfully. "Here we can't—"

At that instant, a deafening metallic blast boomed outside, drowning all other noises. Musya's lips moved, but he could not hear what she said. He could only see her moist eyes getting gradually firmer and losing their radiance. Then the blast broke off, and they stood motionless, holding hands as though to give each other courage.

"It's time. I didn't think it would go so quickly," Musya said quietly. "And you've not even shown me your cabin, commander," she added with a mixture of mockery and sadness. "I must go now."

"There's no hurry. Today we didn't have much time because of the men from the *Uzbekistan*. Generally you can stay much longer. We'll soon have relief trips too, and we'll be together for three days every month. Then we'll make up for it, Musya."

They went out on deck, and Musya leaned on his arm watching the seamen go past. The workmen on the pier were drawing in the pipes, which made long, grating noises at the joints. Women were running down the gangway, holding their skirts as though jumping over water. Husein came up in the opposite direction. His head was now a mass of bandages all converging on the top of his head and making him look like an Arab wearing a turban.

"What are you doing here?" Basov snapped at him. "Didn't we come to an understanding? Listen, Mustapha—"

"I only wanted to warn you—the *Agamali*'s loading at the fourth pier. I just met her lads at the shop. 'We've overhauled our engines again,' they said, 'now we'll show you some speed!' And I said: 'It'll be an interesting sight.' " He shot a glance at Musya and pushed apart the bandages which had fallen over his eyes. "So we'll have to get revs up, Alexander Ivanovich."

Musya ran on to the pier and waved her hand.

"You see that woman off," Basov said, nudging Husein. "She's a relative of mine."

"Oh!" said Husein in surprise, "when did you manage?"

"Go on, get a move on, they're taking the gangway up," Basov said reddening.

Musya smiled and made a sign with her lips.

"Alexander Ivanovich, the pumps are stopped," the motor-man Gazaryan reported, appearing in the doorway of the engine-room.

"Good. Stop the pump motor. Who's on watch?"

"Second Engineer Zadorov. Aye, aye! Stop the pump motor."

The gangway was taken up with a clang. The windlass on the fore-deck gave a whine. The dark narrow space between the side of the ship and the quay broadened, the reflection of the ship appeared in it upside down. White puffs of smoke curled up and melted away over the quarter-deck.